Mar 10, '10

For Julia,

this

Yiddish South of the Border

from one Ostropolsky

to another,

Alan

YIDDISH
South of the Border

An Anthology of

Latin American Yiddish Writing

Edited by Alan Astro

with an Introduction by Ilan Stavans

UNIVERSITY OF NEW MEXICO PRESS

ALBUQUERQUE

JEWISH LATIN AMERICA
Ilan Stavans, series editor

LIBRARY-OF-CONGRESS CATALOGING-IN-PUBLICATION DATA

Yiddish south of the border : an anthology of Latin American
Yiddish writing / edited by Alan Astro.— 1st ed.
    p. cm. — (Jewish Latin America)
  ISBN 0-8263-2348-0
  1. Yiddish literature—Translations into English. 2. Jews—Latin
America—Literary collections. 3. Jews—Latin America—
Intellectual life. 4. Yiddish fiction—Translations into English.
I. Astro, Alan. II. Series.
                    PJ5191.E1 Y54 2003
                    839'.108098—dc21

                    2003010133

DESIGN: Mina Yamashita

Dedicated to

Adam Gruzman, now of Jerusalem,

and

Yitskhok Niborski, now of Paris,

Argentinean Yiddish teachers *extraordinaires*

Table of Contents

x

Introduction

ILAN STAVANS

In the ever-popular *The Joys of Yiddish* (1968), pages 505–6, Leo Rosten offers this definition for *Ladino*:

> Ladino, or Judesmo, as it is called, can be written in either Hebrew or Roman characters. It is generally printed in what is called Rabbinical Hebrew letters, or in Latin characters. In writing Ladino, the cursive Hebrew letters are used—just as in writing Yiddish.
>
> The first book to be printed in Ladino appeared in 1510, in Constantinople, but some Ladino texts date back to the Middle Ages.

My reader is expected to wonder: what on earth does this quote have to do with an anthology of Yiddish stories from Latin America? The answer appears in Rosten's next paragraph, in which he argues that

> Ladino is spoken along the south-eastern littoral of the Mediterranean—normally in Turkey, North Africa and, of course, Israel—and in Brazil and other parts of Latin America.

Elsewhere, Rosten adds: "Sephardim are the least numerous of Jewry's three main groups. The *Encyclopedia Britannica* (vol. 20, p. 228. 1968 ed.) estimates for 1960: 11,000,000 Ashkenazim; 1,500,000 Oriental Jews; 500,000 Sephardim."

In the last forty years, the demographic data have surely changed from those offered by Rosten. Most significantly, the total number of Jews in the world has probably decreased by almost a million, mainly as a result of assimilation and low fertility rate. But this isn't the issue I'm after. Instead, I want to argue with Rosten, the purveyors of the *Encyclopedia Britannica*, and everyone else who falls into the easy trap of counting the Jews of Latin America—some 400,000 altogether, according to the latest estimates—as Sephardim. Despite common belief, most Jews are not Sephardim and Yiddish has indeed existed in those countries. Truth is, at least two-thirds of those in places like Mexico, Argentina, Cuba, Venezuela, and the Dominican Republic, to name but a few of the twenty-seven republics that constitute the region, are Ashkenazim. Just as is the case of the majority of Jews in the United States, their place of origin is the so-called Pale of Settlement in Eastern Europe. The other third is composed of Oriental Jews. Within that designation are Jews in Turkey, who were true Sephardim. Those who are Oriental and not true Sephardim, though they are often lumped with them, are from places like Iran, Iraq, Yemen, North Africa, Syria, and Lebanon. The number of Sephardim in Latin America is actually small. Some demographers at times include in it recently converted Crypto-Jews.

At any rate, Ladino isn't as widely spoken a language in the Spanish- and Portuguese-speaking Americas as Yiddish is. I myself am a product of Yiddish day schools in my native Mexico. Similar educational institutions existed—some of them are still active—in other parts of the hemisphere. Likewise, Yiddish theater, newspapers, music, and other cultural manifestations were a staple of the Eastern European immigrants who arrived to those shores in the late nineteenth and throughout the first half of the twentieth centuries, at first staying in peripheral places, eventually moving into metropolitan centers. My own father, an actor, started his career on the Yiddish stage south of the border.

For the most part, the histories of Yiddish and its literature seldom give space to its production in Latin America. I remember my increasing frustration in the seventies when browsing through reference volumes in search of recognizable names and works—little if anything was ever conveyed. I owe to Alan Astro heartfelt thanks for his effort to unearth and translate an array of tales, poems, and essays from places as diverse as Uruguay, Colombia, Chile, and even Texas. In his introduction, Professor Astro lists the scattered omnibuses of Yiddish letters from the region that have appeared in Spanish and mentions the chapter devoted to Latin America in *A History of Yiddish Literature* (1985) by Sol Liptzin. These items were not available to a curious Mexican-Jewish adolescent. The majority of the authors he's chosen, I predict, will be unknown even to specialists and literary historians. Others like Leib Malach have been the subject of scholarly discussions. For myself, I'm happy to recognize the inclusion of poet Jacobo Glantz, the father of Margo Glantz, whose memoir, *Las genealogías (The Family Tree* [1976]), is an important contribution to Jewish-Mexican letters. Likewise, I'm excited to see a poem by Isaac Berliner, whose full collaboration with Diego Rivera awaits proper exposure.

In its content, the mosaic Professor Astro puts together for us isn't always pleasant: readers looking for the type of Magical Realism that has come to be expected from literati in the Hispanic world will be disappointed. Instead, Jews are often portrayed as pimps, prostitutes, and moneylenders. For example, in one of the most disturbing stories in the anthology, "Jesús" by Pinkhes Berniker—which I included in *The Scroll and the Cross: 1,000 Years of Jewish-Hispanic Literature* (2003)—a bearded Jewish salesman makes a fortune selling Catholic icons to gentiles. This isn't unexpected, though. Immigrant life in general is miserable, as one sees in the literature produced by those who experienced the journey. In the Jewish novels of Abraham Cahan, Henry Roth, and Anzia Yezierska, the picture is frequently a grim one. Furthermore, the odyssey from Europe to the Pampas was often portrayed in Poland, Lithuania, Rumania, Byelorussia, the Ukraine, and other countries, as an expedition to hell. The only famous Yiddish stories from Latin America I'm able to make people invoke are the handful of ones by the masters Sholem Aleichem, Sholem Asch, and Isaac Bashevis Singer.

They are set in, or at least refer to, Argentina (and on occasion in an eternally rainy Brazil) and invariably deal with the Jewish prostitution ring—*la trata de blancas.*

"The corpus of Yiddish writing in Latin America, as elsewhere, is surprisingly vast," Astro states. Indeed, the total number of volumes published—original works, translations, reprints of Eastern European and American masters—might never be known. But judging by his selection, the intellectual engagement of the Jewish immigrants with the land across the Atlantic was extremely rich. One of Astro's acknowledged primary sources is the multi-volume series of Yiddish literary works edited by Samuel Rollansky in Buenos Aires and released under the aegis of the Argentine YIVO. Rollansky is known to have been careless in his editorial ministrations. I've heard from readers that the stories he selected are at times truncated. Still, unless and until the originals are found, his effort is a valuable source. But Professor Astro's research has pushed him in countless other directions. One of the entries selected comes from the journal *Goldene Keyt.* Others are taken from compendiums like the *Yorbukh fun literature, kunst un gezelshaftlekhayt fun yidishn yishev in Argentine* (1945). A substantial number of them come from individual books, like Borekh Bendersky's *Geklibene shfriftn* (1954), Abraham Josef Dubelman's *Der Balans* (1953), Peretz Hirshbein's *Fun vayte lender* (1916), and Aaron Zeitlin's *Lider fun khurbn un lider fun gloybn* (1967–1970).

What is the function of an anthology? Depending on whom you ask, you're likely to get different responses. Personally, I would list four objectives: to offer a context, to create a portable library, to open unexpected vistas, and to insinuate new readings of classic texts. This one succeeds in at least the first three of these objectives, but more fundamentally this anthology documents that Yiddish—or, in one of its Spanish spellings, *idish*—also flourished in Latin America, leaving behind powerfully artistic testaments.

Editor's Introduction

In the last decade or so, interest in Jewish writing in Latin America has grown, as evidenced by such works as the 1,200-page anthology *El gran libro de América judía*, compiled by the Peruvian Jewish writer Isaac Goldemberg; critical studies such as Noami Lindstrom's *Jewish Issues in Argentine Literature* or Nelson Vieira's *Jewish Voices in Brazilian Literature*; and, indeed, the various books that make up the Jewish Latin America series published by the University of New Mexico Press.

The authors covered in these works use Spanish and Portuguese, but—with the exception of a Sephardic minority among them—they had ancestors who spoke Yiddish. Yiddish is, of course, a Germanic language written in Hebrew letters, enriched with Hebrew, Aramaic, Slavic, and Romance vocabulary. It was spoken by the Jews of Eastern Europe and is still used by some (ever fewer) of their descendants. UNESCO classifies Yiddish as a "seriously endangered" language (see Salminen in the "works cited" section to this preface).

Starting with the arrival of Eastern European Jews in the 1880s and continuing through the first three quarters of the twentieth century, many Latin American republics—most notably, Argentina, Brazil, Cuba, Mexico, and Uruguay—fostered a significant Yiddish-language literature and press. Some examples: an anthology of Yiddish literature in Argentina published by the Yiddish daily *Di Prese* in 1944 numbered some 900 pages (Suscovich); two retrospective volumes published in 1972 and 1973 by the Buenos Aires branch of the YIVO Institute for Jewish Research contain over 600 pages of Yiddish fiction and poems from Brazil and Chile (Rollansky).

Such anthologies reflect only the tip of the bibliographical continent formed by the hundreds of Yiddish books published in

Latin America. It is a largely unexplored continent. Exceedingly few scholars of Latin America, including the Jews among them, know any Yiddish, besides some words, perhaps, picked up from their families or during their studies in the New York area. Thus a vital source of insight into the immigrant experience has all too often been left out of works on Latin American Jewish literature.

Yiddish South of the Border is the first anthology ever of translations of Latin American Yiddish works into English. There are few collections of Spanish translations of Latin American Yiddish writers (such as Eduardo Weinfeld's *Tesoros del judaísmo* dating from 1959 and *Crónicas judeoargentinas 1* published in 1987); I know of no such volumes in Portuguese. A chapter on Latin America is included in Sol Liptzin's *A History of Yiddish Literature,* and some information on local Yiddish cultural history appears in the articles on specific Latin American republics in the *Encyclopaedia Judaica* (Cecil Roth). There is also an excellent overview by Eliahu Toker of Argentinian Jewish literature in Spanish and Yiddish, published in *Pardès,* a French journal of Jewish studies.

The corpus of Yiddish writing in Latin America, as elsewhere, is surprisingly vast for a minority literature. The Yiddish author L. Shapiro, resident in the United States, lamented in 1934 the high number of graphomaniacs among his confrères (125). Less polemically it can be argued that the Yiddish writers' ardent impulse to create reflected such factors as the following: a desire to continue the traditional text-based religious culture along secular, artistic lines; the role of literature in the Yiddish world "as a kind of substitute for a national homeland" (Ertel 133); and the awareness among Yiddish writers in the Americas that theirs would be the last generation to speak the language in their new countries, which demanded a high degree of assimilation. This feeling of being "the last of the Mohicans" became even stronger after the Nazi Holocaust, with the near-extinction of Yiddish in its native territory.

The Yiddish literature of Latin America is of a piece with its counterparts elsewhere. *Yiddish South of the Border* presents evocations of urban poverty among displaced Jews, reminiscent of

the work of the Yiddish- and English-language man of letters Abraham
Cahan, whose fiction provided the basis for the acclaimed film *Hester
Street;* or of the Polish Yiddish writer Israel Rabon, author of the
gritty novel *The Street.* The vicissitudes of the Buenos Aires working
class are depicted, for example, in two tales translated here: "In
Opposite Directions" by Hirsh Bloshtein and "The Parrot" by José
Rabinovich. Also included are excerpts from Pinye Ward's memoir
Nightmare, which recounts his mistreatment at the hands of the
Argentinean police and right-wing thugs. In a lighter vein, one can
read the Chilean José Goldchain's "She Wanted To Throw a Nice Affair,"
which features an activist more interested in the social success than the
political relevance of an evening she is organizing to honor the Red
Army. In "The Courtyard Without Windows," Mimi Pinzón adapts
her schoolyears in Buenos Aires into an oneiric narrative that may
remind one of *Call It Sleep* by the American Jewish writer Henry Roth.

In *Yiddish South of the Border,* there are depictions of all kinds of
peddlers and moneylenders, from the archetypal *schlemihls* and
schnorrers to equally renowned Jewish parvenus. In "Gold" by Noah
Vital, two Jewish speculators imagine they are exploiting a naïve
Chilean peasant, only to discover he has one-upped them; in "He
Worked His Way Up" by Goldchain, a Jewish immigrant treats just
as meanly his coreligionists who were supposed to be his comrades;
in "Jesús" by Pinkhes Berniker, we discover an immigrant to Cuba, a
rabbi who hawks, of all things, images of the Christian Messiah, the
Holy Virgin and the Saints; he makes a fortune, because his bearded
appearance reminds the Cuban peasants of Jesus himself! That
Jews in Cuba actually did deal in Christian images is borne out by
historian Robert Levine (37); and in the present volume, we also
discover Jews selling Catholic icons in the Uruguayan Salomón Zytner's
"The Bar Mitzvah Boy" and in the Colombian Salomón Brainsky's
"Temptation." The peddler selling goods on the installment plan,
sometimes called in a mixture of Spanish and Yiddish a *cuéntenik—*
from the Spanish word *cuenta,* meaning "account"—also emerges as
an emblematic figure in Jewish literature in Spanish and Portuguese;
see such works as Goldemberg's *The Fragmented Life of Don Jacobo*

Lerner, Samuel Pecar's *The Forgotten Generation* or Moacyr Scliar's *The Volunteeers;* and the discussions by Leonardo Senkman (133–34) and Murray Baumgarten (70–71).

In the tradition of border studies, I have included here an excerpt of Rabbi Alexander Ziskind Gurwitz' description of Jews peddling among Mexicans in San Antonio, Texas. Further south, Mexican writer Meir Corona's "Quite a Bank" shows us small-time financiers who are, alas, better Talmudists than they are bankers. "Quite a Bank" takes place in the early years of Jewish immigration to Mexico; in "The Tinifotsky Monologues," set in the 1950s, Abraham Weisbaum lampoons a Jewish bourgeoisie who enjoy all the privileges of the European élite in Mexico and shamelessly ape American lifestyles. Insofar as Borges has suggested that "each writer creates his own precursors" ("Kafka" 365), Weisbaum's satires may be said to foreshadow the non-Jewish Guadalupe Loaeza's affectionate attacks on the wealthy Mexican milieu from which she hails.

A humorous critique of the new Jewish bourgeoisie—many of whom kept their socialist trappings from their years as proletarians—can be found in "A Banquet in Mexico City" by Hanan Ayalti, who arrived in Montevideo as a World War II refugee. Moyshe Rubin's "A Ripped Tefillin Strap" and Zytner's "The Bar Mitzvah Speech" present comical sketches on the complicity of nouveau riche parents in the linguistic and religious assimilation of Jewish youth. Such criticism of the immigrant turned parvenu—called an *all-right-nik*—is a staple of Yiddish literature. It segues directly into Philip Roth's denunciation of neo-bourgeois tastelessness in *Goodbye, Columbus.* Yet in the somewhat romantic but realistic "Homesick in Buenos Aires" translated here, the Polish Yiddish man of letters Hersh David Nomberg notes the differences in attitudes (toward money, among other things) between Jews who settled in Anglo-Saxon countries and those who came to Latin America.

Latin American Yiddish literature offers us some astonishing particularities, such as the frequent portrayal of Jews involved in what was prudishly and racistly called "white slavery" in the late nineteenth and early twentieth centuries. As a result of the disruptions in traditional Jewish life wrought by its encounter with modernity, Jewish men in significant numbers became prostitution ringleaders and pimps, and Jewish women were madams and streetwalkers. This state of affairs obtained in Eastern Europe and centers of immigration such as New York, Paris, and Johannesburg. But nowhere were there proportionally so many Jewish procurers and whores as in Buenos Aires and Rio de Janeiro—perhaps a result of Jewish outsiders' being in an advantageous position to exploit the institutionalized hypocrisy regarding sex in Catholic societies. (For an overview of Jews in prostitution see the works by Bristow and Solé.)

The Yiddish writer Sholem Asch, active in Poland, France, and the United States, portrayed Jews in prostitution in his *God of Vengeance* and *Mottke the Thief.* But *Yiddish South of the Border* provides a far greater number of Jewish pimps and whores, as well as their "decent" coreligionists shocked by such turpitude. Such depictions can be found here in an excerpt from the Argentinean Yiddish writer Mordechai Alpersohn's memoirs ("Of Pimps, Prositutes and Other Seducers"), in the Brazilian Rosa Palatnik's tale "An Engagement Dinner," and in Leib Malach's play "Remolding." (For an overview of how Jews in prostitution have been portrayed in Spanish- and Portuguese-language texts, see Glickman, "The White Slave Trade.")

To enhance the *frisson* of transgressing accepted sexual norms, Malach has the "white slave" Rosa cohabitate with a mixed-race politician. The opposite situation, whereby a European man is attracted to a dark-skinned woman, is represented in *Yiddish South of the Border* in two ways: anxiogenically in the tale "The Mulata" by the Brazilian Meir Kucinski, and touchingly in an episode in the Colombian Salomón Brainsky's "Temptation." While Jews in Latin America might well enjoy the class and sexual privileges accruing to Europeans, it should be noted that in one of the *Urtexte* portraying a seduction by a dark-skinned woman—Mérimée's story "Carmen" on which Bizet's opera is based—it is the dark-skinned woman who could be Jewish. This is how the "copper-complected" Carmen appears to Mérimée's narrator:

"So you are Moorish, or. . ." I stopped myself, not daring
to say "Jewish."
"Stop it! You see quite well that I am a gypsy." (621)

But all is not proletarianism, peddling and whoremongering in
Latin American Yiddish literature. Mordechai Alpersohn's memoirs,
for example, have usually been remembered for their depiction of a
far more flattering episode in Jewish history, which also became a
common theme in Argentinean Yiddish writing: the settlement of
large numbers of Jews in agricultural colonies. At a time before sales
and credit were seen as perfectly respectable means of livelihood, the
longstanding involvement of Jews in commerce and moneylending
was felt to be a stigma by all manner of social reformers. Jews, it was
argued, had to pursue farming, the only truly "honorable" occupation.
While the Zionist establishment of kibbutzim in Palestine is the
best-known program for turning Jews into "productive elements,"
similar attempts were undertaken in Ukraine and the American
Midwest. (Jewish farmers in those two settings are depicted in classic
works of Yiddish fiction by Mordechai Spector and Isaac Raboy.)
The grandest scheme of all for settling Jews in farming outside of
Palestine was the Argentinean plan, funded by an ennobled Jewish
railroad millionaire, the Baron de Hirsch. This experiment is evoked
in glowing terms in Alpersohn's memoirs and short stories (see "The
Gauchito Happy Moses" here) and in Borekh Bendersky's tales (of
which two—"The Evil Eye" and "Disturbed Sabbaths"—are included
in *Yiddish South of the Border*).
Yet the veritable army of functionaries created by the baron's
millions reproduced the pattern, all too common in Jewish history,
whereby an élite exploited their poorer coreligionists. This situation
is bemoaned in Alpersohn's memoirs and in the articles here by Leon
Chasanovitch: "Meager Results: Two Decades of Jewish Agricultural
Settlement in Argentina" and "Bread and Honor."
The problematic representation of Jewish farming in Argentinean
Yiddish literature is a clear example of the peculiar interest of the
selections in *Yiddish South of the Border*. Though the most visionary

Yiddish writers demanded a place for their writing on a par with that
accorded other great literary traditions, very little Yiddish literature
was being translated then—and still much has not been translated
now. Few non-Jews could speak much Yiddish, and even fewer had
mastered the Hebrew script the language is written in. In practical
terms, Jews felt completely free to air their grievances in Yiddish.
Their targets could be their own rabbinical and economic élites, or
the criminal elements among their coreligionists, or the Gentiles as a
group—either as anti-Semites all too ready to turn violent, or as the
repositories of ancient religious enmity.

In Yiddish, Jews did not have to engage in apologetics, whereas
Jews writing in Gentile languages often had specific agendas.
Contrasting with Alpersohn's ambiguous treatment of Jewish
agricultural settlement campaign in Argentina or Chasanovitch's
thoroughly negative assessment of it, stands Alberto Gerchunoff's
now classical Spanish-language paean to the so-called *Jewish Gauchos,*
a work whose very title makes clear its attempt to "naturalize" the
Jewish presence in Argentina: the Jew belongs in Argentina as much
as the gaucho, the famed cowboy of the pampas. For those who cherish
that myth (I use the present tense because many still hold it dear),
little does it matter that the Jews on the Argentinean countryside
were farmers and as such the adversaries of the cowboys. That point
is made by a Jewish character in Borges' tale "Unworthy" (353); even
more relevantly, Gerchunoff's own father was killed by a gaucho!
However, the actual novel *The Jewish Gauchos* is far more ambivalent
than the legend it spawned (Aizenberg).

Another historically dubious attempt to naturalize the presence
of Jews in Latin America consisted in positing a link between the
new immigrants from Eastern Europe and the crypto-Jews from the
Iberian peninsula who had established themselves in the New World
centuries before. This was in a sense an inversion of the late nineteenth-
and early twentieth-century campaign by Spanish liberals to extend
the reach of national influence by "re-adopting" the Sephardic Jews
of the Mediterranean basin (González). This campaign later had the
beneficial effect of leading Spanish diplomats—under Franco!—to

issue life-saving Spanish passports to a few thousand Jews in Nazi-occupied Europe.

Some examples of Eastern European Jews in Argentina re-inventing themselves as Sephardic: The author of *The Jewish Gauchos* consistently invokes Sephardic sources like Maimonides and Yehuda Halevy to explain rituals of the Ashkenazim on the pampas; the Argentinean Jewish writer Carlos Grünberg recasts the medieval Spanish poetic genre *mester de clerecía* ("minstrelsy of the [Catholic] clergy") into a modern *mester de judería* ("minstrelsy of the ghetto"); like his model Gerchunoff, Grünberg uses archaic terms redolent of Judeo-Spanish (Senkman 39–57).

Gerchunoff and Grünberg portray Jews in Latin America as continuing the Golden Age of Spanish Jewry. Yet Yiddish writers in Latin America tend to focus instead on what followed: the Inquisition, which they saw as anticipating the way Jews were being mistreated in their own homelands. Thus Abraham Josef Dubelman imagines the diary of new arrival to Cuba:

> July 15, 1919: . . . At two o'clock in the afternoon my feet tread Cuban soil for the first time. With my first step I feel that it is different land, somewhat reddish. If I were superstitious, I would have already found the proper interpretation. . . I hate to think of blood. . .
>
> I have taken a few thousand steps on the streets of Havana. A strange fright pursues me. It is not the fear that strikes any immigrant when he glimpses new land. No. I am afflicted by an anxiety deep within me. Perhaps it comes from trying to think too much of the shrouds of the future, or perhaps I am still tormented by the fear I knew in my village in Poland. For the crime of being a Jew I was punished with a few lashes of the whip just three days before leaving. . .
>
> July 16, 1919: A sunny morning. I once again walk through the streets teeming with Cubans. They seem even good-humored. But I am afraid of their Spanish, though in a hidden corner of my being I feel an impulse to speak Spanish. . .

> I read with Latin pronunciation the names of the streets:
> Jesús María, Acosta, Inquisidor. . . I shudder: the Grand
> Inquisitor Torquemada. . . (217–1)

The uneasy feeling of being in Latin America—the former domain of the Inquisition—is often portrayed in Yiddish poems, two of which are included here: "Churches" by the Mexican poet Isaac Berliner, from a volume illustrated by Diego Rivera; and "The *Gallego*" by the Varsovian Aaron Zeitlin, who took refuge in Cuba at the eve of World War II. "The *Gallego*" depicts an encounter between the poet and a Cuban descendant of crypto-Jews from Spanish Galicia, who turns out to be more profoundly Jewish than the new immigrants who play cards in synagogue! For unlike many Jews recognized as such, Zeitlin's scion of marranos realizes in 1940 that Jews are once again being "led to the pyre."

Zytner's tale "The Refugee" presents a Holocaust survivor brought over from Europe by a nouveau riche relative whose class attitudes disgust him. Kucinski wrote an almost identical story, entitled "The Uncle." Only Zytner's tale is translated here. To include both would have been redundant, but it would have borne testimony to the veracity of the situation evoked: the incommensurability between the experience of the refugees and that of the earlier immigrants. (For a discussion of how Holocaust survivors are presented in Spanish texts in Argentina, see Senkman 137–46 and 375–89.)

A guiding principle for the choice of works in *Yiddish South of the Border*—besides the requisite that they be esthetically the best I could find—is that they should portray Jews living in Latin America. However, the importance of the Holocaust dictated the inclusion of two Yiddish works without a Latin American thematic but nonetheless published in Latin America. These two texts, written shortly after the end of World War II, challenge the "limits of representation" of the Holocaust (cf. Friedländer). In "The Memo from the Thirty-Six" by Ayalti, gassings and *selektzies* in the extermination camps are re-elaborated into a mock-midrashic, almost whimsical tale. And in "When Life Swallowed Up Death," Aaron Leib Schussheim uses a real event as an allegory of the Holocaust and its aftermath. Jewish supersitition held that by celebrating a wedding in a cemetery one could confound the evil spirits responsible for an epidemic. Schussheim recounts how he witnessed just such a ceremony on the graveyard of Oswiecim—the Polish name for the town of Auschwitz. "Life swallows up death," he writes, but that does not mean it lies easy on the stomach. After Auschwitz, we go on living and sometimes rejoice, as at a wedding; but we dance among the dead of Auschwitz.

On July 18, 1994, a car bomb went off in Buenos Aires, destroying the AMIA Jewish community center that housed, among other institutions, one of the most significant Yiddish libraries in the world. This attack resulted in scores of deaths. The center has since been rebuilt on the same site. The books that did not burn, along with new acquisitions, are being placed on the library shelves. Let us read them and rejoice.

Works Cited

Aizenberg, Edna. "Translating Gerchunoff." *Judaica Latinoamericana*. Vol. 4. Jerusalem: Magnes, 2001. 403–9.

Asch, Sholem. *God of Vengeance*. In *The Great Jewish Plays*. Trans. Joseph C. Landis. New York: Bard, 1980. 69–113.

———. *Mottke the Thief*. Trans. Edwin and Willa Muir. London: Gollancz, 1935.

Baumgarten, Murray. "Urban Life and Jewish Memory in the Tales of Moacyr Scliar and Nora Glickman." *Tradition and Innovation: ReXections on Latin American Jewish Writing*. Ed. Robert DiAntonio and Nora Glickman. Albany: State U of New York P, 1993. 61–72.

Borges, Jorge Luis. "Kafka and His Precursors." Trans. Eliot Weinberger. In *Selected Non-Fictions*. New York: Viking, 1999. 363–65.

———. "Unworthy." Trans. Andrew Hurley. In *Collected Fictions*. New York: Viking, 1998. 352–57.

Bristow, Edward J. *Prostitution and Prejudice: The Jewish Fight Against White Slavery 1870–1939*. New York: Schocken, 1983.

Crónicas judeoargentinas 1. Los pioneros en ídish 1890–1944. Buenos Aires: Milá, 1987.

Dubelman, "Di inkvizitsye." Ed. Rollansky, Samuel. *Meksikanish, urugvayish, kubanish. Musterverk fun der yisher literatur*. Vol. 92. Buenos Aires: IWO, 1982. 217–220.

Ertel, Rachel. "Yiddish in France: A Conversation with Rachel Ertel." By Jean Baumgarten. *Shofar* 14.3 (1996): 125–37.

Friedländer, Saul, ed. *Probing the Limits of Representation: Nazism and the "Final Solution."* Cambridge: Harvard U P, 1992.

Gerchunoff, Albert. *The Jewish Gauchos of the Pampas*. Trans. Prudencio de Pereda. Albuquerque: U of New Mexico P, 1998.

Glickman, Nora. "The White Slave Trade in Latin American Fiction." In *The Jewish White Slave Trade and the Untold Story of Raquel Liberman*. New York: Garland, 2000. 28–41.

Goldemberg, Isaac. *El gran libro de América judía*. San Juan: Universidad de Puerto Rico, 1998. 1, 236 pp.

————. *The Fragmented Life of Don Jacobo Lerner.* Trans. Robert S. Picciotto. Albuquerque: U of New Mexico P, 1999.

González García, Isidro. *El retorno de los judíos.* Madrid: Nerea, 1991.

Grünberg, Carlos M. *Mester de judería.* Buenos Aires: Argirópolis, 1940.

Hester Street. Dir. Joan Micklin Silver. Midwest Film Production, 1974.

Kucinski, Meir. "Der feter" ["The Uncle"]. *Nusekh Brazil.* Tel Aviv: I. L. Peretz, 1963. 24–29.

Levine, Robert M. *Tropical Diaspora: The Jewish Experience in Cuba.* Gainesville: U P of Florida, 1993.

Lindstrom, Naomi. *Jewish Issues in Argentine Literature.* Columbia: U of Missouri P, 1989.

Liptzin, Sol. "Yiddish in Latin America." In *A History of Yiddish Literature.* Middle Village, NY: Jonathan David, 1985. 394–409.

Loaeza, Guadalupe. *Las reinas de Polanco.* Mexico City: Cal y Arena, 1988.

Mérimée, Prosper. "Carmen." *Romans et nouvelles.* Ed. Henri Martineau. Paris: Gallimard, Bibliothèque de la Pléiade, 1951. 609–66.

Pecar, Samuel. *La generación olvidada [The Forgotten Generation].* Buenos Aires: Candelabro, 1958.

Rabon, Israel. *The Street.* Trans. Leonard Wolf. New York: Schocken, 1985.

Raboy, Isaac. *Her Goldenbarg.* In P*yonern in Amerike. Musterverk fun der yidisher literatur.* Vol. 19. Buenos Aires: IWO, 1964. 195–292.

Rollansky, Samuel, ed. *Brazilyanish. Musterverk fun der yidisher literatur.* Vol. 58. Buenos Aires: IWO, 1973. 349 pp.

————. *Tshilenish. Musterverk fun der yisher literatur.* Vol. 54. Buenos Aires: IWO, 1972. 269 pp.

Roth, Cecil, ed. *Encyclopaedia Judaica.* 17 vols. Jerusalem: Keter, 1972.

Roth, Henry. *Call It Sleep.* New York: Farrar, Straus and Giroux, 1991.

Roth, Philip. *Goodbye, Columbus.* Boston: Houghton Mifflin, 1959.

Salminen, Tapani. *UNESCO Red Book on Endangered Languages: Europe.* 24 Aug. 2002 <http://www.helsinki.fi/~tasalmin/europe_report.html>.

Scliar, Moacyr. *The Volunteers.* Trans. Eloah F. Giacomelli. New York: Ballantine, 1988.

Senkman, Leonardo. *La identidad judía en la literatura argentina.* Buenos Aires: Pardes, 1983.

Shapiro, L. "Kries yam-suf." *Studyo* 1 (1934): 117–26.

Solé, Jacques. "Traite des Blanches: la mondialisation du trafic." *L'Histoire* 264 (2002): 54–59.

Spector, Mordechai. *Der yidisher muzhik. Musterverk fun der yidisher literatur.* Vol. 15. Buenos Aires: IWO, 1963.

Suscovich, Salomón. *Antologye fun der yidisher literatur in Argentine.* Buenos Aires: Di Prese, 1944. 942 pp.

Toker, Eliahu. "Identité et langage dans la littérature juive argentine." *Pardès* 21 (1995): 115–24.

Vieira, Nelson H. *Jewish Voices in Brazilian Literature.* Gainesville: U P of Florida, 1995.

Weinfeld, Eduardo, ed. *Tesoros del judaísmo: Extractos de obras de escritores judíos de América Latina.* Mexico City: Editorial Enciclopedia Judaica, 1959.

Acknowledgments

I would like to thank Debbie Nathan and Moisés Mermelstein for translating some selections in this anthology. Seth Barron offered valuable stylistic suggestions.

Research for this book was supported by a grant from The Memorial Foundation for Jewish Culture and by a sabbatical from Trinity University.

Every effort was made to contact copyright holders of the material used. I gratefully note those I was able to find in the end section on sources. All omissions that come to my attention will be corrected in subsequent editions.

ARGENTINA

I

Of Pimps, Prostitutes, and Other Seducers

EXCERPT OF A MEMOIR BY MORDECHAI ALPERSOHN

[*Mordechai (or Marcos) Alpersohn (b. 1860 Lantskorun, Ukraine, 1860; d. 1947 Argentina) acquired a traditional education and tried his hand at writing in Hebrew before emigrating to found one of the first Jewish agricultural settlements in Argentina. His* Memoirs of a Jewish Colonist, *published in Berlin and Buenos Aires in 1922–28, became a best-seller throughout the Yiddish-speaking world, earning him the label "the Jewish Robinson Crusoe." In that work, Alpersohn denounced the attitude of* noblesse oblige *and the sheer corruption of the German and French officials of the Jewish Colonization Association. In addition, he authored several plays and short stories.*]

We saw some ten richly-dressed women, accompanied by fat-bellied men in top hats, standing at the green metal gate of the immigrants' hotel. Through the iron railing of a fence, they began pleading with our wives and offering chocolates and other candies to our children. One by one they approached the guard with muttered requests. He kept shaking his head and waving "no" with his hands. I realized that under no circumstances was he about to let them in.

Some of those individuals, who to judge by their accent were Polish Jews, recognized relatives and other acquaintances among the immigrants.

They started sobbing, and their tears gushed onto the iron railings. It was hard to say whether those were tears of joy or sadness.

Through gestures, I attempted to ask the guard at the gate why those ladies and gentlemen were not allowed in. He gave me a strange little wink, grinned, turned his head of curly, black hair, and roguishly intoned, "No, no, no!"

Thereupon arrived a red-headed, freckle-faced young man, carrying a stack of papers under his arm. He identified himself as Baron Hirsch's agent. Respectfully, the guardian opened the gate for him. Speaking for Dr. Loewenthal, the young man announced that in a few days we would be sent to the tracts of land that Baron Hirsch had acquired for us. "We have to formalize the purchase through the government," he said to us in a confidential tone, "and you're off!"

The young man then launched into a speech, wherein he lamented that the committees in Galicia and Germany had rushed things by sending us over too soon. He enjoined us to avoid contact with the Jewish ladies and gentlemen who stood at the gate and by the railings. "They are impure!" he stated emphatically. "Don't let your wives and daughters take to the street!"

The young man continued: "There are hardly any decent Jews here, just those impure souls, the dregs of humanity. Because of them, the few Sephardic and English Jews one finds are ashamed to acknowledge their religion." He then spoke with the hotel employees, before departing.

No sooner had he crossed the threshold than a hubbub arose. A little Jew—who had earlier warned us to avoid eating a certain dish, lest it contain horse meat—chimed in with others, supposedly as honorable as he. They began inciting those assembled. "We've been hoodwinked!" they shouted. "They've bought no land at all! The whole colonization scheme is a swindle!"

"They're missionaries," screeched the little Jew, whose pointed beard waggled to and fro. "They want to baptize and convert us!"

From the other side of the gate, the "impure" poured oil on the fire. They brought their colored silken handkerchiefs to the corners of their eyes as they commiserated with the immigrants.

A few Jews with experience sneaking across borders had used false papers to smuggle some pimps and prostitutes into the hotel courtyard among us. These creatures used their whorish lips to paint our predicament as blackly as possible. The more naïve women among the immigrants broke out crying. Several of us protested, chasing out the interlopers. We came to blows, and the guard—who had apparently been bribed—failed to stop the fighting. They managed to trick some pious Polish Jews, wearing traditional fringed garments, into taking their wives, grown daughters, and all their earthly possessions over to the other side, never to return. Then the excitement died down.

The following morning, Dr. Loewenthal came to the immigrants' hotel. In my entire life, I shall never forget the figure cut by that tall, stately Jew with the mesmerizing black eyes, whose gaze none of us could bear for more than an instant. Each and every one of us went out to the courtyard, surrounding him. He simply waved his hand, and an awesome silence ensued.

"My children!" he said, speaking to us plainly, in Yiddish. "The good-hearted baron has sent Sir Cullen and me in search of refuge, in a free country, in some corner of the wide world, to establish a home for you and all of our oppressed brethren. The Argentine republic—a great, free, and fertile land—seemed to us best suited for that purpose. We have bought property enough to settle you as farmers in this secure and vibrant country. True, the committees in your homelands rushed things a bit. We have not had time to prepare housing for you; in fact, besides the earth itself, we have purchased nothing. But the fault lies not with the committee members. You came in droves, and the authorities in both Galicia and Prussia demanded that we ship you off, before. . .," his tone turned bitter, as he took a deep breath, "before they deported you as undesirables!"

Throwing a penetrating glance over those assembled, he now spoke mildly: "You have already seen why it is impossible to keep you here in the city, while we acquire permanent housing and farming equipment. Decent families must remain far from those who would defile and corrupt them. Yesterday, some of you went down a path leading into a terrible abyss. My conscience impedes me from detaining you here much longer. I have sent forty young men out to the country to find shelter for you, and in a few days you will travel there. I beg of you to be patient, to employ the forbearance with which our people has been blessed. If you endure the first unavoidable difficulties that colonization demands, you shall attain peace and tranquility on your own plots of land. Believe me, brothers, you shall reap the benefits! The baron is guided by a great and noble ideal, born of his love for you. Remain steadfast and do not deviate from the proper path!"

"Send us, doctor! We shall go! Hurrah! Long live the baron!" These cries resounded from all sides.

Dr. Loewenthal departed contentedly. We began repeating his words, offering elaborate interpretations. We prepared for the trip to peace and tranquility on our own plots of land. All was optimistic commentaries and general satisfaction, until the Sabbath.

On Saturday morning arrived a red-headed gentleman, around thirty-five years old, wearing a high top hat similar to a coachman's. A swarthy young man accompanied him respectfully. They were greeted with reverence by the hotel employees. The gentleman in the top hat introduced himself as the rabbi of the local Western European Jews: Frenchmen, Germans, Englishmen and Belgians. Since he spoke only English and Spanish—languages none of us knew—the swarthy young man, who was his sexton and spoke Yiddish, served as the interpreter. We were invited to attend a synagogue service. Some ten of us followed them to a mud- and trash-filled alley. In a narrow, dark room stood a Holy Ark, a lectern, and a few benches strewn with prayer-books.

Such was their synagogue in those days. Now they have a magnificent temple with a cantor and an organ.

Cards were distributed to call us by order to the lectern, according to whether we were Cohens, Levites, or just plain Israelites. The sexton led the prayers and blessed the new month of Elul in the Hebrew year 5651. Besides the newcomers, only the rabbi, the sexton, and a few old men were in attendance.

The red-headed rabbi quickly decamped, whereupon the sexton shared with us some sad tales. Rabbi Henry Joseph, as was his name, lived with a Christian woman; his sons were uncircumcised; they were complete gentiles. The sexton confirmed what we had heard earlier: the Jews here were ashamed to reveal their identity, because the Poles and Galicians among them, who had arrived earlier, were active in prostitution rings. What is more, some of the Russian and Polish families whom Leizer Koifman had tricked into coming had deserted the agricultural colonies at Palacios and Monigotes. Most of them now lived in town. If they themselves did not actually run the brothels, they worked in them as menservants, cooks, and maids.

"And that's the Jewish community of Buenos Aires!" he lamented. "Most of the year we can't even assemble a *minyan*. Only on Rosh Hashanah and Yom Kippur do the pure and impure elements come together to pray. I myself was one of those whom Koifman brought over three years ago."

A shudder went through me as I heard those words. "So you're one of Koifman's immigrants?" I asked in surprise. "Perhaps you know the Weiner family, who came over with Koifman, the Jewish official. Where are they? How are they doing?"

"What's your connection to them?" he asked. "Are you related?"

"Yes. Mr. Weiner is my wife's uncle. For eighteen years they lived in a village, until they were expelled by Ignatyev's infamous decree of 1881. They joined the hundred families who emigrated with Koifman to a prosperous settlement here."

"Your uncle Hirsch Weiner and his son Abraham Elijah are among the lucky ones!" he answered. "In Monigotes they found a mason who pays them a peso a day. They transport mud and bricks to earn their daily bread. Your aunt and her daughter-in-law make around eighteen cents a day doing laundry. But if it had not been for the misfortune that befell the little children of Monigotes, the misery there would not be so great." He stopped speaking, and sighed deeply.

We begged him to tell us all he knew about Koifman's colony. "After all, we're going to settle here. Let us at least be forewarned."

"God forbid something like that should occur again! It simply cannot happen to you!" the young sexton assured us. "Koifman was hoodwinked! But it wasn't for naught that the immigrants wanted to kill him!"

"Tell us! Tell us!" we implored in one voice. And he told us.

"In the villages and small towns, life had become unbearable for Jews under Ignatyev's decrees. In 1887, three delegates were sent to Paris and London. They beseeched Jewish millionaires to arrange for transport of their coreligionists to the United States, Canada, and Palestine. Two of them—Leizer Nisenzon and Moses Hendler from Kamenetz-Podolsk—wandered for one long year, knocking at the doors of Jewish philanthropists. They returned empty-handed. The third delegate, Koifman, was so unfortunate as to meet an individual who claimed to be an emissary of the Argentine republic and who promised everything: land, cattle, equipment, and financial aid for the first period of settlement. Entranced by such largesse, Koifman gathered some hundred families and set off for Argentina, only to find misery. All the promises turned out to be false; it was one gigantic swindle. The families were dumped on the train line between the Palacios and Monigotes stations, without food or shelter. Within one month, more than three hundred children perished from hunger and cold. Many of those families set off by foot to Buenos Aires. Their wives and daughters ended up in brothels. Some of the families stayed in the country, where they suffer unspeakable deprivation. Now word has it that Dr. Loewenthal is going to take them under his wing and settle them in the new colony. They shall finally be rewarded for their suffering!"

We heaved a deep sigh, wiped the tears from our eyes, and returned in sadness to the immigrants' hotel.

That same Sabbath, in the afternoon, we were taken to the train station and sent off to our settlement. That episode was the first link in a chain of woes that would weave through the next thirty years: nearly a third of a century replete with struggle, desperation, humiliation, with rarely a day of happiness. Few of the original settlers attained the "peace, tranquility, and their own plots of land" as promised by Dr. Loewenthal—unless we count those murdered by gauchos and those who died of natural causes, working on their farms. But we are getting beyond ourselves. . .

A streetcar, drawn by a pair of horses more dead than alive, came to the immigrants' hotel. The red-headed agent from Baron Hirsch's office ordered us to board the streetcar for the train station. No matter how intently the pious Jews implored him, "Let us go by foot! It is a sin to ride on the Sabbath!" he responded: "You must take the streetcar. Otherwise, you will miss the train." That turned out to be a bald-faced lie. The train did not arrive until nine o'clock that evening.

The cattle- and poultry-slaughterer Gedaliah Weiner, who was one of our number then, tried to run after the streetcar. His strength was soon at an end. One by one, the pious Jews, with heavy hearts and tears in their eyes, climbed onto the streetcar. They recited by way of excuse the words of the Talmud: "God pardons those forced to sin."

None of this surprised me. Throughout the whole trip I had noticed that the Jewish emigration and colonization officials systematically chose the Sabbath for us to travel or undertake difficult tasks.

Facing the train station, on a field of grass where *Plaza 11* now stands, we sat and waited contentedly, as befits pioneers who are going off to settle their own plots of land. The young people sang Eliakim Zunser's "The Plow." The women bought oranges and bananas for next to nothing, after they had exchanged their Russian kopecks for shiny new ten-cent pieces. For five kopecks they got ten cents, but one hundred rubles brought in a full two hundred ten pesos! The general mood was one of excitement.

The sun shone so brightly that day, and it was pleasantly warm. Leaves were green, flowers bloomed, and we were thrilled. "What do you think of our Argentinean winter?" a young woman called out to those assembled. "Father in Heaven! What a country! What a surprise! Long live the baron and the great land to which he has brought us!"

"Hurrah! Long live Baron Hirsch!" The cry resounded in Yiddish and Russian.

At nine o'clock the train moved, and we were off.

—Translated by A. A.

2

The Gauchito "Happy Moses"

A SHORT STORY BY MORDECHAI ALPERSOHN

Old *reb* Nathan volunteered for a tour of the agricultural colonies in Argentina, to look over the harvests of the Jewish National Fund's fields and to sell shekels—the commemorative medallions whose proceeds supported settlement in Palestine. The organization had appointed a young man to accompany him. The roads were muddy and full of ditches, so they went on horseback.

One dawn, they were riding out near one another toward *La Esperanza* colony. The well-rested and -fed horses rubbed each other's chins merrily, neighed softly, and stamped their feet.

Silently, absorbed in their thoughts, the riders sat in their soft saddles. They looked in amazement into the translucent fog, where the morning revealed itself in a play of daylight and nocturnal shadow. The day was indeed beautiful: bluish, clear. As though emerging from a nightmare, it spread out over the field and wrapped the long rows of wheat, rye, and hemp in a glittering shimmer.

The nascent light in the east was reflected on the small, whitewashed houses of the colony afar; it gilded the small woods and orchards of ripe peach trees. A swallow burst into song, answered by a whole chorus of birds. The young rider was the first to stop his horse. He exclaimed enthusiastically, "Listen to that, *reb* Nathan! How beautiful! The bounty of nature! Look at the hemp, thick as borscht! What gladness, my word!"

"That's nothing," the old man said, with unshakeable pride, "when you think of our Land of Israel. The blessings of plenty pour forth from the heavens there over the entire earth."

"So you think the grain *here* derives its sustenance from the heavens *there?* Isn't that exaggerating a bit?"

"Foolish boy that you are, what's wrong with that?"

"Well, in the Land of Israel there isn't such wide-open space, such rich soil, such lovely fields bringing forth bread."

"Child that you are, our Land of Israel is lovelier, richer. It seems you haven't learned any Torah!"

Feeling insulted, the boy wished to get back at the old man. He grimaced and said, "'Child that you are. . .' That's what you old folks always say. You're living in the past, with your memories from biblical times. We are in a free, sun-filled, abundant land—Argentina. We enjoy liberty and sustenance. Such rich soil. . ."

"Don't we have the same *there?*"

"There we have stones and swamps whose clearing and draining will take years upon years of our pioneers' blood and sweat. And how many Jews could actually settle there? It's a poor, tiny land!"

"But what can you do about that? It's our land, the land of our forebears! Our Father has bequeathed us a small legacy, but a good one, a precious one. It belongs to us, and we shall revive it, rebuild it!"

"A legacy! Quite a legacy! It pains me that God did not give our ancestors Argentina, but Palestine instead!"

"Crazy boy that you are! We are older than Argentina! How long ago was it that they discovered Argentina?"

"'Crazy boy. . .!' You are three times as old as I am, and you've drunk a couple of thousand times as many matés as I have. . ."

He could not finish expressing his thought, for suddenly a sound like that of a crying child reverberated in his ears. He raised his head and caught sight of a small, frightened hare running out of a hiding-place within the hemp. The hare momentarily stood on its hind paws. With large, cowardly eyes it looked at the boy before bolting down the road.

Three wet dogs, panting, with muffled barks, emerged from the grain and raced after the hare. The poor creature zigzagged around, whining. The boy found himself smack in the middle of the pursuit. His horse took fright, started to buck, and reared. In an instant, the boy was on the ground.

"Serves him right!" thought *reb* Nathan, riding over to him. "Leo," the old man called out, "stand up, Leo!"

But the boy did not react. His eyes remained closed; he was quickly fading. The old man pulled at him, trying to rouse him. Then *reb* Nathan heard a voice from behind: "*¡No se asuste!* Don't be afraid!" A dark-skinned *goy* jumped off a horse, grabbed his knife, placed it against the boy's temples, and pressed hard. Leo opened his eyes, looked around, and sat right up.

"*¡Qué vergüenza, joven!* What a disgrace, young man," said the dark-skinned man, laughing, "You let a horse throw you! Just look at your trousers! They're split open."

"There's your punishment for your jewels of eloquence! You shouldn't have spoken ill of the Land of Israel," said *reb* Nathan, laughing.

The dark-skinned man picked up from the ground the logbook of the sales of Zionist medallions, which had fallen from Leo's pocket. He dusted it off, handed it to him, and with his slight voice said to him, "Crawl up on your horse. We'll ride over to the tavern nearby. *Doña* Sara will give you a needle and thread to sew up your pants."

The gaucho's voice and face seemed familiar to *reb* Nathan, but he could not place them. Meanwhile, the boy had regained his composure, and the three of them rode over to the tavern. At the outside counter a young maid stood, bargaining with a gaucho over a pair of knickers—*bombachas*. The dark-skinned gaucho asked her for a needle and some thread. He handed them to the boy, who went off to the shed to mend his trousers.

Reb Nathan and the dark-skinned gaucho entered the tavern. Old Bezaleel, the owner, was busy with some heavyset Italians, who sat at a small table over a plate of sausage. He was serving them drinks, bottle in hand, when he caught sight of *reb* Nathan. "Ah! So early in *La Esperanza!* What brings you here? Peace be upon you!"

The old man explained they were collecting funds for the Land of Israel. When he mentioned the fright they had had with the boy, Bezaleel turned to the gaucho and called out, "Were those your black dogs? You'll have to pay a fine," he said in Yiddish, patting him on the back.

"A fine?!" answered the gaucho, pulling out a five-peso note from his pocket. "Here you go."

Reb Nathan opened wide his eyes and, biting a lip, gazed at the gaucho's brown face.

"Why are you looking at me like that, *reb* Nathan? Don't you recognize me?"

"Who might you be? Are you Jewish? The son of one of settlers in the colonies?"

Old Bezaleel burst out laughing: "It's 'Happy Moses!' *Doña* Mamerta's son. You know, our first midwife, our granny! How many times the settlers fetched her at night on horseback! She delivered all our wives' first children!"

"Well, I'll be darned! So you're the little *goy* we called 'Happy Moses!' Now you've grown into a big *goy!* Do you still sing so well? What have you been up to all these years? What about your mother? Is she still alive? Does she still smoke those little cigarettes of hers?"

"Wait a while, I'll tell you everything. But first I'm going to wet my whistle." He went over to the counter where the maid was standing, ordered a brandy, then another, and a third.

Old Bezaleel leaned over towards *reb* Nathan. "You know who he is, what the women whispered about him back then. . ."

"What women are liable to say. . ."

"Indeed, women. . . But *she* was a pretty one," laughed Bezaleel. "She bragged about being descended from marranos. Her last name was Aguilar, and people whispered that 'Happy Moses' was. . ."

Old Bezaleel did not finish his sentence, for Leo and the gaucho had just come over to them.

"Ask those two *viejos*," said the gaucho. "I paid a five-peso fine because of you. Now we have to make up and become *amigos*. We'll have a good bite together. My dogs hurt you, and I'll give them a lickin', I will. It's not my fault. *¡Caramba!* You don't know me, but my mother and I visited your family before you were even born! Your late father was a good man."

Nonetheless, the boy was angry with him and walked away.

"Let the kid go," said the tavern owner to the gaucho. "Instead, sing us a few measures of 'Happy Moses.'"

The gaucho, already a little tipsy, answered, "I can sing it. I remember 'Happy Moses.' I know all the prayers that Rabbi Abraham taught the children at school.'"

"Are you a Jew?" Bezaleel asked him, winking at *reb* Nathan.

"I don't know. They wrote me down in the civil registry with my mother's name, Aguilar."

"Did you ever ask who your father was?"

"I asked about him, but my mother wouldn't tell me. Before she died, she took a little pouch from around her neck and handed it to me."

He unbuttoned his shirt and revealed a small, flat pouch that hung over his heart.

"Open the pouch. Let's see what's in it."

"*¡No se puede!* You can't open it!" he said, shaking his head. But he soon gave in, took a knife, and slit the pouch open.

It contained a Zionist medallion from Vienna, dated 1908.

Old Bezaleel gave a side-glance to the table where Leo was sitting, and whispered into *reb* Nathan's ear: "They're both in a better world now."

—Translated by A. A.

3

An Evil Eye

A SHORT STORY BY BOREKH BENDERSKY

[*Borekh Bendersky (b. 1880 Remankevits, Ukraine; d. 1953 Entre Ríos, Argentina) emigrated with his parents in 1894 to an agricultural settlement in Argentina. He began publishing in the periodical* Di Yidishe Hofenung *in 1908. Bendersky's short stories, collected into two volumes, reflect the Jewish experience in the Argentinian countryside.*]

Deborah-Gitl woke up well before dawn, unable to fall back asleep. It was Friday, much had to be done before Sabbath eve, and the days had grown shorter. She dressed quietly, opened the curtain covering the window, looked into the darkness and thought, "It's still early, let him sleep. . . He works the whole day, poor thing. . . In the meantime, I'll start the fire."

Deborah-Gitl snuck out of the bedroom and into the kitchen. She lit a lamp, washed her hands and performed the proper blessing, then took some wood chips and started the fire. She placed a large pot of water on the stove and looked at the dough. "The kneading trough is full! May it be preserved from the Evil Eye!" she said, spitting three times to ward off a curse. "I hope there'll be enough flour."

Glancing at the flour sack on the gas canister near the door, she added, "We'll need to borrow two or three tins of flour. Otherwise, there won't be enough to roll out the dough."

When the water in the large kettle had boiled, Deborah-Gitl prepared some maté and went to wake her husband in the bedroom. "Sleeeeping?" she asked.

Startled, Chaim-David muttered, "What?" and then began to scratch his beard.

"I know it's a bother, but it looks as if you'll have to go to the neighbors' to borrow two or three tins of flour. We don't have enough. The dough has risen! May it be preserved from the Evil Eye!"

Chaim-Yankl did not seem very happy about the task his wife had set for him. He made a face, flailed his arms about, then extended them toward Deborah-Gitl as he tried to embrace her.

She pushed him away gently, and said with a smile, "Go on. . . Just what do you have on your mind?. . . We have to get the oven going! The dough is still rising, may it be preserved from the Evil Eye!"

Chaim-David dressed himself, drank down a few matés, and went outdoors to see how much time remained before dawn. A cool, fresh breeze was blowing. The morning star had not yet appeared. From the houses in the agricultural colony glimmered fires, which peered through the small panes of glass into the night.

From the field could be heard the chomping of the horses feeding on the oats. The cows in the corral, seeing Chaim-David going about, sensed that it was already daybreak. Extending one leg, then another, they rose, mooed softly, and turned their heads toward the pen that held their calves. The calves, lowing, began to push against the thick wire enclosure. They looked with eager eyes at the udders full of milk, and licked their muzzles.

The first signs of day began to appear in the east. Chaim-David found an empty kerosene tin, fashioned a handle out of wire, attached it to the tin, and set off to Zalman's to borrow flour.

Zalman's family had also gotten up before dawn, first of all because it was Friday, and, second, because his wife had recently given birth. All the work had fallen upon his aged mother. She ran back and forth between the bedroom and the kitchen, glanced from time to time at the oven, and said, "The fire is burning nicely. May it be preserved from the Evil Eye! Soon we'll have to rake out the ashes. The dough is rising, may it be preserved from the Evil Eye! Soon it will be time to bathe the child. Master of the Universe, preserve him from the Evil Eye! What a jewel he is! If anyone must suffer, let it be me and not him! And his poor mother is wasting away. She hasn't yet eaten a thing. . ."

When Chaim-David arrived with his tin, Zalman had already gone off to tend the cattle and his mother was in the kitchen. Finding no one in the first room, he wandered into another. He immediately realized the mistake he had made, and stammered, "I wanted. . . My wife sent me. . ."

"Please go see my mother-in-law in the kitchen," said the new mother, weakly.

Chaim-David stumbled his way into the kitchen. The old woman measured five cups of flour into his large tin, and he started back home through a colt pasture.

"Will you have something to drink?" asked the old woman, coming into the bedroom. She was taken aback at the sight of the young mother. Her right cheek was flaming red! What a fright!

"Do you have a fever?" the old woman inquired, laying her hand on her daughter-in-law's forehead. She began muttering spells, spitting, yawning widely, in an attempt to nullify the Evil Eye.

"No, nothing is wrong," said the young mother, smiling as she sipped some tea.

"Nothing! I only wish it were nothing! Father in Heaven, may it afflict Chaim-David, his head, hands, feet, body and soul! Because he's to blame! He gave you the Evil Eye! Master of the Universe, may his eyes be poked out!" The old woman, at wits' end, began running back and forth across the room. If only Zalman were there, she would know what to do. But where was he?

Finally, he came back, riding on his horse. No sooner had he passed through the gate than his mother ran up to him and in one breath told him what had happened, and how it was all Chaim-David's fault. "May his ribs burst open, Father in Heaven! How can a Jew have such eyes? Wait, wait, don't get down from the horse, I'll get the scissors. He can't have gotten far yet. Ride up to him and get some of his hair. That always does the trick! Go, my son, go quickly. Time isn't standing still. The sooner we start working, the better."

Zalman begged, "But Mother, what's wrong with her? Tell me exactly what happened!"

"Don't ask!" the old woman screeched. "I'm telling you, just go!" Tears welled up in her eyes.

Bewildered, Zalman remained on his horse. The old woman handed him the scissors, and he galloped off across the field.

It was already daybreak when Chaim-David started home with the tin of flour. The sun shone like the smile of a child, and whatever it lit up smiled back. The field lay in anticipation of the day's events.

Chaim-David, crossing the field, observed his cattle, his prize possession, and reckoned that his debts were mounting even as little money was coming in. On the other hand, it was sinful to complain, because things could be worse. Therefore, it behooved him to thank the Lord and extol His Beloved Name.

Chaim-David put down the tin of flour, cleaned his hands with the dew on the grass, and assumed a pious countenance. He began reciting the morning prayers by heart, interspersing them with his own thoughts.

"*How goodly are Thy tents, o Jacob. . .* Those are the houses in the agricultural colony, spread out so far from one another. . . *Thy dwelling places, o Israel. . .* We dwell far enough from each other so as to avoid quarreling. . . *And I, Thy servant, through Thy great mercy, shall come into Thy House. . .* The synagogue right in the middle of the field. . . *I love the edifice of Thy House. . .* I should love it, since I carried my share of bricks and sand to build it, and donated two boards for benches! *And I pray to Thee, o God. . .* This is all for Your sake, Master of the Universe. . . *Thy help is true. . .* And I could truly use some help. . ."

Chaim-David, filled with festive devotion, spontaneously entoned a hymn: "*Master of the Universe, Who reigns supreme. . .*" He finished with the verse, "*Thou art with me and I fear no one.*"

The last words wavered in the air as Chaim-David became aware of a rider galloping toward him. At first, he thought it was a boy from the colony riding about, but then he saw the rider gesturing menacingly. He grabbed the tin of flour, and began to stride hastily.

Suddenly things began to spin. He made out something gleaming in the rider's hand, reflecting the bright sunlight. But all was not yet lost. Casting the tin of flour away—no small sacrifice!—he started running breathlessly.

However, when he heard pounding of hooves and the panting and gasping of a horse right behind him, he knew he stood no chance. He no longer felt or heard anything, not even Zalman calling out to him, "Wait, stand still, you bandit! Murderer! You killed her!"

He lay in a stupor on the ground.

To this day no one knows how it happened. Foolishly enough—as it turned out—Chaim-David had recently had the hair on his scalp cropped closely. So was it because he refused to give up even a single hair from his beard that Zalman cut off half his moustache? Or did Zalman simply take the scissors and cut off the first strand of hair he got hold of? No one knows, and neither of them ever spoke about it.

One only hears what happened after Chaim-David came home. Deborah-Gitl, pressed for time, was besides herself with rage. The oven had already gone out. The dough had overflowed the edges of the trough. "It should have been rolled out hours ago, and there was no flour!" That is why, when she saw her husband enter empty-handed, she started hollering. "What are you doing, standing there like a golem? Speak! Where is the flour? Look at him, he's laughing! What do you have to laugh about?"

Answering nothing, Chaim-David drew a few steps closer to his wife. Only then did she see that he was not laughing at all. He was missing half his moustache, shorn to the very skin. And from afar, it looked as if he were laughing.

The next morning, at the Sabbath service in the synagogue, Zalman was called up to the Torah to pray for the complete recovery of the wife *"amidst all the sick of Israel."* All the faces were solemn, except Chaim-David's. He stood there, pale, his prayer shawl wrapped about his head and shoulders. His eyes were filled with fright and sadness, but half his mouth was grinning.

—Translated by A. A.

4
Unrestful Sabbaths

A SHORT STORY BY BOREKH BENDERSKY

Every Sabbath, old Dobra arises from bed earlier than on the other days of the week. As soon as the slightest patch of blue can be seen through the windows, she rouses herself, washes her hands as she performs the proper blessing, then murmurs silently a prayer of thankfulness for the new day. She puts on her Sabbath finery: a dark blue cretonne dress with small white polka dots, and on her head a silk scarf with large yellow flowers, a gift from a grandchild in the city. Involuntarily, she glances through the open door into the kitchen, where water is boiling in a teapot over the fireplace. She sighs to herself heavily: "Fine things I've lived to see."

Dobra grabs the Yiddish prayer book for women and, placing it under her arm, slips quietly out of the house. Since it is still too early to go to synagogue, she stops by to see a neighbor, with whom she is friends. Zelda, an old woman like herself, runs a beautiful home. Having transferred ownership of their large farm to their children, Zelda and her husband, Daniel, lead a peaceful existence, tending some dairy cows and a small garden near the house.

Dobra takes a bit of stew warming over a fire lit before the Sabbath. She speaks of what weighs upon her heart: "Back when I had my husband, may he now be in Paradise, my home was a proper home. Sabbath joy made life worth living. Now, my children. . . Heaven forbid I should hold anything against them; they treat me very nicely. But when the Sabbath comes, I don't know what to do with myself. Six days, they sleep late; they practically sleep the day away. And then, on Saturday, devilishly enough, they wake up before dawn and light a fire as if to spite the Sabbath. A knife in my heart! Such things I would wish only on my enemies! What can I do? So I get up and leave the house nice and early, to avoid seeing them sin. But no matter how soon after daybreak I wake up, the fireplace has just been lit and they're drinking maté. Fine things I've lived to see!" Dobra sighs and shakes her head.

The two old women take a little tea, then set off on the road with their ragged Yiddish prayer books under their arms. Dobra and Zelda speak of the good old days as they slowly approach the synagogue that stands right in the middle of the agricultural colony.

Daniel and Zelda work in the garden every morning until the day becomes too hot, and resume every evening as the sun begins to set. Their garden is one of a kind in the colony, for who else still tends a garden with such care? Old Daniel not only makes sure that all sorts of vegetables flourish, but also that the rows of plants be straight and that no grass spring up among them. He stands at one end of the garden and Zelda at the other, each holding the end of a taut string. Daniel closes one eye, cocks his head to the right and to the left, hollering all the while, "A little more this way! A little more that way! Pull it tighter! Loosen it!" Then he adds, angrily: "You old cow!" The road thunders as Zelda stalks furiously into the house. Soon she comes out again and returns to work.

The garden produces an incredible variety, ranging from onions to radishes, from parsley to horseradish for the Passover Seder, as well as other greens the names for which Daniel does not know in Yiddish. "I have it written down somewhere," he answers when asked what he is growing. But his neighbors' cattle are a constant source of trouble. At night they sneak through the wire fence into his garden and wreak havoc, trampling even more than they eat. In the morning, when he sees the damage, Daniel feels as though the cattle had trodden upon his very heart.

A plan slowly comes to him. He sets into the ground a stick as tall as a man, tying another stick onto it breadth-wise so that arms appear to spread. He adorns the figure with some old clothes—a pair of pants, a jacket, a hat—so as to scare off the cattle. "Let 'em think it's me!" But that's not enough. So he places another such figure further away and, unwilling to part with more of his clothes, dresses it in a worn-out housecoat of Zelda's. He adds a head made of straw, which he wraps in one of her old scarves.

That Saturday old Dobra rises early, hastily puts on her best clothes, tucks the women's prayer book under her arm, and sets off to visit her friend, lest she herself see her children desecrating the Sabbath. But what is happening at Zelda's? Astonished, Dobra catches sight of her in the garden, doing something with her arms. "Zelda? I've come to wish you a good Sabbath. But why are you in the garden?" But Zelda answers not, remaining silent as though Dobra could not possibly be addressing the question to her. Now Dobra glimpses, a little further in the distance, old Daniel, gesturing vaguely with his arms. "A good Sabbath, *reb* Daniel. But why are you in the garden, today of all days?" *Reb* Daniel remains stuck in the ground, motionless, not even deigning to turn toward Dobra. This she finds most aggravating: "What are you so haughty about? Now you too are working on the Sabbath. Fine things I've lived to see!" Faced with their utter disregard, Dobra angrily foregoes her weekly visit to their home and sets off to the synagogue alone.

Every Sabbath since then, as soon as day begins to break, Dobra can be seen going by herself along the road toward the synagogue. She is wearing her dark blue cretonne dress with the small white polka dots, on her head is the silk scarf with the large yellow flowers, and the tattered Yiddish women's prayer book is tucked under her arm. Gently but quickly she strides, stopping nowhere, not even throwing a glance towards Daniel and Zelda's home and garden. Silently, she pours out the promptings of her heart to the Master of the Universe: "I thank Thee, dear God, for all these things. May these unrestful Sabbaths that I must suffer serve in Thine eyes as an atonement for my sins. Doubtless I have deserved no better."

—Translated by A. A.

5

In Opposite Directions

A SHORT STORY BY HIRSH BLOSHTEIN

[*Hirsh Bloshtein (b. 1895 Keydan, Lithuania; d. 1978 Czernowitz, Ukraine) was the son of a poor tailor who died when he was twelve. His first publications appeared in the Warsaw Yiddish daily* Moment. *In 1925, he emigrated to Argentina, where he worked in left-wing newspapers, taught in schools for workers, and published stories and poetry. In 1931, Bloshtein was deported from Argentina for his communist activities and settled in the Soviet Union, where he became an established Yiddish writer. He was an active contributor to the Moscow Yiddish monthly* Sovetish

Heymland *starting with its inception in 1961. A volume of his poetry,* Bam Lirishn Kval *("At the Lyrical Spring") was published in Moscow a year before his death.*]

They would run into each other twice a day: early in the morning, going to work; and in the evening, coming back. They would see one another on the same sidewalk, but they were headed in opposite directions—his factory was to the east and her office to the west. They would look at each other for just a moment, then pass by—hurriedly, so as not to punch into work late and lose half a day's pay.

They worked in the same places for about a year, so the fleeting moments of their mutual glances linked up to become hours. The hours spent looking were etched in their memories, and they had grown accustomed to each other. Deep in her being she held a picture of the tall, broad-shouldered, somewhat stooped young man with the black eyes and the thick, curly hair. As for him, he counted among his rare intimate relations the slim, blond girl with the lively gray eyes, which sparkled from under an elegant, pink hat. But neither of them knew the other's name, because they never exchanged a word, going as they did in opposite directions, dogged by their work. So he would quickly disappear to the east, and she to the west.

Occasionally he failed to see her, and he felt something missing then. A moment in his day would be gray and empty, yet that moment was perhaps his favorite time because of the secret pain it caused. Standing at his work on one of those lonely, bland days, he would think from time to time about how she must be sick, or how something bad had happened to her at home, or that she'd been fired from her job. In any case, the fleeting, meaningless moment stayed and caused him pain.

He tended to be a quiet young man, shy and retiring. He marveled at the boldness and impudence of the pals he ran with, who followed girls down the street and showered them with the cleverest, raciest pick-up lines and wisecracks. If he, Chaim, had possessed a mere tenth of their nerve, he could have stopped the slim, pretty girl long ago, and they would already have had a friendship going for who knows how long, since he had already liked her for a while now—a long while.

But he couldn't change the way he was: bashful, lacking in boldness. Only the night knew of his desire. He tossed and turned then in his hard, iron cot, with the blankets pulled over his head, while she gleamed in his dark life with her radiant hair and smiling eyes. She would never know about those nights, when his big, dark, hairy hands turn girlishly soft and white—and he kissed hers. She would never know that he even made up a name for her, the loveliest one he knew: his youngest sister's name, Rosie. That was what he called her, and she answered, with such a light, melodious voice.

She didn't know—and she never would —that he was looking for her. He never missed a lecture or show at a workers' organization, secretly hoping he might run into her. In such a place they were bound to meet someone whom they both knew and who could introduce them to each other. But soon a year had passed since he started seeking her, and she was nowhere to be found. She appeared only in the mad, yearning nights, when young blood glowed and rushed and merged with her eyes, her hair. And afterwards came two moments: one in the morning, one in the evening. They pricked sweetly at a distant, delicate corner of his soul and glimmered to a spark, which then faded.

A few weeks into the second year, on a spring day, two gray moments came: one in the morning and one in the evening. Next day the same thing. And the weeks worked their blunt pull on him. The spring turned gray and sad. The nights hurt with their yearning. His eyes sank ever deeper in his head and became ever bigger.

Chaim did not know where to look for her, and often he had the terrifying thought that she might have a lingering illness—or maybe she was dead?! But he kept going each day to the same sidewalk. He did this even when the downturn in his trade threw him out of work. At dawn he would run around looking for employment—and at the appointed hour, he would go to that sidewalk.

But she was never there.

One day, after a long period of fruitless job-hunting, he got lucky. He found work in a unionized shop at fairly good wages. But he still was not happy. The nights did not cease yearning, or tearfully gleaming in her glow.

Then came a Saturday, the day everyone gets off early and shop workers get their pay. Chaim went to the payroll office to get his envelope from the boss's son, who distributed the wages. And there she was, sitting next to him, as blond and slender as always, beautifully dressed—radiant.

Chaim felt something rip in his spirit, and a prickling, twisted feeling zigzagged through his hands and feet all the way to his heart, then out to the surface of his body in tiny, cold droplets. His feet trembled, and he avoided the eyes of his friends, who must have noticed he had gone pale.

It took him only a couple of moments to take his money, a couple of eternities, long, distraught moments. But in those two moments, Chaim met her eyes, and it seemed to him that she looked at him and turned red. . . It seemed also that she pulled her hand from the boss's son's hand—and on a finger of each one's fine, soft hand was a simple, shiny gold ring.

Chaim hurried from the payroll office and wandered off aimlessly, grieving and distressed as though betrayed. He walked with broad but shaky steps. A long chain fashioned from a year's worth of moments, two every day, was covered with deadly rust, cutting sharp and deep in his delicate soul—and it hurt him.

He decided he would never again go to that sidewalk where they once passed each other every day, yet from the first were headed in opposite directions. It also was clear that he would never again work in that shop, and he searched for some excuse to give his friends about why he quit his job.

He stopped automatically at a large newsstand and bought a whole pile of papers, new and outdated—then quickly went home, where he locked himself into his dark little room and with leafed through the pages with feverish fingers, looking for engagement and wedding announcements. His crazed heart yearned to know her name, the name of his first lover, whose voice he had never heard and would never hear.

Thus did fragile feeling entangle for a year on a piece of sidewalk in the big, rich-versus-poor, poor-versus-rich city. Two people had been headed in opposite directions, and one trod on the other's jumbled heart—wounding it, making it bleed.

—Translated by Debbie Nathan

6

Meager Results: Two Decades of Jewish Agricultural Settlement in Argentina

A REPORTAGE BY LEON CHASANOVITCH

[*Leon Chasanovitch (b. 1882 Shirvint, Lithuania; d. 1925, Valkhov, Ukraine) was a name assumed by Kasriel Shub in his work as a writer and Labor Zionist leader. Arrested in 1906, Chasanovitch escaped deportation deep into Russia by fleeing the country. Ultimately, he lived in such diverse locales as Cracow, Vienna, Toronto, New York, the Hague, Stockholm, Berlin. Sent by the Labor Zionists to Argentina in 1909, he called for organized resistance by the Jewish settlers there against the corrupt, aristocratic officials of the Jewish Colonization Association, who had him deported as an anarchist. Chasanovitch spent the last years of his life working to improve the lot of the Jewish farmers of Carpatho-Russia.*]

Twenty years ago [*in 1888*] glad tidings traveled, with the speed of the wind, throughout Eastern European and especially Russian Jewry. As each Jew told his fellow of the good news, his heart quivered with joy; desperate masses became drunk with hope. On every street corner, in spacious bourgeois homes and dark cellar rooms, in great

cities and in far-flung hamlets only one subject was discussed: the
Jews had a new redeemer, who would deliver them from poverty,
decrepitude, and oppression. Long centuries of wretchedness and
weeping were to end. The news arrived like a bolt of lightning into
the deepest dark of night, illuminating the lives of those who had
ceased to believe in themselves and in the world.

It was the right moment to enact a fundamental change in the
situation of the Jews, whose hardships had grown unbearable. In
Russia they faced economic destruction and had no legal protections.
Their livelihoods were shaken to the core. The pauperized Jew became
a widespread social type. Unemployment was commonplace. The
Jewish *luftmentsh* came into being. Government-sponsored anti-
Semitism, in the form of exceptional decrees, threatened to drown
the Jewish masses in a sea of misery.

In Argentina, instead of exceptional decrees of a despotic empire
and the arbitrariness of its police, there were the legal protections
afforded by a liberal republic. Instead of poverty, there was prosperity;
instead of pursuing small-time brokerage and other precarious
occupations, Jews would secure useful and honorable work in farming.
Instead of inhabiting dirty alleys, dark cellars, and damp garrets,
they would live outdoors, in the air and sunshine. They would no
longer be subject to hatred and scorn, but would enjoy sympathy
and respect. Such was the great ideal that loomed before the Jewish
people, drawing their ardent enthusiasm, infusing new strength into
the weakened, captivating the minds and souls of those who had
thrown down their arms in despair.

Everyone knows the identity of the man who revealed that ideal to
the Jewish masses. It was the gentle Baron de Hirsch, who devised a
great Jewish dream and planned to fulfill it by bestowing a kingly gift
on his people. Yea, the Baron de Hirsch wanted to realize a dream that
went beyond all pragmatic considerations. His sole intent was to rescue
his people—a people with whom he had little direct acquaintance.

The dual nature of the Jewish character showed itself in him with
all its contradictions. The moneyed Jew, the railroad speculator, who
had amassed millions with little concern for the means employed,

became a great philanthropist. The lord who oversaw a vast financial empire with utmost rationality, considering every factor, weighing every obstacle, suddenly lost all sense of measure in striving to help his coreligionists. In order to save an entire people, he came up with fantastic schemes that anyone would declare to be utter madness, if millions of pounds sterling had not stood behind them. He sought to devise a magic formula that would revolutionize the life of an entire people and restore in two decades what two millennia had destroyed. The messianic impulse, which always hovered in the Jewish collective consciousness and more than once brought forth daring mystics who tried to bring the heavens down to earth, had bored its way into the heart of a Jewish millionaire, an educated European, who strove to bring redemption in the form of a resettlement program grander than the world had ever known.

Hirsch planned to relocate to the Argentine republic no fewer than three-and-a-quarter million Russian Jews over the course of a quarter-century. Twenty-five thousand were to be sent in the first year, and the number settled would increase each year thereafter. The Englishman Arnold White went so far as to propose that fanciful plan to the Russian government, in negotiations he held with them as Hirsch's representative. . . .

Hirsch's aim was no less than to solve the Jewish problem. If his project had been implemented, that problem would have disappeared from the czarist empire, where the overwhelming majority of our people lived. In the first quarter-century of the plan, half the Jews would have left, so that those remaining would not exceed the number Russia could digest. If necessary, still more could emigrate.

But that was not all. Argentina, having become home to a large, flourishing, powerful Jewish peasantry, would turn into a center of Jewish influence and might. In one or several provinces, Jews would constitute a majority and be accorded a broad measure of autonomy. Argentina would become a point of attraction for Jews of the entire world, a place of political and economic ascent for the Jewish people. All needy and persecuted Jews would take refuge there. Because a single Latin American republic would have siphoned off the poor

Jews of Eastern Europe, those left behind would feel less pressure to compete furiously with one other. Simultaneously, Jewish prestige throughout the world would be enhanced. The entire web of anti-Semitic slurs about Jewish exploitation and unwillingness to work would be belied by the eloquent Argentinean Jewish example. The whole world would see what Jews could attain when they are free, what a godsend they would be for a land that allowed development of their healthy instincts. In other words, settling Jews in Argentina would benefit not only those immigrating there, but also those who remained in the Old World, by improving their status and ultimately vouchsafing them peace and tranquility.

The Baron de Hirsch was so convinced of the total success of his undertaking that he feared he might lack human raw material if he recruited settlers only among the significant number of Jews ready to emigrate. So he arranged with the Russian government to allow his Jewish Colonization Association to work within the czarist empire itself, easing constraints on departing Jews. The Russian government, seeing Hirsch's plan as a simple way to get rid of the unpleasant Jewish problem, granted exceptional privileges to whoever left under the aegis of the Jewish Colonization Association. He received for free the *vikhodnoye svidyetyelstvo*, the certificate stipulating that its bearer was "leaving Russia forever" and absolving him from all legal obligations, such as military service or the fines imposed on relatives of those not registering for conscription.

How magnificently Hirsch imagined this all. . . .

No less than Hirsch himself, the people believed in his mission. In their souls, something occurred reminiscent of the messianic fervor aroused by Shabbetai Tsvi, with all the attendant mystical and religious trappings. It had been hundreds of years since the Jewish public had been so enthused, so shaken, so captivated as it was by the Argentinean adventure. Not only the masses were enthralled, but the Jewish intelligentsia as well. Blood went coursing through the benumbed body of the Jewish people, its pulse beat loudly, a fiery spirit enlivened all its limbs. Entire Jewish neighborhoods became obsessed with Hirsch's plans, and the Jewish press ran headlines and reports about the South

American republic. News, rumors, and legends about Argentina circulated throughout the Jewish ghettoes. A far-off land on the other side of the Atlantic, beyond the equator, whose name the masses had previously never heard, was spoken of by one and all. Suddenly they seemed not only knowledgeable about Argentina, but also personally acquainted with it. Fantasy came in handy, filling in gaps in the information available.

Indeed, the people believed in their redeemer, the Baron de Hirsch. With a wave of his hand, he infused thousands—nay, hundreds of thousands—with readiness to cut all ties to their old country, give up their businesses, sell for next to nothing everything they could not carry with them, and set off to the end of the world. Some left even before he instructed them to. Fearful lest they be overlooked in the tumult of the new exodus from Egypt, they took their wandering sticks in hand and arrived unsummoned to Hirsch's offices abroad, which were besieged by thousands and thousands of newfound Argentinean "patriots." Argentina fever had gripped the masses and drove them on. Hirsch's agents had to issue repeated warnings against premature departures. The farmlands had to be "prepared," they claimed, in order to calm crazed emigrants ready to jump the gun and bring about some catastrophe. But as often before, the prophet was caught unawares by the force of his own prophecy. His disciples were ready to follow him anywhere, but would not listen when he pled with them to stay put. He was forced to send them to Argentina even before the most basic arrangements could be made for their arrival.

The Baron de Hirsch sacrificed a large part of his fortune trying to implement his settlement project. In order to ensure the existence of the enterprise beyond his death, he established the Jewish Colonization Association as an English joint-stock company in 1891. He endowed its founding with a capital of two million pounds sterling, or fifty million francs, which he later increased to ten million pounds, or two hundred fifty million francs. Shares of its stock were distributed to the Alliance Israélite Universelle, the Anglo-Jewish Association, and the Berlin, Frankfurt, and Brussels Jewish communities.

These various organizations—the depositories of Hirsch's great bequest to the Jewish people—choose the board of directors who plan the Jewish Colonization Association's aims and activities, ratify or reject the administration's agenda, hire and fire the top administrators. It is the ultimate court of appeals for all matters pertaining to the association. Or that is the way things are supposed to work. In actuality, the board of directors hardly exercises its rights, except for holding a short annual plenary meeting, purely formal in nature. They entrust a board of paid administrators with full power, which the latter use and abuse to their hearts' content.

The Jewish Colonization Association, founded principally to settle Jews on Argentinean farmland, still has that aim as its priority, though it has also dispersed its resources on fruitless projects entirely foreign to the baron's original intent. In a few years from now, to celebrate the twenty-fifth anniversary of its founding, the association ought to have brought three-and-a-quarter million Jews to Argentinean agricultural colonies, creating a new land of Israel. We may therefore ask how successful that Jewish Colonization Association has been in fulfilling founder's will.

I am not about to demand from them a reckoning of all the three-and-a-quarter million Jews they were supposed to settle in Argentina. It is not the association's fault that Hirsch entertained such naïve and fanciful hopes, exaggerated the means at his disposal, and underestimated the obstacles his plan would encounter. Relocating populations is a difficult and tricky endeavor for any people, and all the more so for the Jews. Even a strong and wealthy nation, with a well-oiled state apparatus, a disciplined, educated corps of civil servants, and a long-standing tradition of farming, could only through careful, slow and gradual efforts settle new frontiers. So we shall not hold the Jewish Colonization Association accountable for three million of the three-and-a-quarter million Jews it was supposed to relocate. We shall limit ourselves to asking about the remaining quarter of a million, or even some fewer. But we have a right to demand some significant accomplishment from an association that has had at its disposal such colossal means and a population so eager to be resettled. So what are the results?. . .

The Jewish Association Colonization's last annual report, which appeared in 1908, presents the following population breakdown for its seven settlements in Argentina:

Moisesville. . . . . 3,810 inhabitants
Mauricio. 2,314
Clara. 4,538
San Antonio. 943
Luisville. 2,999
Baron de Hirsch. 892
Santa Isabel. 275
Total. 15,771

We see from this that all the agricultural colonies in 1908 were home to fewer than sixteen thousand souls, a number inferior to the Jewish population of one Russian provincial town or in a single street of Vilna.

—Translated by A. A.

7
Bread and Honor

A REPORTAGE BY LEON CHASANOVITCH

[*Writing in 1924, the author reflects upon his struggle with the Jewish Colonization Association, established by the philanthropist Baron de Hirsch to oversee Jewish agricultural settlement in Argentina. The organization's officials were often domineering and sometimes corrupt.*]

The Yiddish press is not at the level it should be. Our reporters and editorialists have become infected with the cynicism and lack of seriousness typical of newsmen of other nations. The results? Jewish society has remained backward. Ignorance regarding the gravest problems facing us today runs rampant. Institutions that have outlived their usefulness and grown rotten to the core remain in operation. . . .

The Yiddish press must fulfill its mission in Jewish communities throughout the world, and the role it has to play in Argentina is of particular importance. During my visit, I saw the scorn provoked by the image of Jewry as decadent. In Argentina, Jews were simply identified as part of the underworld. In no other country is it so justified to feel shame at being a Jew.

For that reason, when a group of upstanding citizens asked me to suggest a name for the newspaper they wished me to edit, I answered, "Bread and Honor." They greeted the name with enthusiasm. It became a battle cry against all those elements of the community who had darkened the lives and ruined the reputation of Argentinean Jewry. . . .

Certain officials of the Jewish Colonization Association had been so "kind" as to finance room and board for me on a battleship in the Buenos Aires harbor, and incidents I experienced there were indicative of the terrible association of ideas elicited by the word "Jew" among non-Jews in Argentina.

I had been so fortunate as to earn the trust of the ship's captain. Several hours a day he would converse with me about all imaginable topics: German militarism, Argentinean nationalism, the role of Jesuits in society, the Jewish question. During one of our chats, I placed my hand in my vest pocket and pulled out a simple watch on an ordinary brass chain, a gift from a friend in New York. The captain exclaimed, "This is the first time I see a Jew without a golden watch."

"Were you to visit us in Vilna or Warsaw," I answered him, "you'd see thousands of Jews without golden watches."

"Is this possible?" he exclaimed in surprise.

Later, the moral support of the Jewish Colonization Association had arranged a trip for me back to Warsaw on a Dutch steamer, at the expense of the Argentinean National Treasury. A Russian socialist revolutionary, traveling back to Europe in similar conditions, asked me angrily, "By what right do the Jews in Argentina call themselves *rusos*, thereby sullying the good name of the Russians?"

Since I was in a sarcastic mood, I answered, "In revenge for the

Kishinev pogrom."

"Really. . . I'd never have expected such chauvinism from a Labor
Zionist!" my naïve fellow traveler exclaimed hysterically.

Extraordinary efforts were required to cleanse the reputation of
Jews in Argentina and South America generally. A great battle was waged
to remove impure elements as far as possible from the rest of the Jewish
population. When the history of that battle is written, it will provide
one of the strangest chapters in the chronicles of the Jews.

The recently-implanted Jewish community of Argentina must often
expend considerable energy to establish institutions that in other lands
are taken for granted. In 1909, while I was visiting the Baron de Hirsch
colony, I received a telegram from a *Sociedad Israelita* of which I had
never heard, in a place—Coronel Suárez—equally unbeknownst to
me. They wished to invite me to give a talk. My friends at the Baron de
Hirsch colony, standing around me, dismissed the telegram with a wave
of the hand, and sought to dissuade me from going to such an
insignificant Jewish settlement. I answered that if people I did not know
in the slightest called out to me, they must be in dire need of me. I felt
bound to travel to them, no matter how few they were.

It was a long, difficult trip, mostly on narrow road, across the burning
hot pampa. I arrived Friday night, just before the lighting of Sabbath
candles. A group was waiting at the station, including an honorable
Jew with a long beard, the kosher-meat slaughterer of the village.
Forcefully, he grabbed my suitcase from my hand, lest I carry it.

"My dear fellow Jews," I asked, "what do you desire of me?"

"A cemetery."

"What?!"

"You heard right, a cemetery. That is what our community needs
most of all!"

"How can I get you a cemetery? I would never do anything to
bury another Jew. . ."

"But we are commanded to ensure proper burials for our
coreligionists!"

On the way from the train station to my host's home, they
recounted the tragedy that had stricken their families, who numbered

fifty if I recall correctly. They had settled in that out-of-the-way village after the pogroms of 1905 and 1906. Unable to purchase land for a cemetery, they rented an area for a few years' time. When the lease was up, they unearthed the remains of their loved ones and sought out a new place of rest, only to disturb their graves again to transfer them to a new home. . . What those community activists desired of me was a lecture on the importance of a cemetery, a lecture that would stir the inhabitants of that small village to contribute the needed funds.

I sympathized with the aching souls in Coronel Suárez, but I had to explain that a lecture on such a topic would simply not issue forth from my mouth. After lengthy negotiations, my hosts accepted my proposal: I would give a talk on "The Tasks Facing Argentinean Jewry," after which the local leaders would make an appeal for funds for a cemetery.

On Saturday night, the entire Jewish settlement—men, women, and children—gathered into a well-lit hall. After my lecture, the head of the *Sociedad Israelita* made a short speech on the cemetery question, and funds were raised there and then. The gratitude of the local activists went beyond words.

There is, however, another organization, administering the Jewish people's greatest fund, supplied by the gentle Baron de Hirsch to make his dream come true. If *that* organization had only realized his dream, the reputation of Argentinean Jewry would perhaps be greater than that of any other Jewish community in the world. Herzl writes in his journal of a conversation with the visionary Baron de Hirsch, who planned to charter a magnificent English ship to transport one hundred journalists with him to visit the Argentinean Jewish agricultural colonies and tell the world what Jews can accomplish when given freedom.

No such ship ever set sail, and not only because those two unique men could not communicate with each other, or because Baron de Hirsch died prematurely. Rather, it is because the Jewish Colonization Association has no reason to be proud of its Argentinean colonies. It has little to show the world in exchange for the colossal sums of money invested. I am firmly convinced that a thousand times more would have been accomplished, if—instead of being used to finance a senseless feudal philanthropic system, the likes of which has never been seen in the history of migratory ventures—Baron de Hirsch's millions had been invested according to sound capitalistic principles, but without exploitative aims. In that case, Baron de Hirsch's grandiose plan of colonization would have resulted in one of the greatest feats in Jewish history.

—Translated by A. A.

8

The Builders
of a Jewish Future

A REPORTAGE BY PERETZ HIRSCHBEIN

[*Peretz Hirschbein (b. 1880 Kleshtshel, Poland; d. 1948 Los Angeles) was a miller's son and a yeshiva student who began writing in Hebrew and Yiddish at the age of eighteen. A novelist and playwright, he is best-known for his Yiddish pastoral drama* Grine felder *("Green Fields"), which opened at the Irving Place Theatre in New York on May 30, 1919. It was later made into a popular film that is often projected at Yiddish cinema festivals today. Hirschbein's Argentina trip of 1914 resulted in the first of the many travelogs he ultimately published. He settled in New York in 1930. In this piece Hirschbein describes how one early Jewish agricultural settlement in Argentina was brought under the aegis of the Baron de Hirsch's Jewish Colonization Association.*]

With bent backs, gray beards, faces wrinkled and tanned, and a proud, confident gaze, they stride resolutely over their fields. Such are the first Jews from Russia, who have come to Argentina to seek their fortune.

It was not the Baron de Hirsch's endowment that laid the cornerstone of Jewish agricultural settlement in Argentina. Rather, credit must be given to the Russian government, whose terrible decrees of the 1880s "encouraged" the Jews to pull up stakes and move to the wild lands of the Southern Cone. They were accompanied by their hopes for a better tomorrow and by the lashes of their oppressors' whips. Coolly and calmly the first settlers recount their bitter days of wandering, an experience that was new for them, but which the Jewish people had known for millennia.

"In 1887," one of them recalls, "the Russian government started carrying out its decree against the Jews in Congress Poland, in the district of Podolia. Jews were no longer allowed to reside in villages within fifty versts of the border. In that district, in a small village named Staraya Huta, near Smotritsh, lived two Jews, Pinhas Glazman and Joseph Ludmer, who faced exile. In a nearby village called Kernetshov, a Jew named Leizer Koifman, the lessee of an estate, was also required to leave. These three men, good friends, deliberated together and decided one of them should go off to seek land they could settle. Ludmer's brother-in-law in North America suggested Argentina as a possible destination. He recounted how he had tried with several others to live as farmers near Minneapolis, where they were badly treated by the local authorities.

"So the three villagers pooled their funds and sent Koifman off to meet with the Alliance Israélite Universelle in Paris. He spent eight months there. The Chief Rabbi of Paris, Zadoc Kahn, along with a fellow named Lubetski, negotiated on his behalf with the Alliance. It was decided that he should travel home and gather some one hundred families, who would set out to Argentina to become farmers.

"Once home, Koifman and his two friends publicized the project and assembled some eighty-eight families. On June 15, 1889, we started out on our journey. Upon our arrival in Berlin, an immigrant aid society informed us that Argentina was not letting any Jews in, and therefore we could purchase tickets only on vessels bound for North America. Left hanging in mid-air, we decided, after much discussion, to send emissaries once again to Paris. Five men—Isaac Rechter, Peretz Feigenbaum, Zalman Aleksnitser, Leizer Koifman, and an agent of the Alliance Israélite Universelle—went to the French capital and told Chief Rabbi Zadoc Kahn what had transpired.

"Precisely at that time, the Argentinean government had established in Paris an agency charged with encouraging immigration to its shores. The Jewish emissaries decided to request the Argentinean consul to let Y. B. Frank, an employee of the immigration bureau, to arrange the sale of twenty-five acres of land for each family. Consequently, his government would recognize us as honest farmers, worthy of being allowed to immigrate. They put down four hundred francs for each plot of land. This deal was sealed on July 5, 1888. The contract was sent to Herr Sigismund Simmel in Berlin, who was charged with sending our group to Argentina.

"But upon arrival in Buenos Aires, we were not let in, because it was presumed we were white-slave traders. When the captain showed receipts for the land purchase, we were permitted to go ashore, but were informed that the terrain bought in Paris had been settled long before. The money would be returned, but we would be given no land. Later, we learned that the agricultural minister, convinced Jews could only deal in women's flesh, deemed it dangerous to let us establish a colony and preferred scattering us around the country.

"Adrift once again, the new arrivals started to look for Jews in Buenos Aires. Finally, we came across three gold merchants: two Germans, Lambert and Hildesheimer (first name Moritz); and a Rumanian named Hochenstein. These three upright individuals sought out an important landowner, Pedro Palacios, who suggested a few people go inspect the property for sale. They traveled for an hour and twenty minutes by rail on the line that just then was still being built between Buenos Aires and Tucumán.

"When our emissaries caught sight of the vast terrain going for just twenty-five pesos an acre, they were overjoyed. Little did they know that the usual rate was two to three pesos an acre! On August 28, 1889, they concluded a contract with *señor* Palacios, who sent us off to the train station that bore his name. He was supposed to provide food. No houses had yet been built. For six full weeks we settlers were kept in a large tin granary near the train station, still partially under construction. Once a month, each immigrant received a sack of rotten maize and another of worm-infested flour, until we were settled on the land.

"During that period over one hundred children died. Half the families still ived in the granary; the other half had been taken to the next station, Monigotes, which in turn became a burial ground for Jews perishing from hunger and various illnesses. We all might have starved, if not for the engineers who were developing the railroad. Having learned hungry people were there, they threw small rolls from the windows of the train every time they rode by. Other passengers would help us out as well, throwing crackers. Young and old would rush on top of each other to grab the food cast from the train windows.

"When we were finally brought to our land, we started building houses of earthen bricks, covered with straw. But terrible rains that year flooded our little homes. When we needed wood, we had to go some thousand yards away where there were some small trees. But the area was so overgrown with high grasses that we would get lost and wander for days. No settlement was nearby. In order to avoid starving, we would feed on the raw flesh of partridges we caught in the grasses.

"So things went for a year's time. Palacios, the landowner, started to outfit us, supplying one Jew with a pair of oxen, a second with a yoke, and the third with straps to harness the animals. What could we do? The fields were not fenced in, and the unrestrained oxen ran off—as did some of the people!

"At that time, thirty-five families gathered together in our synagogue built of earthen bricks. We swore to God not to abandon our third cemetery, but instead to bring here our loved ones buried in Palacios and Monigotes. We would found a colony and ease the way here for our brethren back in Russia.

"Leizer Koifman had abandoned us. People wanted to kill him for dragging us so far and causing such misery. He later showed up, but he couldn't make a go of it here. Some children of the remaining thirty-five families began to drift among the Christian colonists scattered around there. They would wander for ten days or two weeks until they found a settlement, where they would earn some bread. Fathers and older sons worked building the railroad, and younger children were employed taking pigs or sheep out to pasture. At that time, a sack of first-class flour cost twenty-eight pesos, and flour mixed into pig feed cost six to seven pesos a sack. Needless to say, we ate flour of the second kind. We would wash out the empty first-class flour sacks and make garments for the Sabbath; everyday clothes were sewn from sacks of second-class flour. There was no religious instruction, except for what fathers would teach their children on the Sabbath.

"The situation grew worse and worse in the next few years, until the first settlers got together and wrote letters crying out for help to Jewish newspapers as well as to the Alliance Israélite Universelle in Paris. . . .

"In 1893, Dr. Loewenthal suddenly arrived from Berlin with two other men. They took lodging from a merchant who had built a small house. Without letting on who they were, they explored the area for a couple of days. Dr. Loewenthal then revealed he had come on behalf of the Jewish Colonization Association. He returned to Europe for four months. Upon his arrival back among us, he said the terrain we had chosen was no good; twenty-five pesos per acre was too expensive; at that price, we would never finish paying off what we owed to the present landowner; Carlos Casares' land, to the south of Buenos Aires, was better and more centrally-located. . . But we called an assembly, where we decided to stand by our oath not to leave.

"Dr. Loewenthal then suggested settling nearby, at the Sunchales station. Those who volunteered to go there would be given food, a small plot of land, and agricultural training. His intention was to lure people away, and in some cases it worked. But those who remained won out.

"In the end, Dr. Loewenthal bought the land from Palacios, and he even brought back the privileged 'raisin Jews' from the Sunchales station. (We called them 'raisin Jews,' because the only delicacy we could afford in those days was a plate of raisins and rice.) And that is how we became foster-children to the Baron de Hirsch."

—Translated by A. A.

9

Homesick in Buenos Aires

A REPORTAGE BY HERSH DAVID NOMBERG

[*Hersh David Nomberg (b. 1876 Amshinov, Poland; d. 1927 Warsaw) was a Yiddish and Hebrew essayist, journalist and short-story writer, and a member of the Yiddish literary classicist Y. L. Peretz' circle. In 1916, Nomberg helped found the Folkspartey, which worked for Jewish autonomous rights in Poland, and he served as a member of the Polish Sejm (Parliament) in 1919–20.*]

Until the Great War, Jews in Buenos Aires were convinced that their stay there would be temporary. Deep in their hearts, all harbored a secret hope: that the wheel of fortune would eventually turn, and they could go back to their homelands. In the meantime, they lived, they married, and even their children married. Their business grew and they got rich, or they toiled in a *taller*—a workshop—and died of tuberculosis. Their hair turned gray while they waited, yearning.

Their homesickness was vague, as befitted those whom chance had flung so far afield, to a strange sky and foreign stars. The sky might be deep blue in Argentina, and the evening stars might glitter brightly, yet their hearts were haunted. They found it hard to accept that things were as they were and that Argentina was where they would remain; that the brief years fate had doled out to them would be spent here.

After all, a kind of tidal wave had cast them here. Seldom was Argentina the destination they as individuals would have chosen. Some had come in groups to the first agricultural colonies founded by the Baron de Hirsch. Others fled pogroms. Some could not arrange steamship tickets to New York, or a ship company agent had tricked them. Almost everybody had an odyssey to recount.

All of them were young, fresh, green. It was possible to discern immigrants of various periods: the Baron de Hirsch colonists, who arrived the end of the 1880s; those who came as a result of the Russian revolution and pogroms of 1905; and, of course, the latest ones, from before the Great War. They were like geological strata. Instead of discovering a unified mass, you saw layer upon layer, with little blending. The pimps and prostitutes were on the lowest level. No one knew when and how they had found their way here.

The Polish Jews suffered the most acutely from homesickness. Being a Polish Jew in Argentina is something of a step down. Here, his Lithuanian and even Bessarabian coreligionists turn up their noses at him. Doubtless this is because many of the white-slave traders come from Poland, and the innocent suffer for the faults of the guilty. But part of the problem is that the Lithuanian Jew constantly brags about his learning, whereas the Polish Jew is considered something of a hedonist. He enjoys gathering all his friends and family together for roast goose and wine. He likes to dance a *sher* at weddings, to sing songs, to thump others on the back. The Lithuanian Jew, confronted with such Polish frivolity, feels his face grow tighter and tighter with anger. His serious, dignified character cannot tolerate it: "A Polish Jew!" he roars.

What is worse, the Polish Jew has a weakness for his homeland. No one feels more attached than he does to the woods and creeks of the landscape he grew up with.

A Polish Jew seeks me out. He is from Volomin, a little nothing of a *shtetl* near Warsaw. He has been in this country for twenty years, "But please," he asks, "tell me, as God is your witness, is that tiny patch of forest"—the whole thing amounted to some hundred birch trees right by the railroad tracks—"is that little forest is still there?" It was not far from where he used to live.

"The little forest?" I told him the Germans chopped it down during the occupation.

"A pox on them!" he cursed. He had imagined the Germans were fine people, incapable of doing such a thing.

Another Jew here used to own a restaurant in Warsaw. He has lived for fifteen years in Argentina and has not exactly lost money here. Nonetheless, he offers me proof that this is a God-forsaken land: "Back home, we have the Vistula. Now that's really something to see. Back home, when you cook two pounds of fish, a pleasing aroma wafts through in the neighborhood. Here, you can cook forty pounds of fish and no one smells a thing! The fruits have no scent, and the fish has no flavor. Back home—remember?—a piece of roasted veal would melt in your mouth."

Meanwhile, he has aged, and his senses of smell and taste have dulled. He has been living in Argentina "just for the time being," and has no idea that he has gotten old.

But then came the war. The world was torn in pieces, and the old country was turned upside down. Hope of returning vanished. In each Jew's heart, an inner voice proclaimed the words of the prophet: "They shall build houses and plant vineyards." And so they put down roots.

Buenos Aires offers working people much in the way of cultural life. It is still not completely established, but it holds out promise. There are two daily Yiddish newspapers, some weeklies, a Yiddish theater, libraries, trade unions, social clubs, and mutual-aid societies, as well as other religious, secular, and leftist organizations.

The Jewish masses in Argentina are more advanced than the first immigrants to North America were. The first immigrants to New York and Chicago had not left the old country with a generation of experience as organized workers or as readers of Yiddish literature and the Yiddish press. Immigrants to Argentina came from later generations. They already had gotten some education, belonged to political organizations, and had memberships in libraries.

Within one generation, the Jewish masses here have developed culturally, as is apparent from the kind of lives they lead and the tastes they have acquired. Still, poverty is more severe in Buenos Aires than in New York. Workers' associations and cultural groups lack funding and dynamism. Here you do not find a sense of initiative similar to what the Anglo-Saxon race implanted in North America and instilled into immigrants from other nations.

Here, people drink coffee instead of whiskey. Rather than playing baseball, they buy lottery tickets, bet on horses, and lose fortunes. Gambling has assumed disastrous proportions, wiping out families' resources. The pennies that in other countries are deposited in savings banks are spent here on lottery tickets. Almost every day there is a drawing, and hundreds of thousands wait to hit the *grande*—the jackpot. Men go hungry, let their wives and children starve, but continue betting. Gambling fever here is a curse, worse than weakness for the bottle.

Buenos Aires was built by southern Europeans, whose home is the *plaza*—the town square—and whose roof is made of stars. Life is lived on streets and in cafés. One comes home only at night, or to escape downpours, when the tropical sky spills out like an overturned tub. Family life suffers intensely, because a man here seldom maintains a proper household. Jews, of course, must sense this lack more than others do.

The Spaniards brought their architectural style with them. From the entrance of a usually one-story house you proceed into a rectangular area paved with stones and open to the sky. This is the patio, where everyone gathers. People spend the whole day here because their rooms are small, cramped, usually windowless, and divided from each other by nothing but thin walls. The patio is shared by six or seven families whose doors open onto it. Everyone can be seen by everyone else. All get to smell whatever anyone cooks. Here people woo, fight, raise children—in open view.

This is not our sort of home, where one is enveloped in domestic warmth. So the husbands spend time on the streets, running off to drink coffee or attend some gathering. Meanwhile, the women are kept under lock and key at home, because the custom of the land allows them little freedom. A young woman, not to mention a girl, may not venture into the street. Strolling with a young man would compromise her reputation. And a woman would never show her face in a café.

Yet the sky here is deep blue. The winds blow warm. The breezes tantalize you. Children mature early. Jewish daughters grow lushly beautiful, bronzed by the sun, and their gazes are hot with passion. You see dark, graceful maidens in bloom. Alas, their glowing eyes are surrounded by black circles, the result of the long hours they toil.

Night falls; the breeze grows cooler. Virginal faces yearn, sadly looking out from doors and windows. You might think you've been transported to the Orient, to Turkey or Persia.

A young man approaches and lolls motionless on the narrow steps, while a girl stands in the hallway. Or perhaps he is in front of the window, and she is behind its iron bars. This is how they chat, long and intimately.

—Translated by Debbie Nathan

10

The Courtyard Without Windows

EXCERPT FROM A NOVEL BY MIMI PINZÓN

[*Mimi Pinzón—cf. Mimi Pinson, a Parisian seamstress in French Romantic Alfred de Musset's story by the same name— was the pseudonym chosen by Adela Weinstein-Shliapochnik (b. 1910 Tserkov, Ukraine; d. 1975 Buenos Aires). She arrived in the Argentinean capital at the age of four. The editors of the local Yiddish paper* Di Prese, *who published her first stories in 1926, originally refused to believe that an adolescent raised in a Spanish-speaking environment could master Yiddish style so well. Pinzón's translations into Yiddish include works by the great Argentinean writer Jorge Luis Borges, the Argentinean poet Alfonsina Storni and the Uruguayan novelist Horacio Quiroga; she also translated Soviet Yiddish writers into Spanish. The following is taken from a largely autobiographical novel published in 1965.*]

"The wall"—that is how everyone living on the tenement courtyard referred to the large apartment building.

That building was a universe unto itself, with its own laws, its own customs, its own life. It remained aloof from the other houses and courtyards and the street. And the street, in turn, had no dealings with it. Those on the street did not step foot into the homes of those who lived beyond the wall.

The wall was so remote and foreign to the people living on the courtyard that it became for them something nearly legendary, inexistent. Or if it existed, it did so as something far, far beyond them, both in terms of the space they inhabited and their grasp of the world. Irritated mothers would threaten children who refused to go to sleep: "Just wait. They'll come and get you from beyond the wall, throw you into a sack, carry you up to the top floor, and do to you there who knows what!" The women who would fight over a place at the courtyard sink or over a bit of clothesline to hang their laundry on would take aim at a pushy neighbor or a new tenant with these venomous words: "If *Madame* finds it cramped here, why doesn't she tell her husband to rent an apartment beyond the wall?"

Ethel was aware of how people beyond the wall lived. Each family had their own apartment, with two, three, or even more rooms: separate rooms to eat in and to sleep in. She knew that each family had their own kitchen, with four brick walls, a ceiling, a sink, and a stove with burners. She knew that each family had their own bathroom, with a bathtub and white limestone walls. Ethel knew all of these things, in the way one knows there is someone who rules the land. No one has ever seen him, no one has ever spoken to him, but one is sure he exists.

She had found out about the life of the people beyond the wall from the same source whence she had gradually learned of so many new and wondrous things: from her teacher at school. The school, a tall, gloomy, clumsy building was almost a "wall" unto itself. Her father took her there one morning. Her hair was freshly washed, her clothes were starched, and she was scared to death. There he abandoned her, her heart pounding and her knees rattling, amidst the frightful noise of hundreds of screaming, laughing and crying children.

The teacher with her white starched dress, smoothly combed hair, and tightly-drawn mouth, would grimace a little whenever she addressed Ethel, as though pronouncing Ethel's name brought a sour, sickening taste to her thin, small mouth. Ethel would repeat every day—to the point of dizziness and fatigue—what the teacher instructed her regarding the nation's grandeur, prosperity and vigor;

the deeds of its *próceres*, its heroes. From those lessons it emerged that there was no better, wealthier, more heroic or beautiful land on the face of the earth, and no people more fortunate, intelligent or courageous than those born there.

Ethel also learned from the teacher how people lived in the most diverse cities and countries in the world. There were Chinese who wore long braids, ate rice with a kind of sticks, and dined on bird's-nest soup; there were savages who consumed even human flesh; and no more than two hundred years ago people were so uncivilized that they ate with their fingers instead of forks. It was only two hundred years since something so important as the fork had been invented: this was how the teacher talked, this was the kind of thing she recounted.

There was only one way of life Ethel never heard the teacher mention: the way people ate, spoke, slept and fought in her courtyard; the way the Galician Spaniards, the Italians and the Jews in their various tongues would yell, sing, quarrel and reconcile; curse their enemies; lull their children to sleep; joke with one another and cry over their misfortunes together; beat their wives and mourn their dead mothers. It was as though such people did not exist for the teacher. Or if they existed, they were even more foreign and remote than the foreign and remote Chinese.

Ethel learned from the same teacher that one must always eat with a fork and knife; that one must never, ever, bring the knife to one's mouth; that one must brush one's teeth every day, before going to bed; that it was healthier to sleep one to a room, or at the most two to a room. The windows should be kept open at night, to let fresh air in.

Ethel, sitting in the large classroom with its windows, would almost doze off to the sound of the teacher's drawn-out, measured voice that seem to suck in the luminescence of the early-winter day. Ethel wondered: "How could I explain such things to the people living on our courtyard, who are still so uncivilized that they sleep six or eight to a room, with several children on some makeshift bedding at the foot of their parents' bed—or simply on the floor?"

At that moment, Ethel felt deeply wounded. It seemed to her

that as the teacher spoke, she looked directly toward the particular corner of the room where Ethel sat. The teacher stared at Ethel, because she knew—how could a teacher fail to know?—that Ethel lived with others like herself: savage, uncivilized people, who used forks and knives improperly and toothbrushes not at all, and who did not sleep one to a room near an open window.

So despondent was Ethel that during the break she felt the need to pour her heart out to someone. She shuffled toward a dark-skinned girl with curly, thick black hair and a smiling mouth full of slender teeth. Ethel hesitated because the other girl's smock was not high-collared; it was more of an apron, washed out, mended in several places, full of artful patches. Quite a treasure.

Ethel felt more drawn to this girl than to any other. Of this dark girl with the curly black hair and the smiling mouth full of slender teeth, Ethel would ask the question tormenting her: did all the other children live the way the teacher said they should? Were the people on Ethel's courtyard the only savage and backward ones, or were there others besides them?

Having shuffled over to the dark girl, Ethel offered her a piece of the cookie her mother had given her and took in exchange a bit of sourish but tasty *criollo* bread. Slowly, cautiously, fearful lest the girl laugh at her attempt to speak Spanish and her dumb questions, Esther began to ask in how many rooms her family lived, how many windows each room had—in short, how they lived.

The other girl, chewing the piece of Ethel's mother's cookie, simply looked at her as though she were a savage, even more uncivilized than the Chinese with their braids, or the cannibals who eat human flesh: "What do you mean, how many rooms? Who lives in more than one room? My mother, my two little sisters, my brother and I live in a room built out of wood at the back of the big courtyard. Windows? No, there are no windows in any part of the courtyard, not even in the front rooms that lead out onto the street."

Ethel was so surprised that she forgot to chew the piece of *criollo* bread. The girl laughed, showing all her slender teeth: "Why do you pay attention to the teacher? Do you really think she knows everything? My mother says, 'It's easy for her to talk, that teacher of yours. "Bring a new smock. Buy new notebooks—every day!" I'd like to see that teacher of yours in my place, standing at the sink. Let her try washing four to five dozen filthy sheets every day. Afterwards, let her try pressing them with rusty old irons and carrying them back to the customers who'll give her a hard time: "There's a spot on this shirt. What's this, washerwoman? I ask you: Am I giving you laundry to wash, or just to carry back and forth?"'

"My mother says, 'They pay that teacher of yours to do nothing. Some job she has, keeping you busy a couple of hours a day. It's easy for her to seem smart. She runs through the lesson, then home she goes. Her hands are smooth, her face made up. Let her try plunging her hands for a few days into the boiling sudsy water and into the ice-cold rinse. With the work of her hands let her earn enough to provide four children with food, and clothes, and shoes, and notebooks, and. . .'

"Then my mother cries, lies down with a wet compress on her forehead, gets up, goes over to the sink, washes the laundry, and presses it with the rusty old irons. She spends the whole day either washing or pressing. Does your mother do the same?"

Having answered Ethel's questions, the girl went back to chewing a bit of Ethel's mother's cookie. She looked at Ethel with small, laughing eyes, brimming with friendship mixed with a little mockery, the way an adult—older, cleverer and more experienced—looks at a small, foolish but nonetheless pleasant child.

After the conversation with the dark girl, Ethel became all the more curious about the fortunate individuals who lived according to the principles laid out by her teacher. She longed to sneak beyond the wall and take a look at the happy few. Her heart actually ached from that unfulfilled desire, and her eyes would well up with childish tears—even though she knew that she had next to no hope of having her dream come true.

First of all, her mother almost never left her side, so how could she slip away beyond the wall, where God knows who lived according to their mysterious ways? Secondly, although the high broad gate always stood wide open, its great iron mouth yawning onto the emptiness of a cool corridor, the entrance was zealously guarded by a chubby Spaniard with a large bald pate, an irascible fellow who hated children more than anything in the world. Most of all, he hated the unwashed, raggedy children who stared at "his" wall, "his" polished brass gate, and "his" well-lit small cage, with the glass panes and shiny brass ornaments. He would enter that cage and press a few buttons. It would rise into the air by itself, transporting the passenger to where the chosen few lived.

"Too bad the plague doesn't come upon them," grumbled the chubby, bald Spaniard, his mouth full of curses and sibilant S's, as he polished all the brass and glass beyond "his" wall. Yet it was for naught that he poured out his wrath, since all kinds of plagues already afflicted the courtyard children. They had not been spared a single illness. Colds, the flu, measles, diphtheria always attacked their malnourished little bodies first. At the earliest signs of winter, all the women in the neighborhood would wrap their children in any old clothes they could find, bundling them up in scarves and coats. "Whooping cough, scarlet fever, tonsillitis have already started going around the courtyard," they would warn. And they wrapped their children in ever more rags, convinced that neither the cold nor the diseases that raged in the courtyard could penetrate the layers of cloth.

For his part, the chubby Spaniard who cursed the children so roundly wore no rags. He possessed a short though very thick jacket he wore at night as he walked his dog. Not only the Spaniard was warmly dressed; the dog, low and plump, with short, crooked legs, was covered in a colorful woolen blanket. One evening, or night, Ethel caught sight of the two of them, when her mother, forgetting her own prohibition on Ethel's venturing alone past the courtyard, had sent her to pick up something at the nearby store. The two of them—the Spaniard and the dog—advanced in the same short, measured steps. Sometimes the little dog stopped, now at a tree, now at a lamppost; he sniff-sniffed with his nose, raised a paw; the chubby Spaniard would stand still, waiting patiently for the dog to finish; then they continued on their way. No matter how much Ethel hated both the Spaniard and the dog, she could not help being amused by the scene.

"Just look at how things are," she pondered. "It's not the Spaniard who's walking the dog, but the dog who's walking the Spaniard. Then again—if they're out walking together, that means the wall has been left unguarded. And not just the wall, but also the well-lit cage, the corridor, the steps—everything. Listen, if that's how things are, maybe now's the time to sneak in and take a look at what's going on there."

And Ethel did not think for long. Forgetting—or ignoring—the chubby Spaniard's temper and her mother's blows, she slipped through the great gate into the cold empty corridor. Her heart pounding, her palms sweaty and cold, she moved into the well-lit little cage, quickly slid the door shut and jammed all five fingers into the cold iron grip of the grating. If her muffled groans—for she did not dare to scream— had not brought the Spaniard running to throw open the grillwork, Ethel would surely have left behind a handful of fingers along with her desire to delve into the mysterious happy life beyond the wall.

The violence with which the chubby Spaniard hurled her out the gate, the strange curses that accompanied his physical force, caused her less pain than the black and blue jammed fingers, which *doña* Pilar—to whom she cried out her heart—soaked for a long time in salt water and then wrapped in rags. Although *doña* Pilar looked at her in a nasty way that might suggest she was about to slap her, and although she snarled, "You demon, why are you sneaking into places you don't belong?" she nonetheless wrapped Ethel's aching fingers slowly, carefully. Suddenly she cried out in rage: "May lightning strike that miserable gypsy. Look how loyally he and his rotten dog protect other people's property. Let 'em both drop dead together!"

Then in a uncharacteristically soft and awkward manner she gave Ethel a nudge on the head, which made the girl wonder for a long time after: "Did she mean to caress me?" Then she said to her, "Now go home to Mother."

Luckily for Ethel, the rags unwound before she got home, and her mother realized nothing. It was just before Passover, and her mother was so busy trying to drag some essence of the holiday into the boxlike room with the small wooden stove that she hardly took heed of Ethel's black-and-blue fingers. She supposed the girl had smudged them with ink at school. She was about to get angry, scream at her, "Do you think it's easy to do laundry?" and perhaps even slap her. But immersed in the preparations for the holiday, she soon forgot about the matter.

—Translated by A. A.

II

A Man and his Parrot

A SHORT STORY BY JOSÉ RABINOVICH

[*José (or Yoysef) Rabinovich (b. 1903 Bialystok; d. 1977 Buenos Aires) arrived in Argentina in 1924; a year later, he had already published stories and poems in* Di Prese *and in the Marxist journal* Nayvelt. *The lyrical tendencies of his first works gave way to a portrayal of Argentinean poverty, and by 1937 he no longer wrote in Yiddish. His often caustic work in Spanish is typified by the poetic volume,* El violonista bajo el tejado *("The Fiddler Under the Roof"), which appeared in 1970.*]

It is barely six in the morning and the stars are still out, but Manuel has to get up.

It isn't a job that wakes him. That obligation used to get him right to his feet, but now? Now just getting dressed is drudgery. His pants, his shoes—they resist when he puts them on. His hands have become so powerless that they can hardly drag his clothes on. He and his clothes are mutual enemies. His feet, like an old man's, don't want to walk—they balk. He can't stop yawning. What is he yawning about? Maybe he didn't get enough sleep? On the contrary, he slept too much. If only someone would knock on the door and say "Manuel, time for work!"

He is itching to do something so his hands will turn back into hands. So his body will be hard and strong. So he will stop yawning. So he will be a real man! But since nobody comes to his door or into his heart, Manuel moves like a phantom, with his socks in one hand and a shoe in the other. In his hands his clothes look like rags. His hands, too.

Manuel gets up to make maté for Matilda. He rolls the bitterness inside his mouth and catches it in his throat, unable to swallow, but unable to spit it out either. And the harsh taste refuses to stay in his throat. It goes all through his body and is concentrated around his heart. What a life!

Matilda needs a maté brought to her in bed and put in her hand to drink. His wife deserves this: after all, she is supporting them. It would be so good if he didn't have to do this. His excuse is that she is not sustaining only them but also another life inside her. In such a case, a man should take care of his wife. He dotes on her a bit more to make it easier for her to carry the burden he put in her body.

But ever since he became the housewife and she the breadwinner—even though she still seems like the same old Matilda—something has been piercing him like cats' claws, destroying him. It's a good thing to serve one's wife a maté in bed. It's an honor for the wife and no disgrace for the husband. But the terrible thing is that his wife knew this is only a duty he is forced to carry out because she brings home the rent money. Too, she buys him socks on the street, and she—not he—instructs that money be taken from the box on the table to shop for what they need. That is why it's no good, bringing his wife a maté in bed. Still, he knows Matilda isn't that kind of woman. She cares about him. She doesn't mind going to work, or even that he is unemployed. She doesn't think the things he imagines that she thinks. But she *could* be thinking them. After all, any woman would, and besides, Manuel is forcing her to think that way. It is thus no surprise that his clothes look like rags in his hands when he gets dressed at six o'clock to bring his wife a maté in bed.

The stars are still in the sky, and it is still dark outside. It is winter. If it were summer it would already be light by now, bright and pleasant, and he would not have to turn on the electricity in the kitchen. Matilda can make maté in the dark. Manuel can't, even though he would rather be in the dark. In the dark, the work doesn't seem so distasteful.

There's maté, and sugar too, but no coffee to sprinkle in. What a numbskull he is—they were out of coffee yesterday, too. And she can't drink maté without it. Or maybe she can, but she claims she can't. She usually says that everything he does is fine. But it seems to him that she really feels just the opposite, yet doesn't want him to feel bad that he's the housewife. So she says she can't drink maté without coffee so that he will be encouraged to learn how to run the house.

He sneaks into the kitchen on tiptoe so their parrot won't see him. Damned parrot! They've put up with so much from each other; they've had a longstanding, bitter war. Who will be the victor? Who will survive? Manuel, of course. After all, he has more years left to live than the parrot. Still, the parrot has given Manuel so much heartache, so much real anguish, that he is letting it die of thirst. As long as the parrot screams "Master!" Manuel will not put water in the cage.

The parrot is just another problem. He would let it scream if there were no neighbors in courtyard—would let the bird yell "Master!" until it exploded, and who would care? If no one else could hear, Manuel would not be taking it to heart.

Of course he would not feel happy about being mocked. After all, how can anyone be happy who peels potatoes, lights the stove, stokes the fire, cracks eggs, washes dishes and who also hears—screaming right over his head—"Master! Master!"? It's O.K. when the parrot screeches once then takes a break.

But as soon as it notices Manuel it starts up and will not stop. More than once, Manuel has been so enraged that he has felt like throwing a plate at the parrot's head. He is sure that his neighbors are quietly quaking with laughter. And that even Matilda is laughing. Back before he was unemployed, she never laughed when the crazy parrot screeched "Master! Master!" until it got hoarse. That is because Manuel was the breadwinner then. He liked it that the parrot recognized him. Back then, everyone enjoyed the shrieking, even though there really was no reason to laugh. And now, since he has become unemployed, even Matilda has begun to snicker when the parrot starts in with its cheery screech. The more the bird screeches, the more his wife's snicker reveals its teeth. But would she laugh if she knew about the relentless, bitter war being waged so stubbornly and silently by Manuel, so he won't have to listen anymore—and by the parrot, so Manuel will put a drop of water in its bowl? Would Matilda laugh then?

What is more, if Manuel thought it was merely in the bird's nature to scream, the same way a rooster has it in him to crow, maybe he wouldn't care. The neighbors wouldn't laugh either. But everyone sees and hears how hard it is for the bird, who shrieks "Master!" as tragically as if someone were cutting its throat. The parrot's labored cry to Manuel whenever he goes into the kitchen provokes laughter from wives in the other kitchens—so much laughter that the women could explode from it.

When the bird lets out its mocking fury, Manuel would just as well heave the whole thing, parrot and cage, out the window, and do it so hard that even the Messiah, were He to come, could not revive the bird. But that would be then end of Manuel, too, because people would run after him through the streets, as though he were a madman. Better to quietly carry the parrot out and get rid of it. But people would discover that trick, too.

The parrot has already been without water for three days. Manuel gives it seeds and little pieces of stale bread, but he wouldn't be feeding the bird either if he weren't scared about being seen starving it. So he merely denies it drink. They can see from outside the cage if the parrot has food or not. But no one can see the tin water bowl.

Matilda drinks her maté and leaves for work. Manuel gives her a hug, just as he should. His situation demands it. He receives instructions on what to cook for lunch. He listens, smiling. His situation demands it.

The parrot notices him and starts choking, screeching. "Master!" Manuel gives an involuntary glance at the sky, which is gloomy and on the verge of rain. Something about its appearance presses down on that place, the one in both beast and man, where anguish lies hidden. He goes back in the room, starts making the bed, and notices tiny infant's undershirts beneath the pillows. Matilda had been sewing them before she went to sleep and left them there. Tiny shirts. Manuel starts thinking. He cannot see anything in front of his eyes. Later, when he is again able to see, he rushes to give the parrot a drink of water.

—Translated by Debbie Nathan

12

In Honor of Yom Kippur

A SHORT STORY BY SAMUEL ROLLANSKY

[*Samuel Rollansky (or Shmuel Rozhanski; b. 1902 Warsaw; d. 1995 Buenos Aires) had a traditional Jewish as well as a secular gymnasium education. He emigrated to Argentina in 1922. From 1934 to 1973 he wrote a daily column for* Di Yidishe Tsaytung *of Buenos Aires. Rollansky directed the Argentinean branch of the YIVO Institute for Jewish Studies and authored theater sketches, short stories, essays and histories of Yiddish literature and press in Argentina and elsewhere. He is best remembered as the editor of* Musterverk fun der yidisher literatur, *a 100-volume series of the classics of Yiddish literature.*]

Together with his family, Mendl finally made it over to the home of their old friends, Yosl and his wife. For a long time they had been promising to come over, but never had gotten around to it. Now sitting with Yosl, Mendl apologized: "You understand, we're so busy, and it's so far away."

Yosl concurred, saying: "I've started to believe that living in different areas of Buenos Aires is like being in two different cities. It's exactly one year since you came over, last Yom Kippur."

"It's great to be together," the friends and their wives agreed. "Today we don't have to work, so we can throw a little party. Fortunately, there's such a thing as Yom Kippur, if you work for Jewish bosses as we do."

Mendl and Yosl, who had already been friends back in the old country, had the same political and antireligious leanings. True, they had had their sons circumcised, but not because they wanted to.

"After all," they said, justifying themselves, "there were family considerations, our fathers. . . We couldn't cause the grandfathers such heartache. What could we do, if those were the circumstances?"

Mendl and Yosl were happy to get together on Yom Kippur and reminisce about holidays in the old country.

"We'd eat chocolate cookies that we'd buy from the Russian!"

"People would rip them right out of his hands! His store was packed! All the young people would sneak out of synagogue, and grab a bite."

While they remembered the old days, they watched their wives putting some sponge cake and brandy on the table. Smiling, they pointed out: "It's a holiday, after all! Yom Kippur, to be precise!"

"Do you really think," Yosl confessed, "that if you had come over on some ordinary Sunday my wife and I would have treated you as honored guests? Well, sure we would, but we wouldn't have served up such delicacies. Sponge cake and brandy on an ordinary Sunday? We offer Sunday visitors a cup of tea, a cookie, a piece of chocolate."

As he spoke, Yosl motioned toward the table, indicated with his eyes that his friend should approach, and extended to him a glass of brandy and a plate of sponge cake. Mendl hesitated, as though he wondered whether he ought to imbibe, but then accepted.

"As you no doubt recall," he apologized, "I am opposed to alcohol, but today I won't refuse. I never take a sip of brandy, but in honor of Yom Kippur. . . How many times a year, after all, does Yom Kippur come around?"

Mendl took the drink, sipped it, and his eyes watered. "Wow," he choked, "that's strong stuff!"

Nonetheless, he drank. It burned his palate, but he recovered. Yosl refilled his glass. Though his head felt swollen and stiff as though imprisoned by iron bars, he still couldn't refuse. Yosl smiled at him fixedly. Mendl answered with a hiccup: "Hap-hic. . .py Yom Kiphic. . .pur! Sor-hic. . .ry!"

And Mendl drank. His feet and head felt leaden, but he drank. He sat down when the floor started to bend. In order to take the brandy, he himself had to bend. His sleeve brushed a glass, and the contents spilled on the tablecloth. Mendl heard Yosl's laughter blending into his words: "Yom Kippur, ha! Once a year, ha!"

Sitting at the table, Mendl watched Yosl's wife cut him a piece of roast suckling pig. Mendl's eyes felt dry and sticky. He rubbed them and tried to focus. In his blurred vision, he made out the head of a pig, its chin and big broad lips that seemed to slobber.

"Eat!" said Yosl's wife, elbowing him. "What are you waiting for? An engraved invitation?"

"Me?" said Mendl, with a start, as though he had taken fright. "That's for me? Thanks, uh, but I won't eat that. Not because it's pig, but because I don't eat meat."

"C'mon!" exclaimed Yosl, insulted. "I'd expect that from a religious Jew."

"True, but, no. . .," Mendel argued. "I can't. I don't like it."

"C'mon! Cut it out!" said Yosl, unyieldingly. "Any other day of the year you can do as you wish, but not today, not on Yom Kippur."

Mendel bent to his plate, took a knife and fork, and felt as though he were offering a sacrifice in honor of Yom Kippur.

—Translated by A. A.

13

A Ripped Tefillin Strap

A SHORT STORY BY MOYSHE RUBIN

[*Moyshe Rubin (b. 1856, Izmail, Ukraine; d. 1940 Buenos Aires) had an extensive traditional education that prepared him for the rabbinate. In 1906, he moved to Argentina, where he was involved in Zionist circles and worked as a private tutor. Rubin authored several Yiddish textbooks and school manuals on Jewish history and religious customs.*]

It had been hard for Lebensohn to get the recommendation from a fellow Hebrew teacher at the association, but the first lesson had gone well enough. Though he had not yet shaved off his beard and whiskers according to the custom of the land, he had allowed himself to take off his green hat, and teach his pupils with his head uncovered.

At first he felt a slight shiver go through him. The hair on his head stood on end, as he reminded himself that he, a Hebrew teacher, was teaching the holy tongue while not wearing a hat. He pondered whether he should put it back on and come up with some excuse as to why. Then he reconsidered: it wasn't such a terrible crime for his head to be bare as he taught Hebrew. Indeed, how was Hebrew different from all other languages?

Nonetheless, he felt uncomfortable throughout the lesson he gave to the three lads in the Argentinean household. The eldest looked at him gloomily, scornfully. He was a redhead, and Lebensohn hated redheads; they made him literally sick to his stomach. The redheaded son, not removing his eyes from the gold clock, repeated that he had to arrive in time at the factory to supervise the workers, lest they slack off as usual.

Those last words were like a dagger in Lebensohn's heart. The boy, he thought, was rotten to the core, and the Hebrew language, however it were taught to him, would not improve his character.

The two younger sons—one with quite a sympathetic face and the other somewhat sickly—smiled continually. In their smile he sensed scorn for a new immigrant, who spoke to them not in Spanish but in Yiddish. Nonetheless, Lebensohn felt an obligation to have them appreciate the literary treasures of ancient and modern Hebrew, to show them the splendors that shone in every epoch, the sweet pain, the joyous longing that were hidden deep in the soul of the modern Jew. He wanted to make them yearn for the great prize that the future held out for the Jewish nation. He had begun to explain these things with all the fire in his spirit, but his three pupils soon interrupted him.

"*¡Señor maestro!*" exclaimed the redhead, "we're no longer little *muchachos*. Imagine, telling us such stories. . ."

And the youngest, Marcos, the sickly one with the flaxen hair, started bobbing his head as he explained to Lebensohn that their previous teacher, Notowitz, had gone over that material for the last seven years. "We already know that Abraham was a *judío*, we know that the *judíos* introduced *judaísmo*. Then came Jesus Christ, who brought forth a lot of Christians, who beat the *judíos*. . . Abraham was *rico*, very *fuerte*. He had a lot of *dinero* in the bank. I myself already have a hundred pesos in the bank. And how much do you, *maestro*," he asked as the lesson ended, "have in the bank?"

Such were the comments made by little Marcos, his mother's favorite. Marcos himself showed off to his teacher what a fine boy he was: "I liked *maestro* Notowitz, and the *maestro* liked me. He let me pull on his beard, and that gave him *mucho gusto*."

Despite everything, Lebensohn's teaching had gone well enough. As he came into the room for the second lesson, he found *señora* Granevitch, who wished to observe the class. When Lebensohn explained the message of the prophets—whom they had already discussed a little the day before and who the students had agreed were very interesting—*señora* Granevitch rose from her chair and said with a proud smile on her tightly-drawn lips:

"*Rebbe!* What need is there to teach them such foolishness? We are asking of you only that you take a good look at the calendar, and see how soon the twenty-sixth of December falls, the day Marcos will have his bar mitzvah. You know these Argentinean kids! To teach them to put on tefillin takes at least half a year. Actually, Marcos didn't even want a bar mitzvah. '*No quiero,*' he said, '*y basta,*' and that's that. But then the two older ones calmed him down and made him understand that it was less hard than it seemed. After much wrangling, we talked him into it, on the condition that his two brothers take lessons with him from the same teacher. You see, the older ones don't need to study Hebrew anymore. They've been in the higher grades of public school for four years now!

"That's why I had to dismiss the previous teacher, Notowitz, who had taught them for seven years. They were sick of Hebrew lessons. Do you think I wanted to fire him? Certainly not! Marcos liked him so much, and his beard most of all. He had become one of the family. He thought nothing of bringing me whatever I needed from the grocery store in the pouring rain! And believe me, I felt sorry for him, poor thing, with a sick wife and small children. But what could I do? You know these Argentinean kids! You have to give in to them."

The whole time *señora* Granevitch spoke, Lebensohn sat and looked at her gleaming silk dress, her plump face, her taut lips, and at Marcos, who kept his mouth agape and bobbed his head. But all of sudden he recalled something that jarred him. He—who had found it so hard to bare his head for the first lesson—had already back in the old country stopped donning tefillin and reciting the daily prayers. Ought he now to mask his convictions and teach little Marcos with the bobbing head how to put on tefillin?

"I know," he thought to himself, "that on the day of Marcos' bar mitzvah, I'll earn a pretty penny, provided I've taught him how to put on tefillin quickly and chant his portion from the Haftorah." How could he do something he found so repellent? And yet, to think it over, this just might be his chance to provoke the devil.

"And so, *señor* Lebensohn," he heard the mother saying, "please refrain from all the nonsense and just teach my Marcosito to put on tefillin. And for God's sake, don't burden him with too much chanting. He's such a weak child. It's enough for him just to wrap the tefillin around himself."

Lebensohn agreed to teach him accordingly, and they got down to business. It took a whole month just to get the boy to distinguish between the headpiece and the arm piece, and to know exactly where to place them. Then it was time to show him how to don the tefillin, how to wind them on the hand and on the middle finger. He always got it exactly backwards, winding it twice around the ring finger and once around the middle one. And then he couldn't say the Hebrew for "and from Thy Wisdom": *umeykhokhmoskho*. It came out garbled: *umeyskhmoskho, umeykhosmoskho, umeymokhoskho, umeysokhomkho.* A month went by until he could say *umeykhokhmoskho.* And only then could they start winding the straps, or as Marcos called them, the "little whips."

The bar mitzvah boy noticed how the teacher himself smirked as he showed him how to don the tefillin. And he told his mother, "See how the *maestro* laughs when I wind the little whips."

Once, as he put on the tefillin, the straps became entangled. Marcos got angry and exclaimed, "Such long little whips! They need to be cut down a little."

No sooner said than done. When no one was looking, he sliced off over half the little whips. The next day, when he started winding the straps, one of them broke. The teacher, understanding that this was Marcos' doing, could not contain himself and burst out laughing.

At that precise moment, *señora* Granevitch came running in. She saw Marcos standing there, with one end of the ripped tefillin strap in his hand and the other on the floor. The teacher was laughing. *Señora* Granevitch scowled, and stormed out of the room.

The following day, when Lebensohn showed up for the lesson, Marcos handed him an envelope containing a few pesos owed to him and a note that read, "We will not stand for a *rebbe* who makes light of a bar mitzvah."

—Translated by A. A.

14

When Life
Swallowed Up Death

A REPORTAGE BY AARON LEIB SCHUSSHEIM

[Aaron Leib Schussheim (b. 1879 Redim, Poland; d. 1955 Buenos Aires) was apprenticed to a basket-weaver at the age of fourteen and was one of the founders of the Labor Zionist movement in Galicia. In 1907, he became editor of Der Yidisher Arbeter, *then published in Cracow. Schussheim served in the Austrian*

army in World I and continued his journalistic activity thereafter.
He emigrated to Buenos Aires in 1926, where he worked on the
editorial board of Di Yidishe Tsaytung.]

Have you ever danced in a cemetery around the graves? I have. I did
so with other Jews. We danced in a cemetery around the graves and
on top of the graves to the festive thump of wedding music. This was
in the cemetery of the holy Jewish community of Oswiecim, the town
that lately has become so dreadfully famous throughout the world.

Oswiecim was a not-so-large county seat right on the western
border of Galicia. It was so close to Katowice that even an observant
Jew could walk from one town to the other on the Sabbath; and it
was only a few steps from Ostrova, in Moravia. When Galicia belonged
to Austria, the border post between Galicia and Prussian Upper Silesia
was located in Oswiecim.

I do not know how many people lived in Oswiecim before the
war. Its name does not appear in an encyclopedia recording cities
with populations over 20,000. I think Oswiecim had 15,000 to 18,000
inhabitants, of which a large percentage, perhaps the majority, were
Jews. Yet despite its unimpressive size and lack of industrial
significance, Oswiecim was not just another small town. Its name
figured in Galicia's official appellation, which went as follows: "The
Kingdom of Galicia and the Grand Duchy of Cracow, with the Duchy
of Zator and the Duchy of Oswiecim." So rather than being just a
small town, Oswiecim was an entire duchy.

Incidentally, a dispute raged between German and Polish geographers.
The Germans maintained that Oswiecim—or, as they called it,
Auschwitz—belonged to Silesia. The Polish geographers' reply can be
deduced from the aforementioned official name given to Galicia.

Regardless of whether Oswiecim belonged to Silesia or to Galicia,
one thing was certain: it was a Jewish town—a town of pious,
traditional Jews. In Oswiecim, at least as far as I know, there were no
so-called "Germans"—by which one meant Jews without beards or
ear locks and who wore short coats. There were no such Germans,
except perhaps for the city's Jewish doctor. In Oswiecim I never saw

a Jewish woman go about with her head uncovered, exposing her hair. I believe—I am almost sure of it—that such women did not exist there. Every Jewish woman had her hair cut off after her wedding and wore a wig for the rest of the life—except for the oldest and most pious wives, who covered their heads with bonnets instead of wigs.

During the First World War, I often made brief and lengthy visits to Oswiecim, where my parents lived as refugees. Oswiecim in those war years was perhaps the calmest town in the Austro-Hungarian Empire, especially after German Field-Marshall Mackensen drove the czarist armies out of Galicia onto the Ukrainian steppes. In Oswiecim, people simply did not realize there was a war; practically all the soldiers they saw were on leave. I was one of those soldiers. I took every leave I had in Oswiecim, whose location—perhaps an hour and a quarter from Cracow and about five from Vienna—was most convenient for me.

The tranquility of the town made it ideal for those fleeing the war. Among the refugees there was the acclaimed *rebbe* Shloymele from Sosov, of blessed memory, who performed quite a few miracles while in Oswiecim. From near and far, the lame and the halt sought him out. The deaf and the mute, the blind, girls possessed by dybbuks, epileptics, poor widows with daughters to marry off—*rebbe* Shloymele had to help them all as best he could, with a little help from the forces on high.

In that very town of Oswiecim, I danced in the cemetery, around the graves and on top of the graves. I danced along with other Jews. We sang and clapped hands to the booming beat of the music. That was the way Oswiecim celebrated a wedding in the cemetery.

To that wedding I came as the Balaam of the Bible—may his merits sustain us—had come to the "tents of Jacob and the dwelling-places of Israel." Sent on a mission to curse the Jews, Balaam ended up singing their praises instead. As for myself, I had not come so much to curse Oswiecim as to criticize the wedding to be held in its graveyard. Yet at the wedding I was gripped with emotion and joined in the dancing with the other guests. This is how it happened.

Some time before, I had visited the offices of a Hebrew weekly published in Cracow, called *The Outlook*. Its editor, Shimen-Menahem Lazar—peace be upon him—lamented the superstitious bacchanals that had erupted in several cities. Jews were holding weddings in cemeteries in order to confound the evil spirits and thereby stem the plague of dysentery raging over much of the country.

It was late summer, Rosh Hashanah and Yom Kippur season, during the final year of the war. In Galicia there had been a bumper crop of fruit and vegetables. Suffering, one might say, from a kind of psychological hunger, people set upon the harvest, stuffed themselves, and no doubt disregarded the most elementary measures of hygiene.

A veritable plague of dysentery cut down hundreds of lives. Since doctors could not provide help quickly enough, Jews turned to a more certain method: holding weddings for the destitute in graveyards. Obviously, *that* would work better than medical treatment or hygienic measures.

This practice spread not only into small, culturally backward towns; even enlightened, anti-Hasidic Jewish communities such as those in Cracow and Lvov had celebrated weddings in graveyards as a way of fighting the plague. In Lvov, not one Jewish authority— even among the rabbis opposed to Hasidism—had decried the superstition. The editor of the Hebrew newspaper, Shimen-Menahem Lazar, was a deeply religious Jew, but also a staunch adversary of Hasidism and every questionable folk-belief. He commissioned me to write a mordant attack on the popular ceremony, which he saw as desecrating the enlightened spirit of true Judaism.

A few days after meeting with the editor, I went to Oswiecim, where I found virtually the whole town in a tumult, preparing for a wedding on the graveyard. In Oswiecim the plague had taken a few dozen Jewish lives. The citizens had stoically accepted what they saw as divine justice visited upon them. In a single week—during the intermediate days of the Feast of Sukkot—the chief rabbi had seen his wife and a young daughter die. But he overcame his grief and joined the Simhat Torah procession, dancing with other Jews, several of them also mourners.

Still, something had to be done about the plague. Could death be allowed to rage? Could one merely watch with folded arms? The Jewish community decided to do what others already had done. They sought out a poor young man and a poor servant-girl—an orphan. A match was arranged, and the decision made to marry them in the graveyard.

By the time I arrived in Oswiecim, the town was bestirred as for an event of the utmost importance. This was no trifle: an indigent couple was to be wed. The town notables had to see to everything. Well-heeled Jewish family men went collecting for the dowry. Also needed were wedding clothes, a sable hat and a prayer shawl for the groom, as well as gifts for the bride. A small dwelling had to be arranged for the newlyweds. Pious wives collected money for the bride's wig and wedding-gown. The town notables had suddenly become a collective of parents of the bride and groom. Together, they organized the bride's party on the Sabbath preceding the wedding; the groom was called to the Torah; and pious women saw to the bride's ablutions and prepared the feast for the big day.

The town became so engrossed in the preparations that it forgot about the plague. But the plague did not forget them. It went about its business. Death did not cease snuffing out lives. It became imperative to hold the wedding as soon as possible, and on one fine afternoon it took place. But since the whole town had become the bride's and the groom's family, where could so many gather? Nowhere else but on the town square, the *Ringplatz*.

In Galician and Polish cities, the *Ringplatz* was a rectangle about the size of a city block here in Argentina, or somewhat larger. In the middle was usually the town hall. But in Oswiecim, the *Ringplatz* was completely empty—with not one building in the middle. The betrothed couple was led to the square, where the bride would be ceremonially viewed and veiled as the musicians played.

The *Ringplatz* was crammed full of people. Some Jewish men were wearing their holiday silk-and-fur coats and their sable hats. The groom—dressed like a prince, with a white linen robe over his clothes—waited along with his retinue on the *Ringplatz*. The bride was led in for the veiling. Bride and groom were veritable models of ugliness. Their homeliness seemed to mock the Creator Himself. How could God have made such unattractive people?

After the veiling, the gigantic crowd pushed and squeezed itself into the graveyard, about a quarter hour's walk from the town square. As the musicians played, all those in attendance clapped hands, danced, leapt, pushed, and were pushed. That is how the huge, disorderly mob poured into the place of eternal rest.

The cemetery in Oswiecim lay among fields, and—like the burial ground in Vilna or the old one in Lvov—in shadows cast by thick trees. The graves were hidden among grass and bushes. This site filled the visitors with the spirit of eternity, making them acutely aware of the vanity of life and all its goals, struggles, accomplishments. But on that afternoon, this place of solemn eternity pulsed with unfettered joy for life.

When I entered the cemetery—or more precisely, when I got pushed into it—the bride and groom were already standing under the wedding canopy, erected next to the grave of one of the town's most pious Jews. After the marriage vows had been exchanged, the musicians started showing their skills. The bass tried to drown out the clarinet, and the violin the cello. And the people danced—danced and sang and clapped to the beat of the music, danced and sang joyously where usually the weeping of mourners was heard. There was dancing between the graves and on top of the graves—for who at that moment took heed of the narrow margins separating them? In this dance, the boundary between death and life was obliterated. Death and life flowed together into one eternity. And life swallowed up death.

—Translated by Debbie Nathan

15

Nightmare: Excerpt of a Memoir of "The Tragic Week"

BY PINYE WALD

[*Pinye (or Pedro) Wald (b. 1886 Tomashov, Poland; d. 1966 Buenos Aires) was apprenticed to a tinsmith by the age of twelve. A year later, he moved to Lodz, where he became active in the Bund, the revolutionary Jewish workers' party that was illegal at the time. In 1906, Wald immigrated to Argentina, where he co-founded the Jewish workers' organization* Avangard *and began writing for the monthly journal by the same name.* Nightmare *is his memoir of the* Semana Trágica *("Tragic Week"), a period of bloody repression of Buenos Aires workers' movements that took place in January 1919.*]

January 11

. . .The yard in front of the station-house was crammed on one side with exhausted, dirty, battered, bloody detainees, and on the other with armed, angry-looking policemen. In the middle was a narrow pathway through which I was led to the street.

A truck was waiting for us there: one of those long, wide, square-shaped vans with a motor spewing gasoline vapors. With its iron-clad sides, the truck looked like a big box baking in the January sun. I was put inside, along with more than twenty other arrestees who were seated in two rows, pressed back-to-back and shoulder to shoulder against each other. Dripping with sweat, the firemen worked with great diligence to lash us together with a single thick, stiff rope.

My face began to burn: not so much from the heat in the sun-broiled, iron truck or the pain of the rope biting into my body and making my hands swell, but more from the insult being inflicted on me. We looked like nothing so much as calves trussed together to be led to slaughter.

"Ready!" some commander ordered. Ten firemen with rifles sat on both sides of the truck, and the officer, who was sitting by the driver, shouted:

"Off with your hats!"

The heavy motor gasped, and the truck started moving. With our heads bared under the burning rays of the fiery sun, tied to each other like sheep off to the block, surrounded by guns and angry-looking firemen, we were taken down the Avenida Pueyrredón.

Few people were on the street. They hurried by with frightened faces and dared not even glance in our direction. Our truck stopped by the gate to the police department. We were untied, put in a line between two walls of guns and policemen, and marched into the corridor of the Department for Social Order.

The police yard looked like the general headquarters of a battlefield, with infantry, cadets, firemen and police all around and all fully armed. Jumbled together were officers, captains and chiefs wearing every kind of military and police uniform, with paramilitaries among them. The place was crawling with informers.

The mass of detainees stood under military surveillance: pale, bloodied, dirty, with tattered clothes (some with no clothes at all—they had been dragged out of bed at night), some with bandaged heads, some with open wounds covered with dried, black blood. Others had black eyes, swollen faces, and torn clothing stained with blood and grime. From what battle had they been rounded up?

Even the palm trees in the yard seemed like posts sprouting green swords. Everywhere one looked, the only thing visible was weapons. Soldiers, firemen and policemen with brown, burning faces and sharp eyes, arrived as if returning from combat. Others marched out as though they were being sent into battle.

The crowd of prisoners, who were standing at *plantón*—a disciplinary stance of absolute immobility—showed indescribable forebearance as they suffered the blows rained on them by veritable Junkers and so-called "boys from good families" who beat the seated detainees sadistically, whether or not they moved.

I don't know how, but I ended up first in the line of prisoners who had been brought from the seventh precinct. By now I had no doubt that I was about to be put through hell. I began to feel strangely curious about what it would be like to experience martyrdom in my own body. A desire was growing inside me: to know and feel how much pain a person can bear, and to learn the extent to which one man can hurt another.

I was standing with my face toward the door through which a man from my line of martyrs had been led. I saw how they beat him murderously. He fell over, they pulled him up by the hair, and they beat him some more. He was a tall man, thin, a blond with the face of a Russian.

One's ears buzzed with words and phrases from every conceivable language, uttered by soldiers, robbers, murderers, cabaret boys, pimps, lunatics, drunks. Now and again, two phrases broke though the nightmarish babble:

"President of the Bolshevik Republic of Argentina. . ."

"Soviet dictator of South America. . ."

I wondered: "What in the world is going on here?"

"Your name?" An individual with a black, pointed moustache and sharp eyes interrupted my musings.

I gave my name.

"A Russian, huh?" he muttered, looking at my Argentine identity papers.

"No, a Jew—a naturalized Argentine."

"*¡Argentino!*"

I was led to a cell.

"Here he comes!"

"Why haven't they lynched him yet?"

"Why'd they bring him in alive?"

At the threshold, someone behind me tried to see how hard he could hit me in the head. I felt something burn me. I started to pass out.

The room I was put in was already filled with Junkers, high-society boys and informers. This crowd sized me up with jaded looks and joked:

"Should we cut off his ears first or cut out his tongue?"

"No—first let's pull his hair out by handfuls. It'd be better to crack his skull open and see what a Bolshevik president's brain looks like."

I smiled. The mob glanced at each other and started moving.

"Not now! Not now!" The official in charge of the shift ran towards us. He went into the nearby room, then came right back and led me inside. It was a luxurious office.

The doors were locked. Someone showed me a chair and ordered me to sit down. About ten men surrounded me. One, an officer with a shimmering pistol in hand, sat opposite me and said, "Confess!"

"I have nothing to confess!"

By the time the torture session ended, my right eye was swollen shut. With the left one, I saw that the carpet was saturated with blood, still flowing from my nose and mouth.

"Soak up the blood! The whole office will be ruined!" bellowed the shift officer. I put my white handkerchief to my mouth. It was soon drenched in blood.

"There's the *real* red flag," one of them joked.

Somebody led me to the faucet.

"Did he say anything?" asked another who had just come in.

"Not a word!" was the deferential answer.

Soon came another order: "You've washed up enough. Get going! Hold your head straight. Keep it high!"

Two cadets carved out a passageway among the society boys, the informers, the soldiers and the police, who were pushing through the crowd to get a look. My legs were being beaten from beside me and behind me, but I hardly felt it. I had the impression someone was trying to knock the stuffing out of me.

From the crowd I heard, "The dictator! The president!"

I looked around with the eye that could still see. No one was smiling. But what a joke this was!

I was led back to the first cell. Besides the people I already knew, two men stood inside. One was the blond Russian I had seen being tortured. His skin was yellow and he looked as though he had had some bones broken. Near him was an Italian, a giant of a man. I was put next to them and we made a line. Then they said: "Here is your minister of war and your chief of police. If you so much as look at them, we'll poke your eyes out. . ."

The temperature grew hot, suffocating. The mood was thick with tension.

Our names were noted again and our fingerprints taken. We were not allowed to wash our hands or wipe off the ink. Facing each of us was a fireman with a rifle. We could hear their orders: "Until further notice, don't let them move. They are to be held incommunicado. If they put up any resistance whatsoever, run them through with your bayonets."

As the methodical torture of the "minister of war" and the "chief of police" began, some Junkers stood in front of me. One of them started up. "One way or the other, you won't make it out of here alive."

"Or dead either," added another.

"You're better off telling us the details of the Bolshevik plot."

I kept looking upward, at the spot they had previously told me to look at. I kept silent.

"Look at me!"

I looked at him with my one good eye half open, and stayed quiet.

When the second torture session ended, I felt a rushing in my head. Blood gushed from my nose and mouth until it stopped and dried up.

"To hell with you!"

They made me watch how they tortured the "chief of police" and the "minister of war," who shuddered and cried when they were beaten, and begged for mercy. The two swore they knew nothing, had nothing to say.

Things got quiet. Our interrogators were breathing heavily, as though they had been doing grueling work.

The temperature was suffocating. My nostrils clogged up with dried blood. I barely managed to breathe through my mouth, which made me swallow clots of blood that stuck in my throat. My knees started to tremble and give way. The fireman noticed this. Faithful to his orders, he straightened my knees with his rifle butt.

A parade of new faces then passed by, people who had been waiting outside to have a look at us. One of the internal officers drew himself up in order to make a statement: "Here's the Bolshevik triumvirate . . . This one is the president. . . That's the minister of war. . . He's the chief of police. . ."

The people filing past looked at us with various expressions: studied toughness, cunning, astonishment, sheepishness. The officer "explained" further: "The president threw the first bomb and drank the blood of the soldier blown apart. That's the way they operate. . ."

I felt like laughing, but I have no idea what kind of grimace came out instead. My right eye was swelling over with a bruise, my teeth were knocked out, and dried blood surrounded my nose and lips. I know only that "my" fireman, who was trying faithfully to follow orders, took his rifle and pointed the bayonet at my heart.

Then the big shots started coming: military chiefs, generals, high government officials. One particularly officious-looking man subjected me to an interrogation:

"What nation are you from?"

"The Jewish nation."

"How long have you been in this country?"

"Thirteen years."

"Your religion?"

"Socialism."

He exchanged looks with the others who were following this dialogue, and resumed the questioning.

"So you're a socialist?"

"Yes."

"Do you have anything to tell me about the Bolshevik conspiracy?"

"No."

"Are you afraid to?"

"No."

"Don't you want to make it easier for yourself?"

"No!"

He shrugged his shoulders and left. The parade continued for a long time, with the "explanations," the presentations, the questions.

When all this ended, the doors were closed and internal "order" was restored. I rested my gaze again on the prescribed spot on the wall, and my mind reeled with everything that had happened around me and to me. I was stricken by doubts: had all this really happened? Had I perhaps gone out of my mind after the first torture session? Maybe all this was nothing but delirium, hallucinations.

My ears rang with words like "Bolshevik conspiracy. . . dictator. . . president. . . bomb. . . an oath of blood. " Me! Drinking blood to seal my oath as leader of the uprising. . .

Suddenly I felt as though needles were pricking the swollen parts of my face. My bloodied mouth had ruptured.

I burst out laughing.

—Translated by Debbie Nathan

Brazil

16

Director's Prologue to
Leib Malach's Play "Remolding"

BY JACOB BOTOSHANSKY

[*Jacob (or Yankev) Botoshansky (b. 1895 Tshitshmansk, Ukraine; d. 1964 Johannesburg) studied in yeshivas in Kishinev and Odessa. He first wrote for Russian-language newspapers and in 1912 began using Yiddish as his literary idiom. Botoshansky visited Argentina in 1923 and settled there in 1926. A correspondent for Yiddish papers in Warsaw, Bucharest, Paris and New York, he authored novels, plays and volumes of essays, published through the 1950s.*]

The play *Remolding* represents an important period in Leib Malach's development as a playwright, but that is not the reason I have decided to pen these few lines. *Remolding* was destined to usher in a new epoch in Argentinean Yiddish theater. Therefore, I have permitted myself to write something we always wish to avoid: an introduction.

First, the facts. April, 1926. As is well known, Argentina is an topsy-turvy country, and the beginning of the theatrical season here is in April. *Remolding* had been suggested as a possible play for the Buenos Aires Yiddish Theater, a reading of the script was staged, and the play was selected. Shortly before the first performance, however, the theater owner canceled it, explaining that he could not risk offending the white-slave traders. The author of these lines, a theater devotee and a friend of Malach's, was in charge of dealings with the owner. I was taken aback by such shame-faced cynicism on the part of someone heading a Yiddish theater.

Though still a newcomer to Argentina, I knew that the Jewish community, from its earliest days here, had waged a battle against the involvement of whoremongers in the Yiddish theater, the only public Jewish institution that had not yet rid itself of their nefarious presence. Among those leading that struggle were Peretz Hirschbein and Hersh David Nomberg. Nonetheless, I had not imagined that the white-slave traders actually controlled the Yiddish theater. The report I published on the problem almost resulted in bloodshed. The campaign against the criminal element in the Yiddish theater assumed massive proportions; all sectors of Jewish society and press took part.

The battle is now essentially won, and Yiddish theater in Argentina will in short time have freed itself entirely from so putrid an influence. The *Remolding* affair represented a cultural victory in Argentinean Jewish life generally, and to a cleansing of Yiddish theater in particular.

As director of the first production of *Remolding*, I would like to add a few technical comments. Leib Malach has enhanced Yiddish drama with a new shade of color: a blond hue, a Christian nuance. Not by accident has the author given flaxen hair to his mouthpiece in the play: the immigrant schoolteacher who has fallen in love with a prostitute and helps the girls in bordellos write letters home to their mothers. He embodies the Christian admonition: "Let whoever is free from sin cast the first stone." For him, this is not a purely intellectual matter; rather it bespeaks deep-felt love.

The true hero of the play is a woman of great character and pride: Rosa, the prostitute. How wondrously, how sublimely she struggles to remold herself.

Add to them the figure of Dr. Silva, a mulatto. Entranced with Rosa's whiteness, he sees her as having been "sanctified through sin."

The blond teacher, Rosa, and Dr. Silva are the tragic heroes of the play. Then there are those who rule the abyss: "Mother Hen," the wicked madam of the brothel; "Knife," the white-slave traders' kosher-meat slaughterer; and "Star," the actor. The last two sanctify the dregs of society with religion and art, without which the white-slave traders cannot live.

The other characters, of lesser importance, fill in the background. There are Rosa's relatives, suspended between Judaism and purity. When Rosa goes off to live with the Christian Dr. Silva, she is pure, but not Jewish; when she works in Mother Hen's brothel, she is Jewish, but impure. Her relatives do not know in which direction to be drawn. The presidents of the women's aid societies and the delegates from other organizations portray the small Jewish community's desperate struggle to cleanse itself of those involved in prostitution.

As director, I tried to heighten the "blond" hue of the play, mostly through the use of masks. The blond teacher is made up to look almost like a Christ figure—almost, since he is a Jewish Jesus. Rosa appears as Mary Magdalene. The abyss is dark: "Mother Hen" is made up as a witch; "Knife" is half-rabbi, half-whore; "Star" is a harlequin, with black and red spots on his face. Rosa's relatives are simply greenhorns, immigrants; the lady presidents and other delegates from Jewish organizations are overgrown children.

The whole production follows from the use of masks. It is not naturalistic, but stylized. As the characters arrive on stage, they are accompanied by music, and their movements are like those of automata. For example, in the very first scene, which begins as the blond teacher is writing a letter to Rosa's mother, one hears the melody of "A Little Letter Home to Mama."

I never allowed myself to change the script, but I interpreted it theatrically. The words were not just recited; they were enacted.

The feverish controversy surrounding the play had a definite influence on how I directed it. Very often, the stage was divided into two parts, one white and one black, but that was always done as subtly as possible. In seeking to convey a message, I never neglected theatrical effectiveness.

Tragically, Rosa's "remolding" both failed and succeeded. However, the remolding of Yiddish theater in Argentina *will* succeed.

—Translated by A. A.

17
Remolding
EXCERPTS OF A PLAY BY LEIB MALACH

[*Leib Malach (Malekh or Malaj; b. 1894 Zvolin, Poland; d. 1936 Paris) was the pseudonym of Leib Zaltsman; Malach, his mother's first husband's surname, means "angel" in Hebrew. During World War I he published his first literary piece, a ballad in the Warsaw Yiddish daily* Varshever Togblat. *In 1922, Malach moved to Argentina, and in 1926, he traveled throughout South America and settled for a year and a half in Brazil. Malach's last play to be produced during his lifetime,* Mississippi, *was translated into Hebrew, French and Esperanto.*]

In Rio de Janeiro

Act I. The reception hall of Mother Hen's brothel. . . It is Yom Kippur eve. The blond immigrant schoolteacher arrives from the right, broadly waving a pen in his hand. From the left Rosa shuffles in, her head ensconced in the fur of her lapdog. . .

Rosa: Write, write, blondie. . . You'll inscribe yourself in the Book of Life. Whosoever holds a pen in hand. . .
Blondie: Inscribes himself in the Book of Life?
Rosa: I should be so fortunate. Did you write about the packages I've sent them?
Blondie: Yes, I did.
Rosa: Add something else. . . Wait. . . No, there's nothing new. . . "Regards to Leyzer. . ." Why aren't you writing? Is your mind wandering?
Blondie: The best would be for you to move away, to the States. There are so many Jews there. No one knows anyone else. So many Jews in the States.

Rosa: Oy, you foolish lad, who needs the States and all the Jews there? What's wrong here? Don't we have it good?

Blondie: You know what I'm getting at. There's such hatred here, they don't let you get back on your feet. . .

Rosa: Do I care? If a girl wants to get out of this life, she can. I don't want to pray in their synagogues, so I don't go. I don't pray, anyway. When I die, they can bury me wherever they want, or even throw me to the dogs. . .

Blondie: Nowhere else is like here. There are girls such as you everywhere, in Warsaw, in Odessa, but when they want to make amends, they are welcomed back with open arms, with mercy, not like here.

Rosa: When I go to a dance with the Brazilians, I'm treated with respect. But the Jews turn their heads away. I am not good enough for them and their honorable wives. . .

Blondie: In the States, things are different. Everyone there is equal. You should move to the States. It's a pity to see you cry away your days here. You don't realize it, you're on the inside and can't see out, but you really wish to leave all this.

Rosa: My dear countryman, it's not so easy to get out this life. But I'm not entirely ruined yet. As long as I'm not sick, some decent Jew will someday marry me.

Blondie: Let me be the one, Rosa! If you agree, I have it all planned out. . .

Rosa: Really? Ha! Listen, you immigrant, why didn't you tell me? You want to have a love affair with me. . .

Blondie: A love affair? How can you put it like that? A love affair is so vulgar. You need to be loved in a different way.

Rosa: Ha! Oy, mama!

Blondie: Don't laugh. You need love of a kind that even Dr. Silva. . .

Rosa (covering his mouth with her hand): Shhh. . .

Blondie: No, I don't mean it badly. He's a fine person, but he doesn't love you for the right reasons. He's attracted to you. Something in you draws him to you, and so he likes you. There's nothing else to it. *(Pause.)* With me, it's different. I don't know if you'd want to be with me, to marry me. I don't know if I'd want to, if I'd be brave enough

to. . . You understand, society. . . One is bound. . . But I feel such
compassion for you. No, not compassion, but sympathy. . . I have
such a warm heart, something melts in me. Your pain enters my
blood. You don't feel your pain, but I do. While you are asleep,
even at daybreak, I lay awake and think of you. It seems to me
that you cry then. Don't you cry then?

Rosa: Why should I cry? Have my ships sunk?

Blondie: No, not your ships, but your happiness, your dreams and
hopes. . .

Rosa: So there's no more hope for me? Do you think I live without
hope?

Blondie: You don't realize it. I think: every day a bit of life is over. I see how
your gaze grows shadowy. Even your laughter is so sad. I want so badly
to help you. I love you so, Rosa, but something is lacking. Will!
Courage! If you were to force me to take you out of this abyss, this
impasse. . . If you were to force me, plead with me, constrain me, I'd
do anything. I'd leave no stone unturned. Do you understand?

Rosa: Would you marry me?

Blondie: If your happiness depended on it.

Rosa: So you'd marry me. . . *(She thinks a second, puts her head on his
shoulders; he presses his lips hotly to her cheek.)* Little fool that you
are, what would you possibly do with me? Could you, an
immigrant, offer me silk gowns and a luxurious apartment?

Blondie: Happiness doesn't depend on such things. We could be
humble, poor, but satisfied.

Rosa: Poor? So then you'd send me out to work!

Blondie (with a grimace): Rosa!

Rosa: No, I don't mean you. . . *(She draws his head gently towards her,
caresses him, and kisses his forehead.)* You're so good, so good. . .
But I shall marry a *goy.* If Dr. Silva will have me, I'll marry him.
A *goy* won't mind: you'll be like my little brother. You'll always be
free to come see me! You'll write Yiddish letters to my mother,
whenever you want. Would you do that?

Blondie: As long as it made you happy, really happy. . . But Dr. Silva
can't understand you. One must be able to love not only the you

one can see, but also the you one cannot see, but can only feel: your soul! The way I love you, in my heart! The best thing would be to move to the States. There are so many Jews there. They mix together, and one can emerge, remolded!

(Enter Mother Hen. She is wearing a green velvet dress, with a white silk shawl on her shoulders, and carrying a large candle and a prayer-book.)

Mother Hen: See! There she is sitting, the would-be *shiksa!* You won't go to synagogue?

Rosa: No!

Mother Hen (more to herself than to Rosa): She can't stand being Jewish. . .

Dr. Silva: Today is a holiday for your people.

Rosa: So you know about it. . .

Dr. Silva: The Day of Atonement. I was sure, *dona* Rosita, that I wouldn't find you here today. So I went off to your club, the synagogue. But the lady you work for told me you hadn't come. Don't you pray, *dona* Rosita?

Rosa: No, I don't.

Dr. Silva: It was magnificent there. A world of pure holiness. Light, tears, and lamentations. *(Rosa remains silent. Pause.)* Never have I been so surrounded by a feeling of gentleness and mercy. Your synagogue is a wonderful world. The girls, the women, are white as angels. Oh, the weeping is heart-rending. When we have a holiday, we drink champagne and dance in our clubs. Among you all is whiteness, holiness, light, and tears. . . But you are distracted, pale. You should have gone. Your soul would have been refreshed, caressed with such a tranquil softness. . .

Rosa: I had no reason to go there. I'm fine right here.

Dr. Silva: But there is a God. Surely, there is a God, who shows Himself to the afflicted and humiliated. They cry there, and what are tears, if not God's breath made liquid? That's why the heart is lightened after a good cry.

Rose: Indeed. I've just had a good cry by the candles, as I thought of my mother, but my heart was not made lighter. . . *(Pause.)*

Dr. Silva: Excuse me, *dona* Rosita. I'm not letting you finish what you have to say. . . I've come to ask you to make up your mind about what we spoke about. . . You understand, if you agree to come live with me. . .

Rosa: On the sly?

Dr. Silva: No, not the way others do it, but for real, as my one and only, in my home. It would make me so happy, so happy! *(Rosa bursts into hysterical laughter.)* Perhaps I am no longer of the age when I can express my feelings poetically, but deep inside. . . *(Rosa continues laughing.)* Calm down, child, sit here. *(He places her forcefully onto a chair, and paces back and forth.)*

Rosa: Dr. Silva, you understand, it's hard to accept. You wish to do a good deed. . . *(She bursts out again into laughter.)*

Dr. Silva: Rosita. . .

Rosa: You wish to take me away from here. Do you think it's hard to leave? Not at all; I can go, and that's that! Who'll stop me? But it's hard to want to go. You wish to do a good deed. You understand . . . *(Her voice chokes, and she breaks out crying.)*

Dr. Silva: Poor thing. . . *(He caresses her face.)* My door will be as open to you as my heart. For your going out and your coming in.

Rosa: I am a Jewish girl, not a Russian or a Polish girl, but a Jewish girl. . .

Dr. Silva: I know. Jesus was born to one sanctified in sin, as you are . . . You will be transformed, remolded. Your heart will be open to the longings of your soul.

Rosa: I shall come live with you, Dr. Silva. I can no longer stand to fool my mother. Doctor, may I bring my mother over as well?

Dr. Silva: Of course!

Rosa: I shall come live with you. *(She wishes to kiss his hand, but he does not allow her to; she falls upon her knees, and throws her face into his lap, crying.)*

Dr. Silva: Poor, poor girl. Jesus was born to one sanctified in sin, as you are. You will be remolded, poured from one form into another. . .

[*From Act II (in Dr. Silva's home). Delegates from a Jewish organization seek Dr. Silva's help in passing a law against the prostitutes and procurers that are giving their community a bad name.*]

Delegate: Are they Jews? Israelites? We don't consider them Jews.

Another delegate: They perform ceremonies, they go with Torah scrolls under a bridal canopy through the streets, and people point and call out, "The Jews!" We shall help you, Dr. Silva. A decree should be issued. We shall support you. We do not want to see our names blackened. . .

Delegate: They aren't Jews. We don't recognize them as Jews, even if they go around with Torah scrolls in the streets and establish their own cemetery and their own synagogues. They aren't Jews!

Dr. Silva: It doesn't matter to the congress, *senhores*, whether they are Jews or not. They are a black curse on our young, golden land, whether they are Greek, French, or Jewish. The people here are as multicolored as the heavens at dusk over the Santa Teresa mountains. . .

[*From Act IV (in Dr. Silva's home). Jewish organizations that have accepted Rosa's generous donations have discovered her past and cancel her membership. Already demoralized, she discovers she is pregnant by Dr. Silva, who now offers to marry her. But her mother, who begins the act with the words, "I wish I had miscarried you," imprecates the "bastard that will be dragged forth from her, a creature as black as he." "Mother Hen" convinces Rosa to "get rid of it" and return to the brothel. A French girl working there promises to find a doctor with "golden fingers," but Rosa fears the fate of another whore, a Japanese girl found drowned and whose body was ripped apart by medical students. To complicate matters, the respectable elements of the Jewish community have joined forces with the police in so fierce an attack on the brothels that one pimp calls it a "pogrom." As the curtain falls, Rosa is crazed, imagining the fate she will meet at the hands of the abortionist and his helpers.*]

Rosa: So many golden fingers, so sharp, so pointed. They're pulling at me, ripping strips of flesh out from under my skin, stabbing me. . . *(Her spasms become more rapid, like rolls of thunder issuing forth from a heart ripped open.)*

[*In their Spanish translation, entitled* Regeneración *(Buenos Aires: Pardes, 1984), Nora Glickman and Rosalía Rosenbuj interpret the thunder as a death-rattle ("como truenos cargados; estertores de un corazón que acaba de estallar"[132]); I am not sure that Rosa actually dies.*]

—Translation and notes [in brackets] by A. A.

18
The Mulata

A SHORT STORY BY MEIR KUCINSKI

[*Meir Kucinski (or Kutshinski; b. 1904 Vlotslavek, Poland; d. 1976 São Paolo) studied in a modern Hebrew school and Polish gymnasium and became involved in Labor Zionist causes. In 1935, he settled in São Paolo, where he worked as a peddler and then as a teacher of Yiddish literature. Kucinski published stories and literary criticism in Brazilian Yiddish press organs, as well as authoring several pieces for the* yizker-bukh *(memorial volume) devoted to the Jewish population of his hometown, exterminated by the Nazis. The end of Kucinski's life was embittered by the disappearance of his 32-year-old daughter, Ana Rosa, at the hands of the Brazilian military régime. A volume of his stories has just appeared in Portuguese translation:* Imigrantes, Mascates e Doutores, *edited by Rifka Berezin and Hadassa Cytrynowicz (São Paolo: Ateliê, 2002).*]

Jaime fastened the iron doors of his furniture store with all seven locks at six o'clock in the evening. This was earlier than usual, and he also did not stand at the door—as was his custom—with his keys in his hand, waiting for some final customer to buy something or to pay him an installment.

He immediately went upstairs to his home. In the large rooms, which led one into the other, separated by glass doors, he felt a silence, an emptiness. His wife, Dora, had gone off to a spa with their son, who had just graduated college at a young age; the Jewish newspapers and radio show were filled with messages of congratulations offered by their friends. Perhaps at the spa Dora could find a proper bride for their well-turned-out son, as she had done for their two daughters, who had happily married into such respectable Jewish families. Since Dora had told the black maid to take off until her return, Jaime now found himself alone.

Though fifty years old, he felt like a young bachelor. It was though he had just been released from prison, freed from his chains. He quickly sized up the situation from various angles. To go downtown to a restaurant would be a waste of two hours. It would be better to grab the leftovers in the refrigerator and have the whole evening to relax.

As he gulped down some hot tea, he heard a bell ring. Jaime ran to the stairs, and saw a reddish garment, no doubt a woman's dress, through the glass door. The red hue shimmered enticingly.

As agile as a lad, he slid down the railing and opened the door. Yes, it was a woman, an unexpected guess: *dona* Benedita.

Dona Benedita always made him a little nervous. A poor woman, either a laundress or a factory worker, she had a daughter who seemed to have grown up overnight. Though for years she had been a customer, she would sometimes come into the store even when she needed no merchandise and owed no installments. In the narrow confines of the furniture store, Jaime would feel a warmth as he chatted face to face with her.

When *dona* Benedita came with her daughter, it seemed first as though they were two sisters, and then—all of a sudden—twins. *Dona* Benedita, though a laundress or a factory worker, managed to stay young. Slender and supple, with somewhat black features, she was the result of a mixture going perhaps generations back. The blackness was most visible around her eyes and eyebrows, as a kind of shadow that adorned her noble features.

Her gaze glowed with an inextinguishable lust for life, perfectly suited to her mild, soft and ever-amiable face. *Dona* Benedita was one of those handsome, lovely and pleasant people, with whom it is always enjoyable to exchange a word or a glance. Often, when she left the store, he was overcome by a desire to run after her, keep her there a bit longer. But he managed to control himself, and did not act, God forbid, like a schoolboy. And now *dona* Benedita stood before him, without her sisterly daughter, on the steps of his house, with a white payment card in her hand and an open purse, ready to pay.

"Oh, *cómo vai, dona* Benedita? Come up into the house. I've just closed the store this instant," said Jaime as he bowed, more deeply than usual, and then extended to her a warm, squeezing, hand. "I've been left all alone," he blurted out. "My family's gone off without me."

Jaime took *dona* Benedita by her soft arm and led her up the plushly-carpeted stairs, as though she were some long-awaited guest. *Dona* Benedita was taken aback by the luxurious home and by *senhor* Jaime's explanation of his solitude. Her black, gypsy eyes twinkled, and the shadows around them deepened.

Jaime did not rush to take the money and fill out the card, unable as he was to find a pen and calculate the payment. Finally, he armed himself with courage and, taking the card, asked her in a low voice: "May I perhaps serve you a little coffee, *dona* Benedita?"

The pale pink hue of her face flushed with red, and the shadow around her eyes broadened, practically hiding them. She pinched the card, shoved it into her purse as she took leave, saying "Thank you, *ate logo,* see you soon," as she searched for the stairs.

Jaime accompanied her to the door, but no further. "Here you are. Can you figure out how to open it?" His voice cracked as though sand stuck in his throat.

Soon, the redness of her dress had vanished into the other side of the glass door, and Jaime found himself alone again. The bread and the leftover tea tasted like clay, and he was unable to swallow. He could not feel his tongue, only a piece of leather in his mouth. He recalled the saying:

"The difference between life and death is on the tip of one's tongue."

Now he tried to remember Benedita's husband. Was it not that compact, fiery professional soccer player? The fellow who had once said to him imperiously: "Just take the money. I hate bargaining!"? His voice still seemed to echo in Jaime's ear. A mighty and murderous gentile loomed before his eyes. He felt a chill run down his spine. He ran into the street, hoping to catch *dona* Benedita and neutralize his earlier words with some platitudes. He was sure she had understood only too well what he was after. He could still fix things, apologize, but she was nowhere to be found at the bus station.

It would be better to ride downtown than to remain at home. Traveling in a bus, he could not stop his self-reproach. Because of a sentence that had taken no more than half a minute to utter, the course of his whole life had changed. He would be summoned to the police station. That was just the beginning. The newspapers would write, "A foreigner," or even worse: "A Jew tricks a modest, honorable woman, the mother of a teenage daughter, into coming to his luxurious home." In fact, recently, there had been just such an article about a Jewish businessman, another furniture merchant, even though his Jewish neighbors insisted that it was nothing more than anti-Semitic slander.

Or he could become the victim of constant blackmail. The soccer player would milk the Jew who had desired his wife for everything he was worth.

Jaime wandered into Congregation Ahavath Israel, where his friends from the old country worshiped. It had been a long time since he had attended a meeting of the board of trustees, and precisely on that very day—a Thursday—one was being held.

He sat at the table, and it seemed to him as though the word *mulata* were stamped on his forehead. The trustees discussed an applicant for the position of cantor, and mentioned the towns where he had already sung. When they asked Jaime for his opinion, he once again felt as if he had swallowed sand.

This would be his last meeting. His career in the synagogue, on the bank board, in the chamber of commerce—it was all over now, so shortly after his amazing ascent.

Jaime asked himself: "And what of my career as a father?" He had trouble breathing, as he sat at the green table. How could he shame his son, the recent graduate, the latest and freshest bloom on the family tree? How could he do this to his two daughters, who now occupied such prominent positions in the community?

How hard it had been to climb his way up after his arrival in Brazil! Details of his difficult life began to surface in his memory, now that he stood at the edge of the abyss. First he had worked as a salesman. Then he went out on his own, peddling his wares door to door. Afterwards, he set up the little mattress factory, which then expanded into a store called *El Rey dos Moveis*—"The Furniture King."

His fellow trustees wondered how Jaime, ever the talkative jester, could suddenly seem so preoccupied, inattentive to the important matter at hand—the new cantor. Jaime felt sure they already knew of the catastrophe. He could sense it from their faces, which expressed definite compassion: "That Jaime was such a fine fellow. Too bad he sunk so low."

As he traveled back in the late hours, he clearly made out a group of people, gathering by the closed door of his business. The most popular store in the neighborhood, it stood at the very center of the block it occupied. Those assembled were obviously decrying his behavior. This was just like the case of the butcher who had stalked a married woman, and who was almost lynched by a crowd before being handed down quite a stiff sentence. The incident had taken place not far from Jaime's store. Yes, he clearly made out figures, shadows in the corners of the white building that housed his store.

His coat under his arm, ready for anything, Jaime jumped from the bus and ran to his house, to the dark shadows that stood by his store. All around it was spread a black, nocturnal emptiness. Only a paper rustled softly in the wind.

The door key scraped in the lock like a dried-out bone.

—Translation by A. A.

19

An Engagement Dinner

A SHORT STORY BY ROSA PALATNIK

[*Rosa Palatnik (b. 1904 Kroshnik, Poland; d. 1981 Rio de
Janeiro) taught in a Jewish school by the age of sixteen. In 1927
she emigrated to Paris, where she began publishing Yiddish stories
in the* Handls-Tsaytung; *in 1936, she settled in Rio, where she
wrote for such local and international Yiddish press organs as* Di
Fraye Arbeter-Shtime *of New York,* Der Kontinent *of Mexico
City,* Der Shpigl *of Buenos Aires,* Nayer Moment *of São Paolo,
and* Di Yidishe Prese *of Rio. She published four volumes of short
stories, portraying Jewish life in Poland, France and Brazil.*]

At the corner of the Avenida Atlántica, whence unfolds the broad
expanse of the brilliantly reflective, undulating surface of the ocean,
a brown villa stands under the cool shade of thick palm-trees. The
tall iron gate is open wide, and multicolored streams of water magically
flow from the mouths of two bronze lions. The Venetian windows
are half open and from them issue forth the off-key tones of a genuine
Pleyel piano. The villa stands in the midst of a dense garden. Affixed
to one of the walls of the glass-enclosed terrace is a poster, similar to
a map. It shows a richly-set table, with numbers and the names of the
guests, who are kindly requested to take their places in the great hall.

Senhor Jacob, a short man with a round belly, wearing a custom-
tailored tuxedo, respectfully welcomes his honored future in-laws:
"Come in, *por favor*, come closer, please, please."

Calmly, with deliberate steps, *reb* Dovid approaches the well-adorned
table. His face, bony and narrow, grows pale as he grimaces. His
brown eyes, straining because of the bright light, bespeak a logic all
their own. "Peace be unto you, honored father of the bride! *Mazl-tov*,
dear mother of the bride!"

Dona Marta, the mother of the bride, a massive, forceful Jewess with a head full of dyed, artfully-arranged locks, blushes with embarrassment as she attempts to find the right words to greet her future in-laws. This, despite the fact that she feels quite at home in her flowing lace dress!

Thirty years ago, they had struck it rich. *Dona* Marta had missed the beginning of their good fortune, when *senhor* Jacob—who then went by the name of Yankl the butcher—slid in and out of cheap coffee-houses, wearing a dim, bedraggled suit. He hawked a bunch of brightly-colored neckties with the cry: "Buy them on the installment plan!"

He cursed his miserable trade, and reproached Earth itself for having spawned the infernal land of Brazil. Friends advised him: "Go back to the butcher-block!"

Yankl's sly eyes popped out: "Enough fumbling around in an apron, like a woman! I'm fed up!"

Shortly thereafter, he showed up well dressed and smelling of cologne, in the red-light district, where he had made some dubious connections. Decent people started avoiding him, not even greeting him. Yankl said to himself, "If that's the way they feel, okay by me!"

It was then he wrote back home to his wife: "Don't worry! Thank goodness, there is a God. Soon, with His help, I'll be bringing you over." And when Matta came and saw the narrow streets with the low-built houses, she tightened her black shawl over her eyes: "What is this? Some kind of graveyard?"

But towards the evening, when the sun shone its rosy face on the highest mountain of the Corcovado, entrusting its last rays to the outstretched arms of the statue of Jesus, things began to stir in the low-built houses. A smell arose of flesh and make-up. Matta spat with her fat lips: "Tfooey! Naked *shiksas* in the open windows! So this is the business you've gotten yourself into?!"

"But Matta, dear," said Yankl as he lovingly looked her in the eyes, "It's hardly what I'd call a business. It's just a way to make a little money."

In the Jewish quarter, a tall, new factory soon went up. A crowd gathered around and gaze at it. Cupping their hands over their eyes to protect them from the strong sunlight, they deciphered the inscription: "Casa Jacob."

"Aha!" The Jews were surprised: "So that's it! He's become an industrialist. And we had thought. . . O.K., more power to him!"

Before long, they started greeting him again, smiling submissively as they wished him "*Bon dia.*" Then he received a visit from representatives of a charitable organization: "After all, we are Jews. We need a cemetery of our own, a school, a library. . . What *don't* we Jews need?"

Yankl's neck had grown a little fatter, his face fuller. He bit his lower lip and answered offhandedly: "Eh, of course, you need. . .," as he gladly offered a wad of crisp banknotes with his fat fingers shaking ever so slightly. His roguish eyes looked askance, while he repeated the phrase "Of course, you need. . .," as though he could speak no other words.

The second time the delegates from the mutual-aid society came to him, his name was no longer Yankl, but Jacob. He swung wide the opulent doors, and cried out happily: "Honored guests! Don't just stand by the door, come on in!"

A little later, the Ladies' Auxiliary came to him for funds, with their heads bowed, as though they had wandered in by accident. But the common good came before all other considerations.

Senhor Jacob's efforts on behalf of the community began in earnest when he started to seek a proper match for his only daughter, who had now come of age. The future bride was the spitting image of Matta: the same little bags under the shallow eyes, the pink double-chin with the many folds, and the broad, blunt face. In a low voice Yankl said to his wife: "I don't know who our little daughter takes after. She's a little dull. I've hired for her supposedly the best teachers, and still they can't get a thing into her head."

"Despite that, boys from the best families have sent bouquets for her birthday."

Yankl interrupted his wife: "You're also not too bright."

When the matchmakers began proposing suitors of all kinds—

doctors, engineers, lawyers, professors—*senhor* Jacob declared, "I shall spare no money, I'll give as much as you could desire. But be careful: don't sell me some M.D. who'll sit idly in an empty office because his father-in-law has a fortune. That's not why I've worked my fingers to the bone."

Senhor Jacob made it clear what he was looking for: "I've always had the greatest respect for Hasidim, pious Jews, rabbis, Talmudic judges. They still are worth more in my eyes than those conceited *shmintellectuals*. . . My father and grandfather had always wished their children would marry into Hasidic families. Now I can make their dream come true."

Finally, someone turned up: an unassuming Talmudic judge's pale son, who had fled to Brazil to escape czarist conscription. Now he tried to deal in prayer shawls, High Holy Day siddurs, and Passover Haggadahs.

Senhor Jacob immediately helped bring over the young man's father, who at first looked down at the whole affair, then brushed aside his own objections: "At least, she's Jewish."

Seeing the groom's rabbinical father, *dona* Marta was at a loss for words and unsure whether to offer her hand or simply say: "May our children bring us great satisfaction." The very expression, "our children," made her triple-chin melt with pride. "Our children": what a land Brazil was!

The bride-to-be sat at the piano. Her short legs, which did not reach the pedals, seemed suspended in mid-air. A candy dish stood nearby, and while her fat fingers poked at the higher octaves, her strong teeth audibly gnashed the sugary tidbits.

Soon all were seated at the table. The timid groom with the pale, thin face wore a short tuxedo in which he looked like a poorly made-up actor unfit for his role. Some Brazilian plutocrats took center stage. On the right, there was a well-known banker in a black dinner jacket who sat as stiffly as at a board of directors meeting. The banker's wife, in a long gown, looked at those assembled through a pince-nez, as though she were at the opera. On the left sat the rich Portuguese owner of the largest fruit and vegetable chain in Brazil. His fellow guests were whispering that forty years ago he had arrived as a vagrant—a *malandro*—with a boot on one foot and a gaiter on the other.

There were lawyers, engineers, accountants, and even a Brazilian journalist of sorts, whose desire to hold forth became apparent after his first drink: "May unity and brotherhood reign between all nations," he exclaimed with feeling. *Senhor* Jacob, overcome with gratitude, grabbed the journalist by both hands: "Bravo! Bravo!" And his cunning eyes bulged with pride: "Take a look, people, at who I hang out with."

His friends from the old country sat off to one side. Some of them were well-off, but not exactly wealthy. *Dona* Balbina, formerly known as Basha-Malka, a tall Jewess sporting a wide necklace on her thin throat, pinched Sarah-Bella from behind: "Take a look, but don't faint."

Opposite them, wearing a velvet dress, sat the freckled *dona* Dora, known as Hinda-Deborah in the old country. She said in a low voice: "Yankl the Butcher didn't make a penny on me. I wouldn't have put his meat in *my* basket."

Hinda-Deborah's husband put in his two cents, "You see, it's just a question of luck," only to be interrupted by Basha-Malka's husband: "Luck, *shmluck!* It's more question of smarts!"

Suddenly, *dona* Marta came over to her friends, and said to them loudly: "Please, folks, have something to eat! Why aren't you eating anything?"

Senhor Jacob came by, too: "Really, take something! Would I begrudge you a little food? On the contrary, I have seen to it with God's help there'd be enough for ten weddings!"

Only *reb* Dovid sat quietly, looking at his white hands, from time to time paring his clean nails, as though he wished to remove some dirt that had settled under them. He repeatedly straightened his silken skullcap, lest it slip off his head.

Through the open windows could be heard the violent sound of the ocean, as the waves crashed against the jetties, embraced them, then flowed back out.

—Translation by A. A.

Chile

20

He Worked His Way Up

A SHORT STORY BY JOSÉ GOLDCHAIN

[*José Goldchain (or Yoysef Goldshayn; b. 1901 Bolimov, Poland;
d. ?) emigrated to Argentina in 1923 and settled in Chile in 1930.
In that year, his first story appeared in the weekly* Tshilener Yidishe
Vokhnblat. *In 1946, he published a collection of tales, entitled*
Fun a vayt land *("From a Far-Off Land").*]

The Café Colombia has filled up. All the tables are occupied by the
usual clients. One fellow has come in to get a loan, another to cash a
check, a third to trade a promissory note, and someone else just to get
the latest news of the war. They all feel at home and free to be themselves.
They can have a cup of coffee and sit for a few hours, until it's time to
have lunch, or go to the club, or to play cards until dinner.

But things really get lively when Hershl Khristavayer walks in. His
friends call him by a Russian nickname, "Uncle Grisha." "Khristavayer"
is from the name of his birthplace, Khristavay, a small *shtetl* in Besarabia.
Hershl was one of the first Jews to come to Chile, some thirty-odd years
earlier. Good-hearted and merry by nature, he is the type who considers
himself to be like one of Sholem-Aleichem's "poor but happy" characters—
though in fact he's far from poor. He's a manufacturer who owns his own
house and makes a nice living. Hershl is one of the few Jews in Chile
who despite good material circumstances have remained folksy and not
taken on the arrogance of the wealthy. He's on excellent terms with all,

always has a nice word to put in. Most of all, he's good at telling a story. In fact, he's a master at telling a story, or as he puts it, "weaving a tale." He begins to weave a tale, and all the little tables in the café are pushed together, lest anyone miss a word or one of the colloquial expressions that pepper his speech.

"You get what I'm saying?" That's the way Hershl Khristavayer starts telling a story.

"When I was sailing from Odessa to Chile, I met two young fellows. One was from Bobruisk and the other from Kishinev. Both were political refugees, fleeing czarist persecution. The guy from Bobruisk—Boris was his name—was a cabinet-maker, an enthusiastic guy, with light blue eyes and a black forelock of hair. He didn't know Talmud, but when he spoke of 'Mother Russia' and the *sotsial'naia revoliutsiia,* you could see the kid practically had a degree in political science. Whenever he'd feel homesick for his folks, sisters, brothers and pals at home, he'd sit down at the nose of the ship and croon a revolutionary song like:

> The sun rises and sets
> In my dark prison.

Or:

> You've died a martyr.

"Passengers would then come from all over the ship to hear Boris sing—even from first class. People in third class would applaud, hold him high and cry out: 'Bravo, comrade Boris!' The poor immigrants would feel their own homesickness in his songs and were grateful. The richer passengers would politely invite him into first class, to sing a merry tune for them: 'Please, mister Boris, sing us the *Kamarinskaia.*' Boris's eyes would burn with fire, and his voice would fill with severity as he drove the requesters away, loudly refusing their offer: 'What kind of "mister" am I? I'm "comrade," understand, you bastard? "Comrade!"'

"You get what I'm saying? That's the way Boris was.

"The other fellow, from Kishinev, was a goldsmith by trade. An intellectual, a smallish guy, pale, long-suffering. In every conversation he'd mention a writer: 'Chernyshevskii, in his book *What Is to Be Done?* put it this way. . .' Boris would interrupt him reproachfully every time. 'Why do I care about what this or that writer said? I want to know *your* opinion on the matter, what *you* think about it.' And Boris had a name for him: 'The Long, Drawn-Out Illness.'

"But—you get what I'm saying?—we became bosom buddies, slept in the same cabin, ate at the same table, and always hung out together. The same hope, the same dream, kept us together: that our comrades back home would conquer their freedom, and that we'd return one day to a free Russia.

"The ship sailed on her charted course—you get what I'm saying—and we'd end up separating. Each would follow his own path. As we approached the shores of Chile we grew sad. 'Who knows,' we thought, 'what awaits us in this new land? Will we ever find work? We're so alone, without relatives there, not speaking the language.'

"Reflecting on our lot, the guy from Kishinev called out to us: 'You know what, guys? Why separate? We can stay together just like now. We can rent one room. We'll pool whatever we earn and share all our joys and woes.'

"'Excellent!' exclaimed Boris with revolutionary pathos. 'A commune, comrades! Just like Karl Marx said, a commune!' We shook hands and made an oath to share everything, whatever happened. Happily, merrily, we set foot on Chilean soil.

"And things went as planned. We rented a small, clean room—you get what I'm saying?—brought in little iron beds and started looking for work. Boris found a job the next day; I got a little packet of merchandise together and started knocking on doors, selling things on time; but the guy from Kishinev couldn't find anything in his trade. In those days, Chileans weren't wearing jewelry. But an oath is an oath, and Boris and I shared whatever we earned with the guy from Kishinev.

"On Sundays we'd indulge ourselves by having lunch in a better restaurant and take in a movie, like good loyal friends. One Sunday—you get what I'm saying?—the guy from Kishinev told the two of us to go eat without him. He had been invited over by a friend from home he had run into here, who might help him get work. So we went along with that. What else could we do? We felt bad, though, since we always ate together.

"Anyway—you get what I'm saying?—the guy from Kishinev went off and had a good time with his friend from home. A few days later our roommate came in with something to boast about: a lottery ticket his friend had given him won twenty-five thousand pesos. We were happy for him, but we were about to lose him. Out of gratitude to his friend, he packed up his stuff, moved out from our place and into his friend's house, into a bigger room, and started thinking about some serious business prospects.

"In the meantime—you get what I'm saying?—winter came. Boris lost his job and I earned little. Because of the rains I couldn't go out peddling door to door, and there was no money to pay rent. So we thought of our old roommate and went to ask him to lend us a few pesos until we started working again.

"Our guy from Kishinev—you get what I'm saying?—welcomed us in very nicely, treated us to some tea and jam, and was enjoying his time with us.

"He heard us out and responded calmly, like a father comforting his children: 'Don't worry, friends, the winter will not last forever. Things are tough right now, but don't despair. This is a good country. If you can't find work making cabinets, it'll be in something else. Take me as an example. My trade isn't good here. People don't wear jewelry. Still, when I didn't find work, I didn't worry. I hoped—in fact, I was sure—that I'd work my way up. And now you see how well I've done. So that's why I'm telling you guys to take it easy. You'll see. You'll work your way up too. . .'

"Boris sprang out of his seat and ran out into the street, without so much as saying good-by. I gave thanks for the refreshments, took leave and tiptoed out of the room.

"On the way home Boris wouldn't calm down. 'What a pig that intellectual is! He worked his way up, my foot! Someone gave him a lottery ticket, he won twenty-five grand. . . That's how he worked his way up! What a bastard—you get what I'm saying?'"

—Translated by A. A.

21

She Wanted to Throw
a Very Nice Affair

A SHORT STORY BY JOSÉ GOLDCHAIN

Ida could not fall asleep. All her thoughts were on the gala event that the Progressive Society was preparing to commemorate the twenty-fifth anniversary of the Red Army. Ida was responsible for arranging not only the food and drinks, but also the literary and artistic program.

Suddenly, the event was just one week away, and she still did not know who would be on stage or whether the audience could possibly be satisfied. She tried to think of all the lecturers and artists she knew and could count on. She was familiar with their talents, but for this event she wanted something special. After all, it was the Red Army they were honoring; it wouldn't do just to perform a folk song and recite a bit of poetry. The program had to reflect the grave times in which they were living and the prevailing mood. The musical and declamatory pieces had to do justice to the heroism of the Russian people. But where was proper material to be found?

She had already approached some friends. All were willing to take part. They said: "Give us the music, the poetry, a monologue. We'll rehearse it all and be ready to perform." Still, she could not assemble the materials. She went to the library and found nothing appropriate, asked people around her whether they knew of anything to enhance the program. After all, she was not appealing to them on her own behalf. She just wanted the affair to be as successful as possible.

At wits' end, Ida switched on the lamp by her bedside and tried waking her husband. She needed to confer with him. "Motl, Motl," she said, stroking his hand gently. "Are you sleeping, Motl?"

"What's the matter? What's wrong?" asked Motl, startled, frightened. "Are you feeling all right?"

"Don't get scared, it's nothing," said Ida, calming him. "I feel fine. I just can't sleep. I can't relax. You know I have to prepare the gala event in honor of the Red Army. Time is growing short, and I haven't arranged anything proper yet. Maybe you can help?"

"How can I help?" asked Motl earnestly. "All I can do for you is to turn out the light and go to sleep."

"Sleep! Sleep! All he ever wants to do is sleep!" Ida grew angry. "I don't understand how anyone can sleep these days! Human blood is being shed at the battlefront, and he just wants to sleep."

"And if I weren't sleeping," joked Motl, "would I be retaking Smolensk or Kiev?"

Ida waxed ironic. "So you think you're a wise guy? I can manage without you and your suggestions. You can laugh all you want, but I'm telling you that if the Red Army weren't ridding the world of Nazism, we all might as well throw ourselves into the Mapocho River right here in Santiago!"

Motl implored her: "So what do you what me to do? Just say so, and I'll fly over Berlin and drop bombs! If you want me to serve in the tank corps on the Caucasian front, fine. Tomorrow I'll join up, if you'll just let me sleep tonight."

Ida burst out laughing. "Lucky for you, no one's around to take you seriously. You're some hero, *shlimazl* that you are. He shrieks when he sees a mouse, and he talks about flying a plane. Stop spouting such nonsense about tanks. The Red Army will do quite well without you. What I want you to do is come up with some declamatory material, a couple of poems that reflect the Red Army's heroism. Perhaps you could recite something yourself?"

"I'll tell you the truth, Ida," said Motl, affecting a pleasant tone. "Of course, I'd love to recite something, but I don't know if I can attend. There's so much work now that we have to be there even at night."

"What?" asked Ida, angry again. "You're not going to attend an event that I'm organizing? In that case, don't bother talking to me. I'm through with you for the rest of my life."

"Why for the rest of your life?" Motl implored. "Maybe you won't talk to me just until the war is over. That way I could get some sleep after a hard day's work."

Then Motl said with resignation:

"Okay, tell me what's missing from the gala. Comrade Yankl is opening the program, isn't he? Won't the Chilean writer Finocheti be presenting an overview of the Red Army? Isn't Comrade Sonia playing Russian music? Won't Comrade David be reciting Spanish poems by Pablo Neruda and Yiddish selections by Kehos Kliger? Indeed they are. Won't there be sandwiches and cold drinks? Yes, there will be sandwiches and cold drinks. So what else do you need? A few days ago you went over the whole program with me, so what more do you want now?"

"You're so selfish. You're ready to kill for just a little sleep. I ask you for some suggestions, and you're afraid you won't get your precious eight hours. I want you to be involved, just to help me with what's needed. After all, I want to throw a very nice affair."

—Translated by A. A.

22

Solomon Licht

A SHORT STORY BY YOYNE OBODOVSKI

[*Little information is available about Yoyne (or Jonah) Obodovski, who first settled in Argentina, then lived for twenty-five years in Chile. By 1965 he had made aliyah to Israel. He published humorous sketches about nouveau riche Jewish immigrants, though this story, written between the two wars, evokes the post-traumatic syndrome of a pogrom survivor in his new home.*]

The night had already fallen. The starry sky gazed down, forlorn, on the infinite skyscrapers and the electric signs dazzling with fiery colors, teasing the helpless night, challenging its dominion.

The city was already half asleep. The wheels of an electric streetcar could be heard from time to time, and the hiss of a late train cut into the nocturnal silence.

Solomon Licht was still awake. He leafed nervously through one book after another. A strange indifference kept him from concentrating. A burden lay upon him, filling the void of his small, square room. Each movement, the slightest shrug, cast a mute shadow on the bare walls. His small figure suddenly grew into a huge silhouette. Solomon enjoyed feeling small, even smaller than he actually was. Uncomfortable within the four gray, bare walls, he switched off the light, and climbed up to the roof, where he often secluded himself.

Solomon deeply inhaled the air of the approaching spring, his eyes fixed on the clear starry sky. The night and he, it seemed, were both homeless in the neon metropolis.

As he started to pace the wide roof, memories came to him. He saw himself as a child in the small Ukrainian village, where nature bewitched the spirit, urging it higher and higher. He shuddered anxiously, and stopped. He closed his eyes, as if deciding no longer to view the events of everyday with them. Then he freed his memory to roam the paths and byways of his ever near past.

Almost forgotten episodes, covered in mist, became clear, awakening bittersweet longing within him. The entire village—the inhabitants, surroundings, even the water mill, the croak of frogs and the dreamy sounds of night—wove into his soul. In his spare time, when he could escape the din of the city, he ceased to be Solomon Licht and became the village itself, spreading the luminous bliss and the fragrant freshness of orchards and meadows.

He shuddered with pain. He opened his eyes and resumed pacing, as if warding off an ominous vision that barred his way back to the past. He heard the melancholy chiming of the church bells that resounded with sinister boding in the stillness of the village. A peasant mob formed hastily, armed with knives, axes and scythes. Rifles cracked, as Jews were being chased. A few feet away from him, a fallen friend lay moaning, life draining from his prayerful stare.

Solomon sensed a foggy film over his eyes, and his pace tottered.

Leaning on the railing, he forcefully pressed the palms of his hands against his temples that twitched as though gnawed by worms. He was tormented by the thought that he was no more than a living gravestone to a murdered village. He was still young and full of lust for life, but his shattered soul hovered between past and present. All his impressions intertwined with that past. There, he had left his roots as well as the sun that warmed and nourished them. He could not accustom himself to the present. The big city, with its din, was alien to him. It seemed to be a gigantic larva feeding on the life juices of its inhabitants, rendering them consumptive. Everything here was artificial: the people were like moving mannequins with hollow souls. They lacked the impulse of nature, inner joy, the melody of divine creation.

Solomon wondered whether he was exaggerating. Perhaps *he* was the moving mannequin that staggered at the edge of life, then stood like a weed, transfixed. The theaters and coffeehouses were, after all, always crowded. Laughter resounded everywhere. A good show or movie excited people. For Solomon, however, all this was painful. It seemed to him they strove to fill the emptiness of their souls with noise, and drive tedium out of their lives. That is why they flocked to the theaters and coffeehouses, and delighted in petty conversation.

Solomon pondered: by what means could he reconcile himself? The past was cut off, and the present was a gray routine. Where could he take refuge? Solitude gnawed corrosively at his soul, which howled a bitter lament.

Solomon recalled how the same melancholy seized him in his village. A sad tune would issue forth from him and return to the depths of his soul; or rather, his soul and the tune itself would sing to him until his soul emerged renewed and cleansed. Here, however, the tune was nowhere to be found. Or, perhaps, it was roaming in the amusement halls among the tables in the coffeehouses, but no one could perceive it. It was too still, too whispering. Souls that had been hollowed out like barrels could only respond to deafening noise.

The stars started, slowly, to vanish, and the sky became a black stain that frolicked uncannily with the glimmer of the city's tower of light. A cool dawn breeze loitered about the electric cables. The shine of swinging streetlamps danced on the sidewalks and walls. Fatigue afflicted Solomon in all his limbs. Slowly, he climbed down from the roof. As he stood at the threshold of his room, a force pulled him away. In a short while, he was roaming the streets like a stray shadow.

By the time the sun shone as a red disk on the horizon, Solomon was already far from the city. Two rows of gold-shimmering grassland stretched downhill before him. Birds, chirping as they left their nests, greeted the newborn day. Solomon thirstily breathed in the country air, and gazed in wonderment. He had found himself anew. All the fibers of his body sang with youthful happiness, and his lips murmured a prayer for the unredeemed souls.

—Translated by Moisés Mermelstein

23
Gold

A SHORT STORY BY NOYEKH VITAL

[*Noyekh (or Noah) Vital (b. 1892 Moscow; d. 1961 Santiago de Chile) was brought to Vilna by his parents in 1894 as a result of a decree banning Jews from the Russian capital. He attempted to immigrate to New York at the age of thirteen, but was refused entrance by American officials because of an eye infection. In 1905, Vital arrived in Argentina, where he began writing. In 1927, he settled in Chile, where he became co-editor of the weekly* Tshilener Yidishe Vokhnblat. *In 1946, he published a book of stories entitled* Shtot un feld *("City and Country").*]

Lipman and Zalman got off at a small station in the mountains. A young man in a torn red hat was wandering around the platform. A filthy, scraggly dog sat warming itself in the sun.

"Strange little place," Zalman said, looking around.

"The area where they pan for gold can't be too far off," said Lipman.

The train station was surrounded by greenery, and a footpath strewn with yellow sand led into the mountains, where even from afar you could see the little white houses of the village. The mountains were so close that their verdure shone in the sun. A thin blue mist hovered in the air, bringing with it the scent of fresh grass and dew.

They set off on the path, which meandered through tall grass. Lipman went first, holding his head haughtily and sucking the fresh air into his open mouth.

"Zalman!" he yelled.

"What?"

"Hold onto the money!"

Without thinking, Zalman felt his breast pocket, where he had hidden their entire fortune—three thousand pesos in bank notes—stuffed in a little bag.

Approaching them was a horseman who wore a wide poncho, with a broad-brimmed, fringed hat at his side. Riding up close, he gave them a hearty "¡Buen día!"

"¡Buen día!" the two men answered in unison. "Fine folks, these Chileans," Zalman said, breathing easier.

Now the path led into the mountains. It was flanked by green valleys and streams that rushed through polished rocks.

"There it is. See it?" said Lipman, pointing out a wide valley where a flat, thin river flowed. Several people were bent over the edge. With wide, flat sieves, they sifted the wet sand they had taken from the river. "Panning gold," Lipman called out, as though in a dream.

"Panning gold!" echoed Zalman.

They kept going. Their pace got more hurried. Lipman was always out front; his head seemed detached from his shoulders. If he could, he would have leapt over the mountains and valleys into the magic river of endlessly flowing gold sand. Zalman took up the rear, carrying a little knapsack, his broad shoulders moving rhythmically with every step. Neither noticed their surroundings. From one side a gigantic peak rose up, slicing into the deep fog and its snowy wisps. Behind them were smaller mountains covered with sparse little forests. The white houses had disappeared from view. The men looked around, afraid; but Lipman was not lost, and his steps quickened. The path, now narrower, wound through the mountains, but a little farther it opened onto a flat valley where the white houses lay in two rows. The route now led uphill. The sun was already in the middle of the sky when they came to the village.

"So, wheeler-dealer, where's the gold?" Zalman teased his partner.

"Don't worry, they'll be here soon," Lipman replied. "They've already seen us."

And sure enough, in the evening in the restaurant, someone approached them. He was tall, heavily sunburned and curly-haired, with high boots and a wide hat.

"*¡Buenas tardes!*"

"*¡Buenas tardes!*" they both answered.

In the low-ceilinged room, he seemed even taller. He had to stoop a little. Lipman urged him to sit: "*¡Siéntese!*"

He sat, laid his big-brimmed hat on the table, took from his pocket a little paper and brought it up close to them. He had gold—panned gold.

"*¿Cuánto?*"

It was only a bit of gold, not a lot. Two hundred grams total.

Lipman took the paper and fingered the little grains of gold sand, which shone in the darkness. He felt giddy, as though his head would fly off. He laid the paper back on the table and started bustling around the room.

Zalman looked at his partner and realized this was serious business. He felt warm inside. A drop of sweat rolled down his forehead, burst, and went in his eye. Then another drop, and another. Drenched in sweat, he began fanning himself with his hat.

The Chilean sat calmly. His sun-darkened face was crisscrossed by two deep folds, which made him appear to be smiling and showing his teeth. His sad brown eyes looked clever, good-natured.

Should he bring the gold?

Of course. Why else would they have come here, all the way from Santiago? The Chilean went outside; Zalman shoved aside his chair and started pacing the room. Lipman's face shone: "What did I tell you, huh? Two hundred grams of panned gold! Know what that means, you dolt?" Zalman felt a bit remorseful around Lipman. For a long time Lipman had been urging him, but he had not wanted to go to the gold-panning region. Like someone afraid of death, he had never wanted to get rich quick. He had always gotten by as a peddler, but now he saw that Lipman was right: What did he want to do—drag a sack around, or buy a pinch of gold? He had really done well to take Lipman on as a partner. He would put up the money for the gold, and Lipman would assess its purity and make the deals.

The Chilean came back a bit hurriedly. From under his poncho, he took out a large, dark flask and began dumping glittering grains of gold sand onto a paper. Lipman and Zalman surrounded him. Their eyes got so big that they looked ready to pop out of their heads. Sweat ran down Zalman's face and dripped into his eyes and mouth, leaving a salty taste.

Lipman was already weighing the gold. He finished weighing, and after jotting down some figures he muttered under his breath in Yiddish:

"This *goy* has no head for figures. This is quite a good deal."

The Chilean calmly weighed out a little cup of gold and wrote on the margin of a sheet of newspaper. He poured one small pile after another. Lipman's lips moved as though he wanted to chew something. He was all wound up. Though he was quiet and absorbed in the work, he felt as if everything inside him were talking and moving. His face was thin and yellowish, with a pointed, yellow nose and large grey eyes that crept from his head and gazed out with a question mark.

And Zalman—short, big-boned, with strong shoulders and a square face—stood a bit to the side and watched how Lipman weighed the gold. It was as though he wanted to say, "I'm only a silent partner. It's all up to you, Lipman."

Lipman knew what was needed. He knew especially that the weighing had to be done right, and the calculations, too. When everything was weighed down to the last gram, he started doing the math. He erased, calculated, scratched out, and finally came up with a figure: three thousand two hundred.

The Chilean looked at the sum and calmly poured the gold back into the flask. Lipman started bargaining. He wanted to subtract the two hundred. They had had a lot of expenses, traveling to such an out-of-the-way place—all the way to the gold-panning region.

The Chilean would not give in. His dark, sunburned face smiled. He couldn't lower the price: he had a partner, too. Lipman stuck to his guns. If the answer was no, he could always find someone else to sell him gold. Chile had plenty of gold, and if the going rate dropped, he stood to lose even more. The Chilean went down a hundred, but Lipman was stubborn.

"Give him the hundred!" Zalman said to Lipman under his breath.

"We'll let him leave—let's bluff him!" said Lipman.

Indeed, the Chilean got up. He picked up his wide hat, put the flask of gold under his poncho and headed toward the door.

"Give him the hundred, Lipman!" Zalman yelled.

"All right already!" Lipman headed for the door.

The Chilean came back and put the flask of gold on the table. Zalman quickly took out the little sack of money and counted out three thousand. Lipman took out a hundred and added it to the payment.

The sun was already far behind the mountains when Lipman and Zalman left on the same route back to the station. They walked quickly, not wanting to look ahead or behind them, but the mountains pulled at their eyes. The clouds lay low, covered in purple, like rose-colored tulle hovering in the sky, fluttering beneath a gentle wind. Springs gushed over rocks in the valley below, where the sky took on a violet hue with dark red streaks. It seemed to the two men that they were engulfed in magical flames that lit up around them as they strode. In the distance, they saw two dark streaks moving over a sandy depression on a mountain. Zalman held tight to the flask of gold. He felt light on his feet, as though they were moving by themselves, wanting to dance, to break into a run. His mood was buoyant, joyful. He had worked his way up so quickly—from peddler to gold merchant. And not a small-timer who traded in gold rings or chains. Instead, a wholesaler who bought directly in the gold-panning region. He caught up with Lipman, who had gotten far ahead, his hat pushed up and his head held haughtily.

"Lipman, it's obvious you really know how to do business," Zalman said, giving him a friendly slap on the back. Lipman did not answer. He was calculating how much they could get for the gold, and how much his share would be. In the future, he would travel by himself to the gold-panning region. After all, what did he need that dolt Zalman for?

As they walked, darkness began to descend. A wind came up, almost out of nowhere, blowing in the evening air.

"Zalman, hold on to the gold," Lipman said.

A shiver passed through Zalman's body. He pressed the flask tighter to himself and walked faster. When they spotted the lights of the station, it was already late at night.

They sat in a corner of the railroad car. But Lipman could not sit still; his nerves were propelling him out of his seat. He looked anxiously through the darkness, into the nocturnal quiet, with its aroma of wild flowers.

"Lipman," Zalman called out quietly, "it looks like there are Jews sitting up front."

Lipman glanced around. Two older men were seated, their faces turned away, but Lipman recognized them.

"Gold merchants," he said nervously. "They might horn in on our territory."

Zalman tapped the flask of gold. "There's plenty for everyone," he replied.

Back home in bed, Lipman could not lie still. He felt feverish, and his head ached. His temples pounded like hammers. He thought about everything. About how he would divide the profits and what to do afterward: whether he should take that dolt Zalman to the mines or go alone, and whether to start out small, buying a hundred grams, selling it, then buying a hundred fifty—or, as Silberstein and Starkwasser had done, just start out big.

Occupied with these thoughts, he fell into a deep sleep. And he dreamed. He was in the mountains, climbing higher and higher, until he came to a spring, and the spring was not water but gold. The golden spring bubbled out of the mountains, flooding the area. He was up to his knees in gold; he picked it up by the handful and poured it into his pockets. The gold ran through his fingers in glittering streams—so much gold that it made him despair. So much gold, such a treasure, yet he could take so little of it. He began screaming, calling Zalman. Zalman came with cups and bowls. They put gold in all the cups, in every vessel. "Zalman!" he cried, "take more—as much as you can! Let's put it in our hats! In our shoes!" They dragged heavy sacks with gold, uphill and down, on narrow paths, over abysses that were practically impassible. Lipman grew so tired that he could not go on, and sat down to rest. But Zalman ran ahead with a sack of gold on his shoulders. Lipman stayed by himself, sitting. Nearby were sacks of gold. Suddenly the tall Chilean appeared with a glittering knife and hollered: "Your money or your life!"

"Help!" screamed Lipman, then woke up. He wiped the sweat from his brow and looked around him. It was already well into daytime. He dressed quickly and ran to Zalman's. Together, they walked around the exchange, whispering conspiratorially. But everyone already knew that Lipman had found a partner to put up cash and was now buying directly in the gold-panning region.

At Silberstein's booth, Lipman bent over a table, watching how the gold was assayed. Zalman stood aside, the way a broker should when his partner is the expert. Old man Silberstein poured drops of liquid over the granules. Vapor started steaming out of them, and a greenish foam developed.

"Don't you see? It's brass!"

Lipman bent farther over the piece of paper, and he himself lowered the glass dropper into the vial, extracted some liquid and dripped it onto the gold. Green froth like pus bubbled from the metal.

"Brass!"

With soft steps, Zalman came close. He saw how Lipman was turning yellow, as though stricken with jaundice. Sweat ran into his protruding eyes.

"Lipman!" Zalman was wringing his hands. His voice was distraught, and he started running around the room.

"We've been ruined! We've been slaughtered!"

A crowd from the exchange gathered around Zalman. They wanted to know what had happened. Anyone passing by would have thought someone had just been run over. But those who were up close saw the big-boned, square-faced Zalman, his grey eyes flowing with tears.

"I've been slaughtered," he mumbled.

—Translated by Debbie Nathan

Colombia

24
Temptation

A SHORT STORY BY SALOMÓN BRAINSKY

[*Salomón (or Shloyme) Brainsky (b. 1902 Zhelikhov, Poland;
d. 1955 Bogotá) was born into a Hasidic family but by the age of
fourteen he had come under the influence of secular ideas.
Brainsky embraced Zionism but during a trip to Palestine became
disillusioned. "In the Land of Israel," he wrote in 1926, "they
have completely suppressed Yiddish." Brainsky immigrated to
Bogotá in 1934. His first stories there appeared in Spanish
adaptations by a Colombian poet, Luis Vidales, who did not know
Yiddish but instead reworked Brainsky's oral versions of his tales.
Ultimately, Brainsky published three volumes of fiction, which
include careful psychological portraits of Jews and non-Jews.*]

I

Nathan, the shoemaker from Porisov, a small Jewish village in Poland,
came home one evening shortly before his departure for Colombia
with a Torah scroll under his arm. With a slight shiver, he lay the
holy object down on the table. His wife, Tzipporah, who at that
moment stood skimming the broth, froze with the spoon in midair.
"What can this mean?" her staring eyes asked in silence. What was a
Torah scroll doing in her house? But Nathan—tall and broad-
shouldered, with a dense, pitch-black beard that framed his full, fleshy

cheeks—hardly paid attention to his wife's wide-open eyes. He took off his frock coat, wiped the sweat from his brow with his sleeve, and asked if supper was ready.

"I was about to set the table," Tzipporah said, coming out of her stupor. "But where are we going to eat if a Torah scroll is on the table?"

Nathan quickly picked up the scroll and placed it in the cupboard. Only when husband and wife sat at the table, eating their kasha and broth, did Tzipporah ask whence the holy scroll had come. At first Nathan did not answer, but when his wife repeated the question, he said that an opportunity had arisen to buy it at a reasonable price.

"What is a reasonable price?" asked Tzipporah with amazement. "Since when have you, my husband, become a dealer in Torah scrolls?"

"You've gotten quite good at picking on me!" snapped Nathan. "What a plague of a Jewess you are! You were already told I got it for a reasonable price; now stop pestering me."

From the way the words were uttered, it was clear he could not explain why he had suddenly spent a whole hundred zlotys on a Torah scroll, especially on the eve of such a long trip.

Such were the circumstances that had led to the unexpected purchase: a notification from the post office had arrived that afternoon announcing a certified letter. It occurred to Nathan that this must surely be related to his departure, because the mail he received—such as it was—always had to do with some momentous occasion. He took off his apron, put on his frock coat and went to claim the letter. It consisted of a thick stack of papers regarding his trip. But they were written in Gentile letters, which he was unable to read. He did not trust his daughters to decipher them, even though they had some understanding of the language, so he decided to go to Mordechai Mezritsher, whose son was versed in Gentile matters and spoke many tongues.

Mordechai Mezritsher was a small Jew about fifty years old with a pair of lively black eyes that darted around like birds in a cage. He was pleased that Nathan had come by.

"Ah, a visitor. Have a seat, Nathan. What's new?"

"To be frank with you, Mordechai, I have not come to see you, but your son. I would like to have him read some papers I have just picked up at the post office. People say he is quite the expert in such matters."

"I wish he devoted his mind to the Talmud instead of immersing all his senses in those heretical books. Then I would have a learned son," sighed Mordechai. "Come in, you are needed to do a favor," he called. Mordechai's son was a comely, dark-skinned lad with sparkling eyes, who sewed bootlegs on a machine all day long and studied during the night. Everything became clear to Nathan after the boy deciphered the papers and explained the details to him.

In the midst of their conversation, Israel-Leon, the tailor, stopped by. All three of them prayed at the same synagogue, where many craftsmen gathered. The arrival of yet another guest pleased Mordechai, a joyous and animated fellow who did not frown at a drink with close friends. He asked them to sit down, and wiped the sweat from his face. "It's terribly hot outside," he remarked. "A cold glass of beer would be a delight." So they sent the apprentice to fetch some bottles of beer.

"What do you think of that, Israel-Leon?" Mordechai said. "Nathan is fleeing from us. He just got all the papers." He asked Nathan when he planned on leaving, but instead of waiting for an answer he went on.

"Tell me, dear Nathan, what kind of place is that Colombia you are off to? Do Jews live there? Do they have a rabbi, a kosher slaughterer, a synagogue to pray in? And, finally, dear Nathan—may you ever be healthy—how does a Jew like you, close to fifty years old, decide to escape to the devil knows where?"

"Well, what can one do, Mordechai? It's hard to make a living here. And besides, I have daughters to marry off," Nathan said with a sigh.

They remained seated for a while in deep and heavy silence. Nathan's simple words went right to their hearts. The bitter present and uncertain future of all the Jews in Poland were clear to them. Suddenly, Israel-Leon's voice cut through the silence: "Why should we add more weight to the heart of a Jew who has decided to throw himself into such an adventure? Anyone who wishes to remain a Jew and follow Jewish law can do so, even in the desert. A Jew like

Nathan would not undertake such trip lightly. Do you know, Nathan, what has just occurred to me? It would be a wonderful thing if you could take along a Torah scroll. You're setting off for a land where there will be few Jews, if any. Even if a congregation could be gathered there, who knows if they have a scroll? And perhaps God has appointed you to be the first Jew in that faraway land to assemble a quorum for prayer."

"It certainly would be a wonderful thing," agreed Nathan. "But a Torah scroll could cost several hundred zlotys, and where am I to get the money?" For a long moment the wrinkles on Israel-Leon's brow deepened. Then his face lit up.

"You know what, Nathan? In our small synagogue we have several Torah scrolls. We could give one of them to you, and with God's help you will someday send us money to pay us back," he said.

That very day, between afternoon and evening services in the tailors' synagogue, some ten men gathered. At first, these simple Jews could not grasp what Israel-Leon was asking of them. Just think, to take a Torah scroll out of the Holy Ark and send it off to a remote place! Israel-Leon explained this would be a good deed of which each of them would partake, and they owed no less to one of their members who was about to set off on such a long journey. At that moment, Berl Israel, the main trustee, intervened:

"Listen to me. Nathan is one of us. He has worshiped among us for over twenty years. Many of his hard-earned zlotys lie in these walls and in the holy books we have here. I propose that we ask him for a down payment of a hundred zlotys, and with God's help he will mail the remainder to us later."

Hirsh Odeser, who had been Berl's rival for years, grumbled that a general assembly should be convened to decide the matter, but Berl objected that this was not the time for politicking. They resolved to give a Torah scroll to Nathan, and celebrated with a few drinks. The blessings and well-wishing lifted Nathan's spirit; true joy, the finest wine of all, warmed his heart. He, Nathan the shoemaker from Porisov, might well have the honor of being the first Jew to bring a Torah scroll to a distant, foreign land.

Half an hour after taking leave of his friends and starting home, his merriment began to wane. The three digits making up the number one hundred appeared suddenly before him in the dark. They danced before his eyes, and mocked him with questions: "When did God name you his envoy in charge of supplying Jews with Torah scrolls? It's just a foolish notion that some religious Jew—and an idle one at—has put into your head. Go back right away, return the scroll, and get back your hard-earned zlotys. It would be a far greater mitzvah to leave that money to your wife and children."

He stood there for a while, but suddenly panicked. "Nathan the shoemaker," a hidden voice warned him, "who are you to play with such a holy object? Do you believe you are purchasing mere leather and thread?"

A shiver of dread ran through Nathan's body. "It is wrong to regard such holy objects lightly," he muttered to himself, trying to apologize. He pressed the Torah scroll to his chest and strode home.

So that is how—along with Nathan's shoe lasts, rulers, hammers, pliers and files—the first Torah scroll, wrapped in clothes and bedding, sailed over the stormy waters of the Atlantic to that distant, foreign land, Colombia.

II

The glowing sky hanging over the suburbs on the Atlantic shore poured fire overhead. The burning sun shone on the half-naked black and bronze bodies of porters carrying huge loads. Shopkeepers kept wiping sweat off their faces. Crowds beset kiosks that sold cold drinks. The sound of car horns blended with the loud cries of people hawking lottery tickets and newspapers. Amid this multicolored mass—black faces, curly woolen hair, white pupils of the eyes and thick hanging lips—one could discern the occasional tourist. Tall, blonde, clad in a white suit, with a colonial hat on his head, dark glasses, and a camera hanging from his shoulder, around he walked, contemplating the scene from above, like a wealthy relative attending the wedding of poor kinsfolk.

Under the radiant sky, on the hot steamy asphalt, into the midst of this multicolored cluster, the Master of the Universe had also thrown some fifteen of His chosen people: Jews from towns and villages in Poland, Lithuania and Besarabia. Instead of discovering the legendary El Dorado, where gold is raked off the streets, they found fiery climes that fry the brains, and a frosty cold that ices the heart. The longing for their homeland gnawed and devoured them, but the way back was cut off. So they trod the burning sand in the streets of the poor neighborhoods. They knocked on doors, and with the aid of a few words of broken Spanish peddled merchandise on the installment plan. Slowly, very slowly, they adjusted to the new surroundings.

The narrow and sandy street was crammed with single-story houses, small shops and workplaces. Shoemakers sat on low benches by open doors. The sound of sewing machines, sanding planes, and wood saws could be heard throughout. The hoarse, drunken voice of a man trying to drown his bitter fate in alcohol issued forth from a liquor store. White, black, and bronze women trudged about, disheveled and shabby, and bought from odorous groceries and butcher shops. Naked children played in the hot sand, their dirty faces covered with flies. Dogs, tired from the heat, lay about with outstretched paws and hanging tongues, not even caring to chase the clouds of flies away from their bodies.

In this little street, in one of the workshops, bent over an old shoe, sat Nathan the shoemaker. His shirt, damp and open, showed a mighty, hairy chest. True, only a vestige of his once dense beard remained, a tuft barely covering the point of his chin. Still, it was the same old Nathan, the same full, ruddy cheeks, only tanned a little darker. Hardly a year earlier, shortly after treading for the first time the earth of his new home, Nathan had met the few Jews there. He was shocked to discover how they procured their livelihoods.

Two of them, who befriended Nathan, advised him to become a peddler. Among the wares they sold on credit were not only ladies' underpants and slips, but also crucifixes and holy images. When Nathan saw such merchandise, he fell speechless. Upon recovering, he stammered: "How can a Hasid like you, Meyer-Ber, ordained as a rabbi, and a pious Jew and a Torah scholar like you, Simon, even come close to such an impurity?" In the old country, Nathan, a typical *shtetl* Jew, would actually shut his windows to avoid hearing the impure chants of Christian processionals passing by. He could not grasp others like him could bring themselves to make a living by selling such things.

"Well," said Meyer-Ber, smiling, "making a living may be compared to saving a life, and that is permitted even on Yom Kippur."

Nathan still could not fathom this. An infinite distance separated him from such objects; generations had carved out an abyss between him and them. A voice at once within him and from far away in time commanded him, "No, no, never shall you draw livelihood from *their* holy objects."

After some sleepless nights, Nathan reminded himself that he had brought along his shoemaker's tools, stacked away somewhere at the inn where he was staying. He counted the dollars that he had sewn into the shoulder pad of his coat, and decided to return to his old trade. It was not hard to find a workshop, and a year passed by as he set on his bench, mending the worn-out shoes of his poor neighbors in the *barrio*.

One cannot say that the beginning went smoothly. No, it was not easy for him to adapt. First, there was the problem of the language. And the craft itself was different here. But Nathan stubbornly overcame all difficulties. Most of all, God's Holy Name stood by him, helping him to succeed. The poor folks of the neighborhood took a liking to the foreigner with the athletic build, who sat on his low bench from dawn to sunset, smiling good-naturedly with his shining black eyes. The quality of his work was good, and he was willing to lend a few cents with a smile. True, he would not become rich this way. But he made a living, praised be God's Holy Name, and always had a few dollars to mail back home. Nathan had even managed to send some zlotys toward the debt on the Torah scroll. He also deposited several hundred pesos in the bank. Some time later, he would return home and live as God had ordained. "Because," thought Nathan occasionally, "what kind of a life is this in this strange land, far from wife and children, bereft of Sabbaths and holidays, without a synagogue, a rabbi, or a kosher slaughterer?"

At other moments, Nathan thanked the Eternal One for bringing him to this new land. Mostly he did so in the evening hours, as he was about to close his shop. The burning sun would start to shrink, becoming a blood-red disk sinking quickly into the pleasant waters of the sea. At such times, Nathan would sit at his bench, unable to avert his glance from the fiery disk that had already reached the horizon. Slowly, the disk would sink into the water. Minute by minute it descended; soon it had dived halfway into the sea. Only a small part could still be seen, resembling a human head trying to peer over the horizon. Then, suddenly, the entire disk had vanished. Only a faint gleam, like a dying flame, remained to color the sky dark blue. Alone, the edges of the horizon reflected the fiery disk, as night arrived in this part of God's earth.

Nathan stayed seated, unable to take his eyes off the Creator's wonders. Serenity enveloped him, especially when he had had a good day. How much would that day's income amount to, converted to zlotys? Nathan reckoned some thirty zlotys. Wait a minute, he thought, as he recalculated. He had never had a head for figures. Why thirty? More than forty. Back in the *shtetl* he would have been satisfied to earn that much in a week. He thanked the Eternal One for the favor shown him, and his heart swelled with joy and hope. In one more year, he would be able to marry off his two eldest daughters properly, and with God's help, all would turn out fine.

Sometimes, however, he was seized with remorse. It started some two months after he had set up his small shop. One evening, a dark-skinned woman about thirty years of age came into the shop. She looked around as if searching for something. When Nathan asked what he could do for her, she asked in Spanish if the *maestro* could make her a new pair of shoes. He stammered in his broken Spanish that here he only resoled shoes, but in the town he came from he had been the best craftsman, and his shoes were sheer adornments.

"*Muy bien,*" said the woman. Nathan asked her to take a seat. She sat down and Nathan prepared to take her measurements. Not a believer in the new fashion of measuring with a tape, he looked around for a piece of paper. The preliminaries lasted all the longer as his glance began to slide along the stranger's fleshy body. It took him a while to find the right piece of paper, and when he did, it ripped. One could not say that happened intentionally, but everything simply slipped from his hands. His glance fell upon her high and firm breasts, delineated by her tight dress; upon her partially bare back, her round shoulders and naked arms. When he was finally ready, he asked her to remove her shoe, and began to trace her foot on the paper. He felt the warmth of her slight foot on his wide, bearish paws, and a flame rushed through him. His hand started to slide up her leg, higher and higher. Strangely, the woman did not discourage him. Her full body just twitched nervously.

In the course of the few days required to finish her shoes, she came in often. She stayed a bit longer each time, asking innocuous questions. At first, Nathan could not understand why she ordered a pair of shoes from him rather than from one of the big stores. The more he pondered this riddle, the more his imagination presented him the succulent silhouette that ignited his blood with passion. One night, around ten o'clock, as Nathan sat half dozing in front of his shop, she strolled by. The street was deserted. He greeted her, and she stopped in her tracks. He took her by the hand. She looked around, entered the shop, and stayed until dawn.

As it is written in the Talmud, one sin leads to another. Nathan's blood streamed with turbulence, like a violent river that has destroyed the dam that restrained it, leaving the waters unchecked. After all, no hindrances stood in his way. The women of the neighborhood were drawn to him like flies to honey. Especially the dark-skinned women, who invented all kinds of excuses to come to his shop. The radiance of his pitch black eyes and his steely arms inflamed their blood.

And Nathan? He drank from this well like a desert wanderer who cannot quench his thirst. He felt as if he had cast away half his age. His sins, which lay like a load on his back, would frighten him from time to time. But that fear was no more than a shadow that vanished as swiftly as it had appeared. Back home, a Jew was held in check by a wife and children. There, he had been a craftsman who worshiped in a synagogue and fretted about livelihood. But here, where there were no obstacles, a man could do whatever he liked. At such times, Nathan would gladly have welcomed a miracle that would cause his strong body to shrink suddenly and become small and thin.

Days, weeks, and months passed. The Hebrew month of Elul approached. True, in the new land, no signs reminded him of the impending Days of Awe. No one blew the ram's horn or knocked on his shutters at dawn, calling him to worship. But looking at his calendar one afternoon, he realized with a start that in a few days it would be time to attend the first services. He panicked. "Master of the Universe," he sighed, "the Days of Awe are upon us, but no preparations have been made." Indeed, it was no surprise that the few Jews involved in prostitution rings should not care about the Days of Awe. But what of Meyer-Ber the Hasid and Simon the rabbi? Had they also forgotten the High Holy Days?

Nathan removed his apron, in preparation to go downtown, seek out Simon and Meyer-Ber, and discuss the matter with them. Just as he was about to leave the shop, a customer came in with some work that had to be done immediately. Soon night had fallen. The store where Simon and Meyer-Ber were likely to be found had already shut. Nathan, dead tired from the day's work, decided to leave the matter for the morrow, when God willing he would attend to it. At that moment, accursed Satan—who will stick his rotten snout in the way whenever a Jew is about to perform a *mitzvah*—stole into Nathan's heart and gnawed on it like a worm.

Satan demanded an explanation: "In what holy book is it written that you of all people—Nathan the shoemaker—have been appointed by God to organize a Jewish congregation? You brought along a Torah scroll that you had purchased with blood money. If you approach them meekly, you will never recover a single peso. When will you get back the hard-earned money you poured in? How do you plan to repay the debt? If pious Jews like them can trade in images of Jesus and crucifixes, surely you can exploit the situation to recover your money. Don't rush. Take it easy. If they can do without High Holy Day services, so can you."

And because the lust for money is so strong, Nathan heeded Satan's counsel and failed to seek out his coreligionists. Two days passed very slowly, two days that seemed as interminable as the very wanderings of the Jewish people. Nathan's unrest, mixed with helpless anger, grew with each hour that Simon and Meyer-Ber did not appear.

On the evening of the third day, they entered his shop, along with a huge man with a thick, red neck. Nathan recognized the man. Everyone in town knew of his shady dealings, but nobody dared say a word. He was a bully and an informer. On the other hand, he performed favors for his fellow Jews, such as intervening with the authorities on their behalf. He would go down to the port and greet immigrants as they arrived, helping them get the official papers they needed. He also lent them their first pesos. Behind his back, he was called Reuben the Rat, but to his face he was called *don* Roberto. Nathan stared at the man with curiosity and surprise. He reckoned that Meyer-Ber and Simon had come about regard the matter that weighed so heavily on his heart, but what had this character to do with it?

The three of them sat down. Meyer-Ber spoke first. "As you well know, *reb* Nathan, the Days of Awe are approaching. Two years ago there was no possibility of organizing services. Last year, we had the requisite number, but no Torah scroll. Today, however, we have a quorum of Jews—may they multiply—and you have a Torah scroll. Therefore, it would be a sin not to conduct proper services. So we have come to borrow the Torah scroll from you."

At that, *don* Roberto took out one hundred pesos and rasped, "I contribute one hundred pesos from my own pocket."

Nathan listened, but did not answer. For a while there was deep silence, during which Israel-Leon's tightly-drawn face appeared before Nathan. His sad and cloudy eyes spoke mutely to him: "Nathan, God forbid! Do not dare profane the great honor the Lord of the Universe has bestowed upon you. He has charged you with bringing the first Torah scroll to a distant, foreign land, so that Jews there might properly worship during the Days of Awe." Nathan harkened to Israel-Leon's sad voice, and said:

"Thank you very much, my fellow Jews. I appreciate your gesture, *don* Roberto. You may take the Torah scroll. There is no need to pay."

And the first time the melodious call to the Torah was heard in the distant, foreign land of Colombia, Nathan's heart swelled with joy. Silently, he thanked the Eternal One for the privilege granted him: to bring the first holy scroll. And a silent happiness warmed his soul, for God had helped him withstand the temptation to trade for money this very great *mitzvah*.

—Translated by Moisés Mermelstein

Cuba

25

Jesús

A SHORT STORY BY PINKHES BERNIKER

[*Pinkhes Berniker (b. 1908 Lubtsh, Belarus; d. ?) was a rabbi's son and studied at yeshivas in Navaredok, Eyshishok and Vilna. In 1925, he emigrated to join his older brother, Chaim, who had started* Dos Fraye Vort, *the first Yiddish newspaper in Cuba. Pinkhes Berniker published stories with Cuban themes in North American Yiddish press organs, such as the Canadian paper* Der Keneder Adler. *By 1931, he had emigrated to the United States, where he worked as a director of a Hebrew school in Rochester. In 1935, a volume of his stories,* Shtile Lebns *("Quiet Lives"), appeared in Vilna.*]

He didn't take it seriously the first few times his roommates suggested that he start peddling images of Jesus, of *Yoshke*, as he preferred to call him. He thought they were kidding. How could they be serious? Were they fools? What could they mean? How could they possibly think that he should shlep the *goyish* icons through the streets of Havana? What was he, a boy, a young lad, who knew nothing of the world? How could they imagine that he—a middle-aged Jew with a beard and side curls, who had been ordained as a rabbi, who had devoted all the days of his life to Torah and to divine service—could all of a sudden peddle icons and spread word of Jesus of Nazareth? No, even they couldn't be serious about that! So he thought, and didn't even try to answer them. He just sighed quietly, wiped the sweat off his face, and sat without moving, sure that they wouldn't bring up such a notion again.

Later he realized he'd been mistaken. Those roommates of his had been very serious. Not daring to propose the idea outright, they had begun by alluding to it, joking about it. He had remained silent and, contrary to their expectations, hadn't jumped up from his seat as though he had been scorched. So they had begun to broach the subject directly, insisting that he not even try another livelihood, even if one presented itself. He, of all people, was in just the right position to turn the greatest profit from peddling the "gods." No one else could approach his success.

"For every god you sell, you'll clear a thousand percent profit." "And the Cubans love to buy gods." "Especially from you, Rabbi Joseph, who look so much like the bastard, pardon the comparison." "You'll see how eager they'll be to buy from you." "And they'll pay whatever you ask." "Listen to me, Rabbi Joseph, just try it! You'll see! They'll sacrifice everything they have for you! People who don't even need a god will buy one from you!" Thus his roommates urged him to become a god peddler. They couldn't stand to see him half starved, in total distress, bereft of the slightest prospects. And they really did believe that selling the gods would solve his problems.

The more persistent they became, the more pensive he grew. He didn't answer them, for what could he say? Could he cut out his heart and show them how it bled, how every word they uttered made a sharp incision in it, tearing at it painfully? How could they understand what he felt, if they didn't know how he'd been trained, what his position had been in the old country? He was consumed with self-pity. The world had stuck out its long, ugly tongue at him. Rabbi Joseph, so diligent a pupil that he'd been hailed as the prodigy from Eyshishok, was now supposed to spread tidings of Jesus of Nazareth throughout the world?!

He couldn't resign himself to his lot. Every day, in the blue, tropical dawn, he dragged himself through the narrow streets of Old Havana, offering his labor to one Jewish-owned factory after another, promising to do whatever it would take to earn a pittance. He was rejected everywhere. How could they let a venerably bearded Jew work in a factory? Who would dare holler at him? How could they prod him, ordering him around as necessary? "How could someone like you work in a factory?" "In the Talmudic academy of Volozhin, did they teach shoemaking?" "Rabbi, you're too noble to work here." They looked at him with pity, not knowing how to help.

"Why? Wasn't the great Rabbi Yokhanan a shoemaker?" he asked, pleading for mercy.

"That was then, this is now."

"And what about now? Wouldn't Rabbi Yokhanan still need to eat?" That was what he wanted to cry out, but he couldn't. He was already too discouraged. The unanimous rejections tortured him more than the constant hunger. And the charity, the sympathy, offered by all became harder to bear. It wouldn't have humiliated him had it not been for the presence, in a faraway Lithuanian town, of a wife and three small children who needed to eat. "Send some money, at least for bread." Thus his wife had written to him in a recent letter. And the word *bread* had swelled up and grown blurry from the teardrop that had fallen on it from the eye of a helpless mother.

Joseph recalled the words from *The Ethics of the Fathers*: "If I am not for me, who will be for me?"

"I must harden myself. I must find work!" He called out these words, forcing himself onto the street. Pale, thin, with a despairing mien, he posted himself at a factory door, glancing around helplessly, hoping to catch sight of the owner. From among the workers, a middle-aged Jew ran up to the door and pressed a few pennies into his palm. Joseph froze. His eyes popped out of his head; his mouth gaped open. The couple of cents fell from his hand. Like a madman, he ran from the factory. Late that night, when his roommates returned, he pulled himself off his cot, stared at them momentarily, and said, "Children, tomorrow you will help me sell the gods." They wanted to ask him what had happened, but, glimpsing the pain in his eyes, they could not move their tongues.

Binding both packages of gods together, he left between them a length of rope to place on his neck, thereby lightening the load. He had only to hold on to the packages with his hands, lest they bump into his sides and stomach.

The uppermost image on his right side portrayed Mother Mary cuddling the newborn child, and the one on his left showed Jesus already grown. Between the two images he himself looked like the Son of God. His eyes were larger than life, and his face was paler than ever. Deep, superhuman suffering shone forth from him, a reflection of the pain visited on Jesus of Nazareth as he was led to the cross.

The day was burning hot. Pearls of sweat shone on his mild, pale face, and his clothes stuck to his tortured body. He stopped for a while, disentangling his nightmarish thoughts, slowly removing the rope from his neck, straightening his back wracked with pain, and scraping away the sweat that bit into his burning face. He wiped tears from the corner of one eye.

He saw, far off, the low wooden cabins in the next village. In the surrounding silence, from time to time, there came the cries of the village children. Feeling a bit more cheerful, he slowly loaded his body with the two packages of gods. Trembling, he strode onward, onward. He was noticed first by the lean, pale children playing in the street. They immediately stopped their games and stiffened in amazement. The tropical fire in their black eyes burst forth as they caught sight of him. Never had they seen such a man.

"*¡Mamá, mamá, un Jesús viene!* A Jesus is coming!" Each started running home. "*¡Mira! ¡Mira!*" The children's voices rang through the village.

From windows and doors along the road women leaned their heads out, murmuring excitedly to one another: "*¡Santa María!*" "*¡Qué milagro!*" "*¡Dios mío!*" They all whispered in astonishment, unable to turn their straining eyes away from the extraordinary man.

Joseph approached one of the houses and pointed to the image of Jesus, mutely suggesting that they buy a god from him. But the hot-blooded tropical women thought he was indicating how closely the image resembled him. Filled with awe, they gestured that he should enter. "*¡Entre, señor!*" said each one separately, with rare submissiveness. He entered the house, took the burden off his neck, and seated himself on the rocking chair they offered him. Looking at no one, he began untying the gods. No one in the household dared to sit. Along with some neighbors who had sneaked in, they encircled him and devoured him with their wide-open eyes.

"*¿Tienes hijo?* Do you have a son?" a young *shiksa* asked, trembling.

"I have two," he answered.

"And are they as handsome as you?" asked another girl excitedly.

"I myself don't know."

"*¡Mira, él mismo tampoco sabe!* He himself doesn't know!" A strange shame overtook the girls. They looked at each other momentarily, then burst into embarrassed laughter: "Ha ha ha! Ha ha ha!" Their hoarse guffaws echoed through the modest home.

"What's going on?" asked the mothers, glancing unkindly toward the men.

"Nothing!" said the girls, embracing each other, then repeating ecstatically, "*¡El mismo tampoco sabe! ¡El mismo tampoco sabe!* Ha ha ha! Ha ha ha!" Their suffocating laughter resonated as each tucked herself more closely into her girlfriend's body.

"And what's your name?" One of the girls tore herself from her friend's embrace.

"José."

"What?" asked several of the women in unison.

"José."

"José-Jesús!"

The village women began to murmur, winking more than speaking.

One of the *shiksas* was unable to restrain herself: "And what's your son's name?"

"Juan."

"Juan, Juan," the *shiksas* began to repeat, drooling. Embarrassed, they pushed each other into thenext room, wildly, bizarrely.

There was a momentary silence. Those watching were still under the spell of what had taken place. Joseph, however, was out of patience. "*Nu, ¿compran?* Are you going to buy or not?" he asked, raising his eyes, filled with the sorrow of the world. He could say no more in Spanish, but no more was necessary. Every woman purchased a god from him by paying an initial installment—from which he already cleared a handsome profit—and promising the rest later.

Home he went, with only the rope. All the gods had been sold. He had never felt so light, so unencumbered. He had no packages to carry, and a hope had arisen within him that he would be forever free from hunger and want.

Later he himself was astonished at how he had changed, at how indifferently he could contemplate Jesus' beard. He went to a Cuban barber and had his blond beard trimmed in the likeness of Jesus.

"Your mother must have been very pious!" said the barber to him, with great conviction.

"How can you tell?"

"When she conceived you, she couldn't have stepped away from the image of Jesus."

"Perhaps." Joseph was delighted.

How could he act this way? He didn't know. The Christian women, his customers in the villages all around, waited for him as Jews await the Messiah. They worshiped him, and he earned from them more than he could ever have dreamed.

They had no idea who he was. He never told them he was a Jew, and he still wondered how he could deny his Jewish background. He learned a little Spanish, especially verses from the New Testament, and spoke with the peasant women like a true *santo*, a saint. Once, when a customer asked him, "*¿Qué eres tú?* What are you?" he rolled his eyes to the heavens and started to say, drawing out his words, "What difference does it make who I am? All are God's children."

"And the *judíos*? The Jews?" asked the women, unable to restrain themselves.

"The *judíos* are also God's children. They're just the sinful ones. They crucified our *señor Jesús*, but they are still God's children. *Jesús* himself has forgiven them." He ended with a pious sigh.

"And do you yourself love the *judíos*?"

"Certainly."

"*¿De veras?* Really?"

"*¿Y qué?* What of it?" He put on a wounded expression and soon conceded, "My love for them isn't as deep as for the Christians, but I do love them. A sinner can be brought back to the righteous path through love, as our *señor Jesús* said."

"*¡Tiene razón!* He's right!"

"*¡Y bien que sí!* And how!"

"*¡Es un verdadero santo!* He's a true saint!" All the women drank in his words.

"Have you yourself seen a real Jew?" Their curiosity couldn't be sated.

"Yes, I have."

"Where?"

"There, in Europe."

"What did he look like?"

"Just like me."

"Really?!"

"Yes, indeed."

"*¡Si él lo dice, debe ser verdad!* If he says it, it must be true." The peasant women winked at each other, and their faces grew intensely serious, as if in a moment of great exaltation. Joseph fell silent, engrossed in his thoughts. He let the peasant women examine some sample gods, for now he simply took orders, which he filled by mail. In the meantime, he took stock of his situation, how much money he had in the bank, how much he was owed, and how many more thousands he would earn in the coming year if business improved by just fifty percent. "Who needs to worry?" A smile lit up his face as he felt these words in his heart: "I give thanks and praise to Thee, almighty God, who hast given Jesus unto the world."

A new god peddler showed up in the same area. Day in and day out he dragged himself from one village to the next, stopping at every home. He scraped the scalding sweat off his face and neck as he knocked, trembling, on the hospitable Cuban doors.

"*¿Compran algo?* Will you buy something?" he asked, gesturing broadly. Solidly built mothers and passionate, well-formed daughters looked at him with pity, comforting him and caressing him with the softness of the Spanish tongue and the gentleness of their big, velvety eyes. They gladly offered him a handout but shook their heads at his gods. "I'm sorry." He got the same answer almost everywhere.

"*¡Compra y no lamentes!* Buy and don't be sorry!"

"You're right!" answered the women, with a slight smile. He stood with his distressed face and heavy heart, looking at the peasant women, unable to understand why they were so stubborn.

A few children gathered around him. They stared at his earnest face, carefully touched the frames of the unveiled images, and began playing with them. "Tell your mother to buy a *santo!*" he said, caressing one of the children. The child stopped laughing. His glance passed from the god merchant to his mother. It was hard for him to grasp what was happening.

"How sweet you are," said the mother, affectionately embracing her now serious child.

"I have a child just like him in the old country," said the god merchant, about to burst into tears.

"*¡Mira, parece una mujer!* He's acting just like a woman!" The peasants were astonished to see the shiny tears forming in the corners of his eyes.

"Should a man cry?" "And he's supposed to be the breadwinner for a wife and children!" "How funny!" A few girls, unable to restrain themselves, laughed in his face. Ashamed, he glanced at their widely smiling eyes, felt his own helplessness, and went away. His feet had grown heavier and his grasp of events slighter. Nonetheless, arming himself with courage, he went from village to village. He knocked on every door and humbly showed his wares: "*¡Compren!* Buy something! If you help me, God will help you. And I sell very cheap!"

But he seldom came across a customer interested in his low prices. Almost everyone was waiting for the *santo*, the holy peddler, who bore a great likeness to God Himself. They dismissed the new god merchant out of hand: "I don't need any." "I'm very sorry." "We've already bought some from someone else." He already knew all their answers by heart.

"Are gods the only thing to peddle?" Such was the bitter question he asked his fellow immigrants every day.

"Do you know of something better? Food isn't about to fly into your mouth. And what are you going to do with the gods you've already bought?"

"*¡Hay que trabajar!* You've got to work!" exclaimed one of his countrymen, eager to show off his Spanish.

"But my work is in vain!"

"Right now your work is in vain, but it will pay off in time," said his friends, trying to console him.

"In time, in time!" he muttered nervously, not knowing at whom.

It had grown dark in the middle of the day. The clear, tropical sky had suddenly clouded over. Waves of heat rose from the ground, and the air became closer and denser. At any moment buckets of rain could fall. *Campesinos*, riding into town, became uneasy lest the storm catch up with them. So they pushed back their gritty straw hats, their *tijanas*, fastened the palm-leaf baskets full of fowl on one side of their saddles; secured the cans of milk on the other side; and urged the horses on with all their might. "*¡Pronto!* Faster! *¡Pronto!*" "Soon there'll be a deluge!" "You'll get soaked with all your gods in the middle of the field." The riders took pity on the poor foot traveler as they dug their spurs ever more deeply into the sides of their horses. But he scarcely moved his feet, hammering his steps out heavily. It was already past noon, and he hadn't sold a single god.

Arriving at the next village, soaked to the bone, he caught sight of an open door leading into a home full of people. Sneaking in, he put down his pack of gods in a corner behind the door. As he started removing his wet clothes from his even wetter body, he heard a woman speaking: "Here's five dollars; send me a *San Antonio* like that next week." "And send me a *Jesus by the Well.*" "I'll take a *San Pablo*. Take three dollars in the meantime, and I'll pay the rest later." "Make sure you don't forget to send me a *Santa María.*" "And I want a *Mother with the Son.*" The women shouted over each other.

He could hardly believe his ears. He thought he was dreaming one of his sweet nightly dreams, in which he saw himself amid circles of peasant women ripping his godly wares out of his hands. He had believed that such good fortune was possible only in a dream, but here it was happening for real. "What can this be?" He wondered why he hadn't yet looked into the opposite corner of the room, and he took a few steps toward it.

He stopped in his tracks, stupefied. All his limbs began to shake. He tried to hide his surprise, for never had he seen a man who looked so much like Jesus. "So that's it!" he murmured to himself, as he watched Joseph rolling his eyes from time to time toward heaven, blessing the peasant women as a *rebbe* blesses his Hasidim. "Aha!" He was astonished at the reverence the village women bestowed on the stranger. "No, no, I could never become such a showman!" He stepped off to one side to keep Joseph from noticing him.

His last bit of hope had run out. "*Y tú, ¿de dónde vienes?* And where have you come from?" The peasant women were surprised to see the new god peddler, after Joseph had left.

"From Santo Domingo."

"You've just gotten here?"

"No, I'm just about to leave."

"Did you see our *Jesusito*?"

"You mean the *vendedor*, the seller of the gods?"

"Yes. Doesn't he look just like Jesus?" asked the peasant women, offended.

"Like Jesus? But he's a *judío*, a Jew!" These words came flying out of his mouth with unusual force.

"*¡Mentira! ¡Mentira!* That's a lie! A lie! You yourself are the *judío*, and a dirty one at that!" cried the peasant women in unison, pale with emotion.

"*¡Palabra de honor!* I give you my word of honor that he's a *judío*!" The new god peddler couldn't restrain himself when he realized what a terrible impression the word *judío* made on them. But his claims were all in vain. The village women still didn't believe him. He couldn't make them understand. "*¡No, no puede ser!* No, it can't be." "*¡Vamos,* *vete de aquí!* Come on! Get out of here!" They couldn't stand to hear his words any longer.

He fell silent and left the house, but not the village. He sought out some young men and bought them a round of drinks. As he sipped black coffee by the white marble table, he told them that the god peddler with the face like Jesus', who overcharged their mothers for the pictures they bought from him, was a Jew, a descendant of the ones who had crucified Jesus.

"*¡No hable boberías!* Don't talk nonsense!" "*¿Cómo es posible?* How can that be?" "*¡No me lo diga!* Don't tell me." The young men didn't want to believe him. As their stubbornness grew, so did his. Finally, he told them of the first Jewish commandment. He left twenty-five dollars with the owner of the café and swore that the money was theirs if he had been lying to them. The cash had the right effect. It was as though the young men had been touched by fire. The blood rushed to their faces, and they drank themselves into a stupor.

Joseph hadn't yet arrived at the first house in the village when a lad ran across his path. "*¡Oiga!* Listen, sir, my mother wants to buy something." The boy breathed with difficulty, hardly able to utter these words.

"*¡Bendito eres, hijito!* Blessed art thou, my son!" Such was Joseph's gentle answer.

"*¡Por aquí es más cerca!* This way is shorter!" said the little *goy* as he strode over the field, with Joseph trailing behind him.

Soon they were far, very far, from the village. The boy had already pointed out that "right over there" was their house. Although Joseph saw no house "over there," he still suspected nothing, assuming that his eyes were not as keen as the little *goy's*.

"*Oiga, santo, ¿tú eres judío?* Listen, Your Holiness, are you a Jew?" The earth had suddenly brought forth, before Joseph's eyes, a robust young Cuban. Joseph gazed in surprise. For once his quick tongue failed him. When he finally could say something, it was too late. He was already splayed on the ground, with several *goyim* pinning down his legs; one held his head and two his arms. He screamed bloody murder, thrashed with his feet, pulled with all his might, but to no avail. They were stronger and did what they had to.

When they found out that he was indeed a Jew, they left him lying there, half naked in the middle of the field. Every one of them spat in his face, hollered "*¡Judío!*" and ran to the village to tell of this wondrous thing.

The village women refused to believe even their own children. And for a long, long time they wouldn't patronize the new god merchant, for they hoped that *Jesús* would come back. But Joseph never returned.

—Translated by A. A.

26

The Faith Healer

A SHORT STORY BY ABRAHAM JOSEF DUBELMAN

[*Abraham Josef Dubelman (b. 1908 Reyvits, Poland; d. 1990 Florida) emigrated at the age of thirteen to Cuba, where he worked in a village store. Dubelman began writing a year later and ultimately became a major contributor to the biweekly* Havaner Lebn. *He published three volumes of Yiddish stories, and after his immigration to Miami in 1961, a book in English entitled:* On The Straight Path *(New York: Vantage, 1979). "A Dybbuk" was one of A. J. Dubelman's many pseudonyms.*]

I

Morning had begun to sift through the slatted door of the hotel room where I was staying. That meant day would soon be coming! All night, the mosquitoes had made sleep impossible, and I had fried in the stuffy, tropical heat.

I got up and stepped out of the hotel. The early-morning breeze was moist and cool—pure refreshment after a night of suffering.

Everything seemed reborn, and the small-town, good-natured Cubans approached me with their infinite eagerness to be of service.

"Are you looking for the *polaco, señor?*"

"For my *paisano.*"

"Over there, where you see the green door, is where he lives."

I thanked them and the Cubans were happy to have helped. I went on my way, to the only Jewish business in town. The proprietor, an old Jew, met me by the door.

"Peace to a Jew!"

"Peace!"

"Where are you from?"

"From Havana. But it's worth traveling so far to meet another Jew."

His face lit up. He ran his hand through his gray hair, and his light-colored eyes had a gentle, yielding look. His face, wrinkled with age but even more from suffering, turned hospitable.

"Why are you standing at the door? Come inside! We hardly ever see a Jew around here." He started spewing out words, thrilled the chance to speak Yiddish with someone besides his wife. He began telling me how lonely he was in this miserable little town, where he had already spent eighteen years, unable to leave.

A customer came in. The Jew's mien quickly changed, and a studied, saccharine smile stretched his lined cheeks. The bargaining began. A pair of pants went into the customer's hands, then back on the shelf. The Jew kept up a running *spiel,* recounting the history of the pants, pointing out how exceptional the fabric was, and also the workmanship. In the end he made the sale. He felt guilty in my presence and tried to apologize:

"I came to this town the way one comes to an inn, just for the night, as it were. I thought I'd stick around to make a little money before moving to Havana or back to the old country. As it turned out, I ended up settling here. But what kind of life is this? You become a yokel. There's no one to speak Yiddish with. Back in the old country, I was used to living among Jews, stopping by the synagogue to pore over a page of the Talmud. But here? You can't even keep kosher. You have a livelihood, but it doesn't do you a bit of good."

I started to reassure the Jew a little. "It's the same wherever you go. You have to stay confident. Be patient."

But my words made not the slightest impression on the lonely Jew. He kept talking: "My wife is an utter wreck. She's ill, broken-hearted from homesickness. We don't even have children for her to devote herself to. She's no longer a *mentsh*, my Hannah. If you'd only known her when we first got here. Like the bloom on the rose she was. But now?"

The clerk came into the store, and the Jew invited me home with him. "Come into the house. Seeing another Jew will do my poor old wife good."

I went for his sake. Inside, a visibly aged woman came up to us and tried to smile as she said, "Have a seat."

II

Their dwelling had three rooms. In one were two beds and some chairs; in another was only a table with chairs. The table was covered with a white cloth on which stood two old-fashioned candlesticks, covered with molten wax. Finally, there was a living room with some rocking chairs and, in a corner, a cabinet that housed old, yellowing religious books. Portraits of the couple's parents hung on the walls. The stately appearance of Jews with long beards and earlocks lent the room a special charm. I looked at their engaging faces, which gazed down at me with their astute eyes.

"Are these your parents?"

"Over there," said the Jew, becoming talkative, "is my father, may he rest in peace. He was a clever man. I'm afraid to look him in the eyes. Do you think I don't know that today is the Sabbath? But what can you do? I try to stay as observant as possible, but we are in exile."

Meanwhile, his wife stood sighing. "This is my mother, may she inherit Paradise. A saintly woman she was. You can't imagine what she had to live through."

Suddenly, the woman caught herself as though she had just remembered something. She opened the back door, bent down, and picked up a glass that was standing by the entrance. The glass was filled with water and various herbs. The water looked greenish and murky, like swill. The wife closed her eyes and started moving her lips in a whisper. Then she started to drink, grimacing from the intense bitterness. The whole scene bewildered me. I was unable to contain my curiosity. "Is that some kind of medicine?" I asked her.

"It relieves my sickness just like that!" She started to redden and hesitated to tell me more. I insisted, acting very interested. She clearly believed that I myself wished to be cured of some illness, and she opened up.

"I had been sick for quite a long time. To tell the truth, I don't know what was wrong. I went to all sorts of doctors. They were always giving me different medicines, but nothing helped. And now, I just take this potion—a glass of water with herbs—and I'm all better."

Unable to restrain myself, I broke out laughing. She became more serious, uttering an oath: "On my word, as today is the Holy Sabbath throughout the world, it has helped. There was a time when I didn't believe either. I too laughed. But God's power is hard for mere mortals to comprehend. The first time my neighbor came here and told me about this, I ran her out of the house. But now I've seen it clearly with my own eyes. This has nothing to do with ordinary people. This is not about doctors. This is from God. When my neighbor took me there the first time, I was afraid. What was going on there? What had I gotten myself into? And let me tell you, the first time you see him, you'll be plenty frightened, too. All kinds of things were hanging on the walls. Dried herbs. A bent, rusty knife. Little idols made of various objects. Frightening. On an old stool covered with thick fur sat an elderly Negro. He was wearing several amulets around his throat. He looked at me with piercing eyes. My neighbor led me closer to him. He wouldn't stop looking into my eyes.

"'Are you a foreigner?'

"'Yes. I'm a Jew.'

"'A Jew?'

"'You know—a daughter of Israel?'

"'Why have you come to me?'

"'I'm ill. My friend told me that you can heal.'

"'I can't heal you just like that.'

"'Why not?'

"'You have to believe.'

"'In your god?'

"'No, that's not it. You can believe in any god you want. But you also have to believe in me, in my medicine.'

"'I don't place my faith in humans. I believe only in God!'

"'Then the medicine won't work. You must consider this carefully. Sometimes, a man can also bring about a miracle. I take your belief and pass it on. You mustn't lie to me about what you believe. Otherwise, I can't hand your belief over to the *espíritus*. You must have faith. When you believe, then come to me.'

"The neighbor broke in: 'Healer, she is obedient. She will believe! She's a decent woman. She won't lie. Please help her!'

"The faith healer looked at me again with his piercing eyes. I thought to myself, 'Who knows God's ways? This *goy* could well be one of the hidden saints whose merits maintain the world.' He asked me again, 'Do you believe?'

"'I believe!'

"He started chanting various spells. I couldn't make out a word. Then he examined my fingernails and started rubbing them with a small bone. I felt an intense pain. Again he asked if I had faith. And when I assured him I believed in him, he began to smile, all the while using a red scarf to dry his shiny forehead. Then he took all kinds of dried herbs from the walls, and from a wooden box he gave me some crushed bone.

"'Take this home with you, *cristiana*. Every evening, you must prepare a glass with these herbs and put it by the door. The *espíritus* will come looking for it. In the morning, drink it up. Have faith, and you will get well. Do this everyday. But don't forget, before you drink, recite that you believe with all your heart, with all your soul, and with all your might.'"

III

The evening had begun to fall. The setting sun flecked the sky with red. The townspeople had begun closing their shops, leaving doors half ajar, in anticipation of a last-minute customer. The Jew, too, stood by his half-closed shop door and hoped for latecomers, but none came.

He looked at me: "Perhaps you'd like step into the house? I've got to stay here for a little while yet." I understood that he felt a bit uncomfortable counting the day's receipts in front of me, so I went in.

His wife asked me to sit down. She glanced up at the sky, then turned to me.

"The stars are already out, aren't they?"

I looked. "You can see them now."

"Since the Sabbath is over, I shall now recite 'God of Abraham.'"

She went to the faucet, wet the tip of her finger, and intoned the prayer. After she finished, she heartily wished both herself and me a good week to come. I looked at this curious woman, and I couldn't keep from asking, "If you're such a devout Jew, how can you go to a faith healer?"

She stared hard at me. "Do you think I go around crossing myself?"

"You're worshiping two gods. What you're practicing is idolatry. The faith healer is not a doctor. A Jew should not believe in superstitions, in magic."

The woman had a guilty look on her face: "One feels so lonely here, so far from other Jews. One must believe in something. All is not lost. God rules the world."

Her reply made me uneasy. I started to encourage her to leave the town and move to Havana. Then her husband came in and wished us a booming "Good week!" as though he had just returned from synagogue. He lit a candle and began the Havdalah service.

I felt somewhat suffocated. I went out to the courtyard to look at the night. In the distance you could hear frogs croaking, and dogs from the surrounding villages bayed at the moon. The night grew darker. From the Jewish home issued forth a graceful voice, lowly chanting the prayerful words, "He who separates the holy from the profane. . ."

Off to the side, behind the door, stood the glass of water mixed with herbs, which the faith healer had prescribed.

—Translated by Debbie Nathan

27
The Gallego

A POEM BY AARON ZEITLIN

[*Aaron Zeitlin (b. 1898 Uvarovitsh, Byelorussia, 1898; d. 1973 New York) was a Hebrew and Yiddish poet, dramatist and novelist active in Warsaw before the start of World War II and in New York thereafter. He combined a keen knowledge of European classics with an assertion of faith steeped in the Kabbalah. At the outbreak of World War II, Zeitlin spent several months in Cuba awaiting a permanent U.S. visa. There he penned some poems on Cuban and Hispanic themes that he assembled under the rubric* In goles Kuba *("In Cuban Exile").*]

The old *gallego* asks: "Are you a *judío?*"
"Certainly."
"If so, perhaps you know who I am?
A Jew or a Gentile? That Catholic wife of mine
curses me, because I descend from Marranos.
I seldom go to church. So she says to me: 'It's
because of your sins, you accursed non-Christian, that
our daughter stays single.' She'll be the death of me,
that wife of mine, who kneels before idols and kisses
the hands of priests. So, let the devil take her.
Nor am I a Jew. There still burns within me
an old dread, and I can't understand
your Kol-Nidre, here in Havana.
On your Yom Kippur here, no tears are shed.
You know no fear of inquisitors.
Most of all: there's no fear of God.
whenever you have time, you play cards,
And there

up there, God sits and grows wrathful. So what.
"And what has become, tell me, what has become
of you *judíos?* No trace of fear.
No fear whatsoever of God
or (excuse the comparison) of inquisitors
who can suddenly raid your hideout.
What hideout? Which hideout? Today it is bright out
and your temple's nice and roomy.
I, on the other hand, am still afraid. I dream
at night of autos-da-fé: I'm led to the pyre."

—Translated by A. A.

Mexico

❦❦❦❦❦❦❦❦❦

28

Churches

POEM BY ISAAC BERLINER, ILLUSTRATED BY DIEGO RIVERA

*[Isaac Berliner (b. 1899 Lodz; d. 1957 Mexico) was sentenced
to forced labor by the Germans during World War I. In 1919 he
published his first poems. Berliner immigrated in 1922 to Mexico,
where he became one of the founders of the local Yiddish cultural
life. In 1936, the volume* Shtot fun palatsn *("City of Palaces")
appeared, with poems by Berliner and illustrations by his friend,
the Mexican artist Diego Rivera.]*

The bells up in the steeples
still call the faithful to prayer, —
Every mute church
like an old graybeard turned to stone.

Their bodies faded by four centuries,
all full of wrinkles and grooves,
staring darkly through the gray spectacles of time
in amazement.

The calm pace of time
can't stamp out blind faith—
Petitioners still kneel and petition
at the open church doors.

And in every glance of the petitioners
there is a prayerful little flame, flaming away,
of holy Jesus religion,
hope and faith, as it did then,

When the armor-clad bronzed bodies
in armor of iron and steel
went striding through these streets here
with calm, measured strides.

The gruesome Spanish knights—
the ultra-Catholic guards
of the holy church fathers
and monks all hooded and black.

And I still seem to hear the singing,
the choirs of pious nuns,
the Spanish inquisitors
with eyes that are glazed at prayer.

—Your light lights up all abysses,
oh, holy Jesus on high—
Your name, so great and so holy,
defiled by a servant of yours.

—Oh, purest one, Virgin Mary,
begrudge him not, cleanse his soul.
Let the holy flames of the pyre
wash away his sins. . .

And I still seem to see them leading
a victim through streets large and small,
the curses, the jokes and the laughter,
of the pious crowd in his wake.

And I still see the faggots cracking
along with the bones and the ribs—
and the burned victim collapsing
with the word of God on his lips.

—Translated by Mindy Rinkewich

29
Holiday in the Streets: The First Anti-Semitic Demonstration

(June 2, 1931)

A POEM BY JACOBO GLANTZ

[*Jacobo Glantz (b. 1902 Nay Vitebsk, Ukraine; d. 1982 Mexico) was born on an agricultural settlement granted to Jews by Czar Alexander II and began publishing poems in Russian at the age of fifteen. He was shortly imprisoned by the Soviets before emigrating in 1925 to Mexico. Besides several volumes of Yiddish poetry, Glantz' creative output included poems originally written in Spanish as well as collages, paintings and sculptural works exhibited at national and international venues. His daughter Margo Glantz, a celebrated writer in Spanish, recounts in her memoir* Las genealogías *an anecdote that the poem translated here foreshadows: her father was almost lynched by local fascists in 1939, possibly because he looked like Leon Trotsky—a resemblance noted by the poet's friend, Diego Rivera. Trotsky was murdered the following year in the Mexican capital.*]

"Drive out the Jews!" (from a poster)

On a broad plaza, lined with trees and planted with flowers,
Next to the ancient gray cathedral,
I walk, thinking painful thoughts,
Avoiding the turbulent press of the crowd.

Has the desperate poverty of the gloomy city districts
Driven them into the open square?
Have the starving masses, clothed in shawls, come
Begging for urbane mercy in the cold?

—No, it's neither the sorrow of hungry days and leprous nights,
Nor the wick of rebellion in the darkness of the masses.
It's old poison poured into new, clay vessels,
Like boiling sulfur on stagnant water.

By the rusty old gate of the cathedral,
Purebred Catholic ladies watch the parade with glittering eyes.
Pale women in poor blouses lie, faint
From the sultry, stifling charcoal fumes.

Life strides with hurried, dizzying steps,
Stops at a point, then it wheels.
Nearby is an emaciated Jew,
Who fixes his straying glance on empty heavens.

The tropical noon, fishing-pole in hand,
Catches shadows on the street, like running deer.
The shadows over the walls of the cathedral
Thin out, then disappear.

The Jew—submissive, silent—reads the screeching posters
And looks at me as though I were a stranger,
Tired eyes, like two exclamation points, stand out:
"Each generation seeks to wipe us out!"

—Translated by A. A.

30
Quite a Bank

A SHORT STORY BY MEIR CORONA

[Meir Corona (b. 1891 Shedlets, Poland; d. 1965 Mexico) was ordained as a rabbi and spent five years as a pioneer in Palestine before settling in the mid-1920s in Mexico City. There he was involved in the Jewish community as a teacher and journalist. His often whimsical fiction was collected into three volumes published during his lifetime.]

There's a stale, sour stench: a miscellany of heaped-up vegetables and fruits, cheese, fried fish, sweaty bodies, thighs, urine, and belching drunks. The smell sneaks harsh but titillating into the nose on a cold spring day. On this street the apartment complex is located.

A dank, dirty corridor leads to the first courtyard, home to a soda factory. Past the gate and the toilet for the entire building, a hallway leads to the second courtyard. There, a dark, narrow, twisting staircase takes you to the door of the bank. It has no sign, and none is needed. Even without one, many of Mexico's Jewish merchants and factory owners already know about the bank.

Its proprietors are two partners with capital worth half a million pesos. But their partnership is not based on the bank or the capital. Each one works separately, with his own capital for his own clients—arranging discounts, drawing up promissory notes, making loans, and so forth.

The partners also have different ways of keeping their books. One does the accounting in Hebrew, in a long, narrow book. He has a single book for all the customers, with each customer taking up two pages. The page for expenditures reads *Nosatti*—"I have given"—and the page for receipts bears the inscription *Qibbalti*—"I have received."

The other partner prefers a Germanized Yiddish, transcribed in

Hebrew letters. He uses a separate notebook for each client. The pages for expenditures read *Hinaustragen*—"carry out"—and those for receipts are titled *Einnehmen*—"take in."

One afternoon, the shoe wholesalers Baumholtz and Langer knocked on the door and walked into the "bank"—a large, rectangular room that apparently once had been whitewashed. The shoe dealers looked around, amazed by the furnishings. In one corner of the room stood two little iron beds, arranged at a ninety-degree angle, like the Hebrew letter *daled*. On the wall over one bed hung a portrait of the kindly old Austrian Kaiser Franz Josef; over the second bed was a picture of the stern old rabbi from Kovno, *reb* Isaac Elhanan Spector. Both pictures clearly showed the effects of houseflies that, apparently without the least respect for the Kaiser's medals or the rabbi's learned visage, had for years enjoyed free run of the place.

Opposite the intersecting beds, in a second corner, stood a wardrobe that looked ancient and second-hand. By the window between the wardrobe and beds stood a small, white table with a newspaper spread on it, and on top of that two and a half rolls and a sliced herring. Around the little table were three simple, white chairs. Two had all four legs, and one had three. Its fourth leg had fallen off and been replaced by a box underneath.

Once inside, the two shoe dealers found only one partner, the Germanic bookkeeper—a tall, blonde, broad-shouldered young man. He was sitting on one of the little beds with a shoe off and his pants leg rolled up, soaking his foot in a bowl of water.

"Good day, Mr. Fishman. So Mr. Tannenbaum isn't here?"

"Good day to you, men! Tannenbaum is here, surely. He just stepped out for a minute to buy something. Have a seat while you wait. He'll be right back."

They sat down and armed themselves with patience. One took a newspaper from his pocket to read. The other had Yehoyesh's Yiddish translation of the Bible, which had just arrived from the States. He opened it and glanced at it. Then they heard hard, slow, heavy steps on the stairway, matched by the rhythmic beating of a stick. Tannenbaum came in. He was a slightly hunchbacked man whose hair was already

gray, and who leaned on a thick cane in his right hand. In his left hand
he was carrying a seltzer bottle. With a smiling, happy face he turned
to the visitors and panted to them in a hoarse voice, "Ah, welcome!
Nice to meet you, esteemed guests! What's the good word, fellows?"

And without waiting for a reply, he turned to his partner: "Just
look, Fishman, at the bargain I picked up. You hardly ever find
anything like this. Take a look!" He lifted the bottle and showed "the
little tube of the siphon inside. It reaches all the way to the bottom so
you don't waste a drop!"

Then, he turned back to the guests: "What are you reading? Is it good?"

He took the book in hand and opened it to the title page: "Ah! The
Bible in Yiddish! The Talmud says that when Onkelos translated the
Torah into Aramaic, there was an earthquake that covered four hundred
square miles. You can find that in the tractate *Megillah*."

"As far as I'm concerned," Langer answered, "the *entire* earth can
quake, as long as I can read the Bible in my own language."

"But let's get to the point," Baumholtz interrupted him. "We
came to get a loan from you, Herr Tannenbaum—two thousand pesos
on two promissory notes. I will sign one of them, and Langer will co-
sign; Langer will sign the other, and I'll be the co-signer."

The old man looked fixedly at both shoe dealers and measured
them up, as though trying to read from their faces whether or not it
paid to do this kind of business with them. Finally, he smiled shyly
and answered: "You know where the Talmud speaks of carrying things
on the Sabbath? It mentions 'two kinds that are actually four.' In this
case, it seems that two are actually one!"

Langer interrupted him: "That's why we've come not about the
Talmud, but for promissory notes. And we didn't come on the
Sabbath, but during the work week."

"Especially during the work week, I like every promissory note to
have a separate co-signer. As for the rate, you probably know that
these days I won't take less than three percent."

Then, in order to sidetrack the conversation, he turned to Langer:
"Please tell me, Herr Langer, since you are such an avid reader, if perhaps
you could find me Droyanov's *Treasury of Parables and Proverbs*. I've been

looking for that book for such a long time. I simply have to read it. In exchange, I could lend you one of my books."

The shoe dealers glanced at each other. They were not about to be tricked into changing the subject. With open contempt, they answered, "We'll make a separate visit to discuss literature. Right now, we're here for money."

In the end, they settled things—both the promissory notes and the interest rate.

Then Langer and Baumholtz hurried out, holding their noses in the reeking courtyard. They were scarcely two blocks away when they realized someone was calling them. They looked around and saw old Tannenbaum running after them, yelling, panting, and waving.

"Oy! Baumholtz, this means trouble!" said Langer. "I'm afraid the old moneybags has gotten cold feet."

"Oy! This is terrible!" echoed Baumholtz, in a frankly terrified voice. "Now what do we do?"

When Tannenbaum caught up and managed to stop gasping long enough to catch his breath, he called out: "Gentlemen, listen! I made a mistake! The passage isn't in the tractate *Megillah*, but in *Hagigah*!"

—Translated by Debbie Nathan

31
The Tinifotsky Monologues

EXCERPTS FROM A SATIRE BY ABRAHAM WEISBAUM

[*Abraham Weisbaum (b. 1895 Konskevolye, near Lublin; d. 1970 Mexico) received a traditional Jewish education and wandered during World War I, ending up in Kharbin, China, where he worked as a prompter in a Yiddish theater. He then accompanied part of the troupe to Shanghai, where he acted, gave private lessons, and wrote for the local English-language Jewish press organ,* Israel's

Messenger. *In 1925, Weisbaum immigrated to Mexico, where he wrote for the monthly* Undzer Vort *as well as other publications. His depictions of Mexican Jewish assimilationist parvenus, which count among the most mordant satires in Yiddish literature, are assembled into two volumes published in 1947 and 1959:* Meksikaner zigzagn *("Mexican Zigzags") and* In meksikaner gan-eydn *("In the Mexican Garden of Eden").*

I. Yente Tinifotsky

Being rich is no picnic. It's no good to be wealthy, especially in Mexico. You get what I'm saying? It's no good!

When people talk to me, they suck up to me, all smiles and flattery: It's *señora* Tinifotsky this, *señora* Tinifotsky that. But behind my back? Oh my God! All the rich women around here are jealous of me. They backbite me from here to eternity. They begrudge me even a piece of bread! So I ask you, does it pay to be wealthy? Is it my fault I'm rich? And what do I get from all my so-called riches? True, I live in the ritzy Polanco neighborhood. In a big, beautiful house. A palace, I tell you! Twelve rooms with a foyer and with a, a, what do you call it here? A *terraza*, yeah. So what do you think I get from all this? A headache, that's all! I wander around like a stranger, from one room to another. I ring a bell for the help and all four maids come running from everywhere until they find me.

Around the table in the dining room, you can seat sixty people. I sit on one side of the table, my husband facing me on the other side, my daughter in the middle, and across from her my boy, my little Salvador. The maid starts serving the food and, poor thing, she has to go 'round and 'round the table. And the chairs! Oh my God! Why did we need those high, heavy chairs? They're so high that when you sit you can't see anyone over them.

In the old days—God forbid they should return!—I cooked stewed beef, barley soup, meatloaf, and sliced the bread myself. I'd make herring with onions, with vinegar. Back then the food used to really taste like something. But nowadays? I know I shouldn't complain, God help me. But the food doesn't taste Jewish now. No way!

So what do I get from all my wealth, from all this glitz, from Polanco? Why should you be jealous? Why? Are you jealous of my cars? My diamonds? What do I get from them? Well at least I get a little enjoyment. I've got people to play poker with. I mean, you have to do *something* to while away the time. A person could go nuts here, wandering round and round all day with nothing to do.

On the other hand, do you think playing poker makes it any better? I mean, everybody and her mother plays these days. You have no idea who you're at the table with. This one woman sits down and puts down a nice, round 25-peso chip. I up her one and put down a 50-peso chip. So then guess what happens? Fifties start flying from all sides, and I decide to show the world that I'm really the famous Yente—Yente Tinifotsky. So I put down a hundred. If it were only so easy for my *children* to give me such pleasure! You heard me—a whole hundred. So then, what do you think? I get matched by this slob of a woman, a pauper, a frump who couldn't even afford to buy my garbage, who any day now will be going bankrupt! So I tell her, *"Señora*, why risk your last hundred? You won't have anything to go grocery shopping with tomorrow. Why stoop so low that even the good works of your ancestors could not make your case before the Almighty?"

She answers me in a huff: "It's none of your concern. Now let's see what's in your hand, *señora* Tinifotsky."

What gall! The little beggar, acting like she's my equal. What a boor! Hundreds! But *I* can put down hundreds! I'm allowed! I'm Yente Tinifotsky! Couldn't you just die from the aggravation? Pretty soon it'll be impossible to organize a respectable poker game anymore. But what else could I expect. The women don't just want to keep up with me, they want to outdo me.

Take what happened recently: I bought myself a Persian-lamb jacket for four thousand pesos. In a few days, I see all the women I know wearing fur jackets. I buy myself a cape made out of six foxes—six! Soon the very same capes are all over the place! A few months ago, that miserable husband of mine went to the States, and bought me a sable. Quite an item. A $15,000 or $20,000 sable, the only one in Mexico! So what do you think happens? I meet up with a woman I know who's got on the same sable. I mean, how am I supposed to deal with this?

So I buy a rug—a carpet—for 8,000 pesos. Back in our *shtetl*, not even the biggest landowner had such an expensive carpet under his feet. You walk so quiet on it, so soft, as soft as on a featherbed. You say you're an expert on carpets? A Chinese carpet is as fluffy and thick and soft as a matzah ball, while a Persian rug is as stiff as an overdone Passover pancake. Back in the *shtetl*, we used to take a shovel, a spade, every Friday before Shabbos, and scrape the mud off the floor, then pour sand on it. But here we walk on carpets. A pleasure! So then what happens? Now my neighbors run out and buy two carpets, a Chinese and a Persian, for ten thousand pesos.

I buy myself a chandelier for the living room for six thousand pesos. Soon I see the same chandelier in another living room. Honestly, it's enough to make you sick! So then I go and have a chandelier custom-made so that no one can copy it, no way. Have a look: big enough and round enough to take up half the ceiling, made of pure crystal and lots of polished glass hanging all over. Yente Tinifotsky is not one to scrimp! She knows how to go all out!

And God, I love diamonds! You think you know something about diamonds? There's blue diamonds, white diamonds, and blue-white diamonds. Blue-white diamonds are the best and the most expensive. The bigger the diamond, the pricier it gets incrementally. Once, in the old country—God forbid those days should ever come back!—my husband-to-be bought me a diamond ring for all of thirty rubles. Today, I wear rings with big diamonds on every finger, and on some fingers two diamond rings. Too bad you can't wear diamond rings on your thumbs. Whenever I wave my hand and flutter my fingers, my diamonds sparkle and flash so gorgeous, so rich, so classy. It's a pleasure to look at them!

On the other hand, I have an uncle, the pious, old-fashioned type. He's always getting after me: "Yente, don't make waves with your diamonds! Yente, dear, why do you have to wear your diamonds when you go to the market to buy a chicken? Why should everyone at the grocery store be looking at your diamonds, your baubles."

I keep my cool: "Uncle, what's it to you if I wear my diamonds when and where I please? And what's it to me if everybody's jealous?

I didn't rob anybody to get these jewels. I deserve to splurge. I will wear my diamonds!

And you don't think I have my share of heartache from that no-good husband of mine? He's got this new idea in his head. He wants to buy a big, Yiddish library, the biggest Yiddish library in Mexico. What a crazy thought! So I go at him with every nasty word in me: "Are you out of your mind? A library, all of a sudden? What do you mean, a library? It's not like you read lots of Yiddish books. When do you have the time to even *look* at a Yiddish book? You're always busy. You're at the business all day. At night you play a little poker. On Sunday, you go out to the country house. The children never pick up a Yiddish book. So why do you need a literary graveyard here in the house?"

So you see, instead of getting a library, I bought a little silver for the house. Yente Tinifotsky's got some smarts. She's got a head on her! Absolutely: a head on her! Once—this should never happen to you!—in the gloomy, muddy *shtetl*, we had four brass candlesticks with copper brims in our house, and a pan for frying fish. Every Friday I had to shine and rub and scour the candlesticks for Shabbos. Oy, was I jealous of anyone with silver candlesticks. Well, these days everything I have is silver. God, I love silver! I have a silver platter, a thick one. Here, have a look. It weighs seventeen pounds. A silver teapot, creamers, forks, knives, spoons. All made of silver, pure silver—*pura plata*. On the buffet, the credenza, the dresser—there's wrought silverware, silver services. It's such a pleasure to look at so many silver things. They gleam, they shine, they light up from every which way. *And he wants a library?!* Silver! More silver! *¡Plata!*

I'll tell you a secret. Just between you and me. Soon it's going to be impossible to live in Polanco anymore. I'll tell you a story. I'll make it short and sweet.

So I'm driving my car and I spot someone I know. I pull up and go over to her with a big hello. "*¡Buenas tardes!* How are you, *señora?* Don't you remember me?"

She looks at me some, gives me the once over, and claps her hands.

"*Señora* T. . ., T. . ., Tee-nee-fotsk. . .?"

"Fotsky," I help her out. "Tinifotsky. I'm *señora* Tinifotsky."

So she tells me she remembers when we used to live in the same apartment complex on Avenida Jesús María. So I ask her what she's doing in Polanco. She tells me she's living here. I can't believe it. I ask how on Earth she would up living in Polanco.

She answers me, kind of angry already, "What are you so shocked about? I used to live on Jesús Maria, then near the Tel Aviv Racetrack, and now I live in Polanco. Why should you live in Polanco and not me? How long did *you* live on Jesús María in three narrow, crowded rooms? Who are you to act so high and mighty? *Señora* Tinifotsky, what a countess you think you've become!"

When I realize I'm dealing with a vulgar little Jewish nobody, I give her an icy *adiós*, and go back to my car. I get home angry, insulted, in a huff, and sit down in the living room, all bent out of shape. That husband of mine is in his fancy armchair, deep in a newspaper.

I'm upset, agitated, and gazing at my gorgeous, manicured nails. God, they're stunning! That's when I realize how much old Yente's changed for the better. These manicured, polished nails once worked overtime, doing laundry, washing floors—oy! Scrubbing pots, burning my fingers on the stove—oy! And today? Fingers like a princess! A queen! See these fingers? To die for! Yente Tinifotsky with polished nails!

"Jacobo. Jacobo!" I say quietly to my husband. "Come here. I've got something to tell you."

He acts like he doesn't hear, the bum, and keeps on reading. So I give out a loud scream: "Yankl! Yankl Blow-It-Offsky! Come here!"

He's terrified. He runs over and puts his arms around me lovingly, looks me in the eyes with a sweet smile. With love, just like it was only yesterday when we standing under our wedding canopy.

"Yente baby, what's wrong? Are you mad at me about something, sweetie? Why so sad, doll? Honey, what's wrong?

"I want you to buy me something," I tell him softly, like I have all the time in the world. "Buy me something, darling!"

"Buy?" He's surprised. "Buy what for you? What could you possibly need? You've got a beautiful house. A car. Diamonds. Servants.

The two toy poodles. A wet bar with a Lazy Susan. Baby, what else can I possibly buy you?"

"Yankl," I say to him softly, tenderly. "I want. . . I want you to buy me something that absolutely no one else has. Lover, precious, buy me a. . . a neighborhood!

He jumps up like he's just gotten scorched, and laughs out loud, "Ha! A neighborhood? You want I should buy you a neighborhood? A neighborhood!"

So I jump up, too, and give a loud shriek: "Why are you laughing, Yankl Blowitoffsky?! Why?!"

Then I say to him softly, tearfully: "You don't have a shred of pity for me. You don't care for me at all. I simply can't bear it. I can't live in Polanco any longer. I just can't! All the bums live here, the beggars, anyone who gets hold of a few pesos buys a piece of land, a lot, a house in Polanco or Lomas. I want to get out of here. Buy me a neighborhood, you hear? I want to live all by myself in my own neighborhood. I want a neighborhood!"

And you'll see: I'll buy myself a neighborhood. Yente Tinifotsky will have her own neighborhood!

II. Yankl Blowitoffsky Gets Some Class

You think I *wanted* to be classy? No, *señor*, no way! What do I know from class? I've lived half my life already, and up to now I never had no class. But now I'm playing a bit part in this class act, like some guy born with a silver spoon in his mouth.

But as you can see by looking at me, I'm just a regular fellow, an average Jewish Joe. True, I'm rich, with everything anyone could need: a factory, an office, some real estate. You know, the whole bit. But I'm also fun-leaving, easy-going, a regular guy. So I'm rich. Is it my fault? Don't tell me I have class, too!

But my little Yente, God bless her, she won't let go of the idea that I have to be an aristocrat or something. And when my missus gets something into her head, it's terrible! No good at all—nossir!

But she's a smart cookie, my Yente. She herself is already such an aristocrat that you wouldn't even recognize her. I'm telling you, a real Duchess of Windsor!

No matter what the occasion, she's always dressed to the nines. She's the best, the prettiest. And the way she walks, like a peacock, like a born countess, one of the Rockefeller women. Always the silk handkerchiefs. And she has a stuck-up way of talking, like a princess. She scrunches up her lips and won't speak a word of Yiddish. A genuine aristocrat, the real article.

The other day she came home with something on her head that looked like a *yarmulke,* like a sherbet dish flying off the top her head. She asks me: "Jacobo darling, do you like my new *sombrero?*"

I answer her coldly: "You call that a hat? It looks like a little boy's *yarmulke.*"

She gets mad: "A *yarmulke?!* Yankl Blowitoffsky, this is the latest fashion. All the classy women are wearing this hat nowadays. You know, Blowitoffskunk, I'm an aristocrat, a woman of means."

Never mind. I know when to shut up. What's it to me if I have a classy dame for a wife? Problem is, my wife wants *me* to be an aristocrat, too—a nobleman. Have you ever been an aristocrat? Ever tried to become one? My little Yente, God bless her, wants to trick me into thinking I come strictly from aristocracy: rabbis, professors, pedigreed pious Jews. She goes out of her way to show off my good breeding, my class, my learning and wisdom. When the prominent Mexicans we know come to our place to have tea, dinner, or a cocktail, my Yente starts boasting to the guests that I studied at two universities, speak six languages, and come from an unbroken line of millionaires and aristocrats. I sit there with my mouth shut. I get so embarrassed I blush. I want to say something, but she won't let me get a word in edgewise. I ask her quietly, "Yente baby, darling, sweetie, lay off the pedigree a little. Go easier on the universities. Say I speak only five languages. Don't mention rabbis! Casting spells would sound less ridiculous. I'm so ashamed I turn red. Let up a little, have some mercy on me, stop with all the classiness!"

But later I really catch hell from her. She cries and screams. She scolds me with her squeaky little voice: "Jacobo, do you know who you are? What are you talking about? Do you think you're still in your muddy little *shtetl?* Yankl Blowitoffsky, you're rich. Yankl, you've got money. You spend your time with movers and shakers. You're not the old Yankl Blowitoffsky anymore! Do you hear? Blowitoffskunk! You are *señor* Tinifotsky, who lives like a baron, a millionaire. Blowitoffskunk, act like a *mentsh*. A *mentsh*, I tell you! You could stand to learn a little something about class."

I start laughing at my wife's shrieks. "Ha! Just look at this little aristocrat of mine. Yente, baby, do you think you can fool your friends from the old country? Oh, such an important aristocrat! Just look, Yente! Oy, God in Heaven, just look how money can buy anything. My Yente, a classy dame! What a joke!"

I laugh, all right, but I'm feeling gloomy, bitter. There's really nothing to laugh at. My Yente's taking years away from my life, torturing me about manners. Here's how she teaches me to be act classy. I'm sitting at a banquet. I get served a piece of fried fish. I take a knife and start cutting the fish, when she tugs at my sleeve. "Jacobo, put that knife down! One doesn't use a knife to eat fish. It's not classy."

I say to her quietly, "Don't start on me with the fanciness. This isn't gefilte fish. It's hard as a rock. Let me eat!"

She takes the knife away from me. No more fish for me.

I go to a wedding, and have to dress up like a count, in a tight tuxedo with a stiff, starched collar that scratches my throat and chokes me so much I start sweating. But after I've got a few drinks in me, I blow off all my troubles and forget about the world. I get warmed up a little. I'm in my cups. I forget I'm a rich man, with a factory, an office, real estate. And that I have a wife with class. I unbutton the tight jacket, loosen my collar and get doing a Cossack dance with the guys from the old country. The floor shakes. Everyone's clapping hands. Step lively, lively! I'm dancing. Flying! Then my little Yente starts with the aristocratic *shtik:* "Jacobo, enough already! Don't forget who you are. Enough, Jacobo, enough!"

Now I raise my voice a bit: "Yente, lovey-dove, don't be so bossy. Quit misbehaving. Stop with the nasty language. Shake a leg, gorgeous, and dance! This is a wedding. It's a *mitzvah* to dance.

Let yourself go, my little aristocrat! It's a *mitzvah*. Music! Music! Let's have another Cossack dance. More music! Another song! Step lively! Lively!"

But what my little aristocrat dishes out later at home, it's better not to know, nossir!

I tell you it's very hard to be an aristocrat. Once I used to get a little pleasure from a glass of tea. I would be brought a shiny, clean glass of steaming tea, with lemon, a lump of sugar, some jam. But these days I drink fancy tea, tea with class. My Yente loves to have "five-o'clock tea," which means I get nothing—no tea! My wife wants to show the guests her new porcelain dishes. The maid brings out a tray with little cups—*tazas*—but by the time she lays out the beautiful little *tazas*, the tea is already cold.

I tell the maid to bring me tea in a glass. My aristocrat of a wife says it's not proper to drink tea from a glass, not aristocratic. But cold tea has about as much flavor as leftover Shabbos casserole. Do *you* like drinking tea out of a little bowl? Not me! Nossir! Five-o'-clock tea is for the birds!

It's hard to be an aristocrat. Two living rooms I've got, and what living rooms! In one there's a fine, soft sofa. It's such a pleasure to lie down on for a while. At the head, I put all the little silk cushions, and take a delightful short nap. Then I hear a shrill little voice: "Oy, what have you done, Jacobo? The sofa, the new sofa! You've messed up the whole sofa, the cushions! Crushed and wrinkled the silk cushions—oy! Just look what he's done with the living room, the new living room—oy! Blowitoffskunk, don't you have somewhere else to sleep besides the new sofa? Oy, oy, oy! When will you learn to act even a little bit like an aristocrat?"

My wife makes an announcement: "Jacobo, we're going on vacation. I've already booked a room in a luxury hotel."

I give her a big thanks for the good news, and ask her, a little nervous: "Yente baby, sweetie-pie, what's the matter? Have you been getting tired? Maybe you're not feeling so good?"

She laughs and answers me sarcastically, "Why should I be tired? I'm not sick, knock on wood. Let the neighbors go on vacation sick. Me, I'm going in good health."

I keep my cool and say, "Yente, doll, just last month you went on a whole week's vacation. What's this vacation bug that's gotten into you? Where are we going? To Veracruz? Acapulco?"

She answers me haughtily that she won't got anywhere such losers go. She's going to a top-of-the-line, luxury hotel. American tourists go there. Millionaires. Movie stars. It costs sixty pesos a day. So O.K., why not? If my Yente says we're going on vacation, we're going on vacation!

They have a special way of feeding you at an aristocratic hotel. It's always the same. The waiter keeps serving me these tiny rolls. Serving them with silver tongs. To look at him, you'd think he was setting down diamonds. I'm dying of hunger, and he keeps giving me a piece of bread the size of an aspirin. I feel sorry for the waiter, so I tell him to just bring me a whole plate of little rolls in one trip. My wife says it's not proper to ask for so much bread. It's not aristocratic. Aristocrats don't eat so much bread.

All day my Yente tortures me with her fancy manners: "Yankl, button your shirt up to your throat. People can see your hairy chest; you look like a bear. Yankl, don't roll up your shirtsleeves so high. Jacobo, buckle your belt."

I sit around lonely, brooding. Suddenly I feel a thump on my shoulder: "Hey, Jacobo! How's it going, *amigo?*"

I turn around and see some fellows I know from Mexico City. I'm thrilled! Soon we're having a few drinks: brandy, beer, sodas. We sit at a table in the dining room and talk a little about business, politics, books, real estate. We tell a few jokes, spicy Jewish ones. It's a pleasure. Things have gotten a little more fun. I've got some guys to play a friendly game of poker with, even to speak a word or two of Yiddish with, instead of walking around like a dummy, like at a wedding where you don't know anyone. Then my Yente comes over, her lips all puckered up, and tells me: "Jacobo, what are you doing? Stop speaking Yiddish! What's going on? What's wrong with you? Don't you know who you are? Oy! Don't speak Yiddish so loud. You're embarrassing me. People will hear us speaking Yiddish! This is an *aristocratic* hotel. You simply don't speak Yiddish here! Oy, the people here are big shots! Here the language is strictly Spanish and English. And you start in with Yiddish—oy! Shhhh! Have a heart. Stop speaking Yiddish. I'm mortified. It's a disgrace. Oy! Shhh, shush, shhhh!"

So does it pay to be rich? I'd gladly give away all the fanciness for one peso. My wife teaches me how to sit, how to stand, how to eat, how to talk, and how to be an aristocrat. Meanwhile, for her to try to be classy makes as much sense as it does to wish someone "Good Shabbos" and then smack 'em one right in the kisser.

As far as I'm concerned, the only true nobility is the ruble. That's right—money. Dough. A pedigree? Aristocracy? Just blow it off!

Listen, Jews—if you've got some money, if God has smiled on you, if you've managed to make a peso and you're rich, have a heart. Don't let yourself be turned into an aristocrat. It's no picnic, believe you me!

—Translation by Debbie Nathan

U.S.A. (Texas)

⧗ ⧗ ⧗ ⧗ ⧗ ⧗ ⧗ ⧗ ⧗ ⧗ ⧗ ⧗

32

San Antonio
Twenty-Two Years Ago

EXCERPT FROM A MEMOIR BY ALEXANDER ZISKIND GURWITZ

[*Alexander Ziskind Gurwitz (or Hurvits; b. 1859 Minsk, Belarus; d. 1947 San Antonio, Texas) was a rabbi whose material difficulties led him to emigrate to the U.S. in 1910. Entering through Galveston, he settled in San Antonio. His two volumes of memoirs portray in stark terms Jewish life on both sides of the Atlantic.*]

We arrived in San Antonio on September 28, 1910. At that time, it resembled all other Texas cities that had recently begun their physical and intellectual development. Not long before Texas had passed from Mexico to the United States, and its cities had gradually evolved so that one would be hard-pressed to recognize them twenty years later. San Antonio has grown in sophistication as well as number of inhabitants, beautiful buildings and large businesses. From 100,000 in 1910, its population has now reached some 300,000.

The city looked half wild, less like a city planted with trees than like a forest dotted with large and small houses and even hovels. Many of the streets were overgrown with wild, prickly trees among which horses, cattle, donkeys and goats fed unmolested. Dirty creeks wound their way through the streets, all of which—with the exception of a few streets with large businesses—would fill with mud after a rain.

There were some places where one could not pull one's foot out of the clayey mud, and the wheels of passing wagons were invisible.

Where now one finds the most beautiful streets with the largest buildings, there stood the poor shacks of the Mexicans, built out of boards like *sukkahs* and covered with rusty tin—a sad spectacle, made worse by the din of wild braying donkeys standing nearby. Some streets were almost completely deserted, except for a few Mexican hovels peeking out from among the trees and the mountains of garbage dumped there from other parts of the city. Biting, flying creatures called mosquitoes teemed in the mud, and in the summer they would keep the residents from sleeping at night and would spread disease.

The population of the city was then, as now, divided into three races: white, black, and yellow, people of all lands. The Anglo-Americans own the largest and finest buildings as well as much land, which their parents bought from the government for next to nothing and is today worth a fortune. They occupy the most important government positions, and run not only local politics but also the banks and the great hotels. Lawyers, doctors and engineers, they are the heads of the city.

After them come the Jews, who fall into two categories: German Jews and Orthodox Jews. The Germans are the rich Jews of the city, and the largest businesses are in their hands. Numbering over a hundred families, some of whom are quite wealthy, they have a large, beautiful temple and a rabbi who follows the Reform ritual. They have little to do with the Orthodox Jews.

Twenty years ago, there were a couple of hundred Orthodox families. One finds a few very rich people with large businesses among them, but most of the Orthodox are small-time merchants, shopkeepers, peddlers. Extreme poverty is rare among them. When a greenhorn arrives, he starts peddling. If he has any wherewithal, he buys a horse and a wagon. He takes his little store with him to the Mexicans and sells them merchandise on the installment plan for very high prices, from which he makes his livelihood. Many former peddlers have now become rich. Whoever cannot afford to buy a horse and wagon carries some inexpensive merchandise in a satchel and does the same thing the others do with a horse and wagon. With time, he becomes a big peddler and then a storekeeper and so forth, and sometimes is even honored with an appointment as president of the synagogue or religious school. Twenty years ago some Jews also worked as fruit peddlers and vegetable merchants, but today no Jews can be found in these trades, which have been entirely taken over by the Italians.

At that time, there was a small synagogue, a decrepit, wooden building. An old sexton, a Russian Jew who had served in Czar Nicholas I's army, would lead Sabbath services before the lectern. He pronounced Hebrew as—you should pardon the comparison—a Lithuanian peasant digs postholes in a field. But he was a fine Jew, with a full, flowing beard that covered his mistakes, so the worshipers were happy with their sexton and his prayers.

—Translated by A. A.

Uruguay

33
The Bar Mitzvah Speech

A SHORT STORY BY SALOMÓN ZYTNER

[*Salomón (or Shloyme) Zytner (b.1904 Bialystok; d. Bat-Yam, Israel 1986) came from a Hasidic home but became active as a young man in Labor Zionist organizations. In 1925 he left for Uruguay. There, he first worked as a traveling salesman throughout the countryside and later manufactured* bombachas, *the traditional gaucho trousers—all the while pursuing his career as a writer. His short stories and journalistic pieces appeared in* Folksblat *and* Haynt *in Montevideo;* Di Prese *in Buenos Aires; and* Naye Tsaytung *in Israel. In 1967, Zytner made* aliyah. *Many of his short stories were gathered into three volumes published between 1955 and 1974:* Der gerangl *("The Struggle"),* Di mishpokhe *("The Family") and* "Tsvishn vent" *un andere dertseylungen ("'Within Four Walls' and Other Stories").*]

In Bernardo Tzalkin's impressive glassware shop, one can purchase as well all manner of religious images, plaster figures of various dimensions, each of which shows the mission and rank assigned to the particular guardian of humankind on this sinful earth. One can also acquire the finest gold and silver picture frames, variously decorated. The shop is as silent and tranquil as a church. The holy statues are placed on shelves at the very front, in diverse poses. Some stretch their arms out in prayer. Others have worried countenances, full of pain, which remind those who enter that earthly existence is meaningless, and that true rewards and punishments will be dealt out only in the world to come.

The decorative frames, sparkling in gold and silver on the walls, can hardly bear to see the sorrowful faces and stooped, bowed, shrunken bodies of the saintly figures, who attract the glances of the passersby. When a customer shows up, a silent, a bitter struggle breaks out among them. Each icon wants all the newcomer's attention and spreads about a godlike serenity, meant to calm the soul in travail. Simultaneously, the brilliant picture frames use their ornaments—flowers of the most diverse shapes, etched in relief—to charm the new arrival. When the shop is empty, the frames look shimmeringly at the oil paintings and reproductions displayed in the great show-window, and await impatiently the acquirer who will deliver them from the suffocating atmosphere.

The oil paintings do not perceive the tumult of the street, the deafening shrieks and roars of motors. They yearn to be covered with glass, surrounded with decorative frames, and hung in dark, commodious rooms with draped windows, around which hovers an air of hospitable tranquility.

Bernardo Tzalkin's shop, his present social position, are the product of a dream come true. Years before, he had gone around with a crate of glass. From door to door he went, asking with a timid voice, blushing all the while, "Maybe you need a window pane?" He trod the streets entire days, hardly managing to cover his expenses, mechanically repeating those few words at every home, every doorway. His thin, drawn-out cheeks, his subdued gaze, his entire demeanor clearly belonged to a man beaten down, who labored hard for each bit of bread, and who lived from one day to the next.

After several years of peddling in the streets, he saw his efforts were fruitless. He sought out a location in a downtown street and set up a glass shop. In addition to glass, he brought in some religious pictures, plaster figures, and frames of various sizes. At first, he himself was shocked by his dealing in icons, from which, as a child, he would carefully avert his glance whenever he saw one. As time wore on, he became accustomed to them. They seemed to him even quite ordinary. The business grew day by day. The religious items were the quickest-moving of all, especially before the holidays. He soon amassed a small fortune, and had an appearance to go along with it. His thin, drawn cheeks filled out, his cautious gaze became audacious and even arrogant. Standing long days behind the counter, he acquired a round, well-fed belly, proudly projected outward, as if exclaiming impudently: "Show respect to Bernard Tzalkin, the big glass dealer! He's no longer the poor glazier who would pace the length and breadth of the city, begging with a meek voice for a little livelihood. Nowadays, people come to him. In the business world his name is uttered with honor and dignity!"

Bernardo Tzalkin was consumed by his shop. Nothing existed for him except glass, frames, and holy images bought by Christian neighbors in honor of their *shmolidays*. . . He wanted people to know just how comfortable he was, how lavish he could afford to be. He had been too involved in business to notice, slowly creeping up, special birthdays of his two children, born before his good fortune. His son was about to turn thirteen, and his daughter fifteen. The time was right to display his largess.

Bernardo Tzalkin had originally wanted to throw two parties: a bar mitzvah for his son, and a *quinceañera* for his daughter. But his wife so upbraided him that he saw stars. She warned him against letting so much money slip through his fingers, and accused him of not knowing the value of a peso. After several evenings of strife and recriminations, they came to an agreement. They would celebrate their son's bar mitzvah and their daughter's *quinceañera* simultaneously, thereby guarding against useless expenses, while attracting twice as many gifts.

Preparing their daughter would not require great effort. They would simply have a white silk gown custom-sewn for her, her hair done up in nice curls, and deck her out for the party. With their son it was a different matter. They would have to drum a bar mitzvah speech into his head, which was not about to enter easily. And as though that were not enough, Bernardo Tzalkin demanded that his only son go up to the Torah, pronounce the blessings, and chant the Haftorah portion taught to him by a teacher.

Bernardo Tzalkin also wanted a picture of his only son, in his little prayer shawl and skullcap, to appear in the newspaper for one and all to see. That seemed to him a compensation for all the years he had dealt in holy images.

His only son—a hefty boy, with full, round cheeks—was completely taken with soccer. He would come home ruddy and perspiring after playing outside with his friends, and would burn with anger at his parents and teacher who demanded he learn the bar mitzvah speech. Most of all, he was annoyed by the Haftorah, of which he understood nothing. The strange words frightened him. He would mechanically repeat them after his teacher, all the while thinking that he could be outside having fun, playing ball with his friends. He would break into a cold sweat as he recited word after word. His teacher gazed at him sympathetically, blaming him less than his father. Upon leaving the house, he would remind the boy to practice his speech on his own, lest he shame himself in front of everyone. The boy would breathe more easily when the teacher was gone, as though he had been freed from a heavy burden, and would escape quickly to his friends outdoors.

Bernardo Tzalkin now kept close watch on his only son. Whenever the boy disappeared from the house, he would go find him in the street, pulling him away from the soccer match just as he was about to score a goal. The boy was angry at having to stop playing, and with bowed head would listen morosely to his father's scolding remarks, the eternal litany: "Did you forget that you have to rehearse your bar mitzvah speech and the Haftorah? There isn't much time left."

The big day was drawing near, and Bernardo Tzalkin had gone all out. He rented the fanciest, most luxurious hall. He arranged with the caterer for a lavish banquet, lest the guests feel cheated. It was, as he whispered to the caterer, a double party, for both his children, and each and every guest should feel satisfied with what was being offered.

He hired a band to entertain the guests, to warm their hearts with the melodies they knew from home. He had invitations engraved in golden letters, which clearly announced that Mr. and Mrs. Bernardo Tzalkin had the honor to invite their friends to a double celebration:

the bar mitzvah of their son and the *quinceañera* of their daughter. On each side of the invitation stood a picture of one of the honorees. The boy, with the prayer shawl on his shoulders and a holy tome in his hand, stared dull and discontented; the girl in her white silk gown had a smile that suggested her childhood had come to an end and a new period of life was about to begin.

A day before the celebration, with all the invitations out and everything in the offing, the boy fell ill. Bernardo Tzalkin paced desperately, anxiously, not knowing what to do. He glanced at his son who lay in bed with a high fever, shivering. His sunken red cheeks, his glassy eyes, his dry lips made it clear that he had a bad cold and would have to stay in bed. Bernardo Tzalkin walked to and fro, wringing his hands in irritation and chagrin, stiffening them as he went over to his son, who lay breathing heavily, almost choking. He threw terrible glances at the boy and hissed into his face, "It's all because of that accursed ball-playing of yours!" Then he added, beside himself, "What are we supposed to do now? What will become of your speech? The guests we've invited? The food that's been prepared?"

His wife sat on the edge of the bed. She glanced anxiously at her son from whose side she did not stir, as she placed cold compresses on his forehead. She hazarded an idea: "Perhaps we could put off the party until a later date? You see how bad off the boy is. He's burning like fire."

"What do you mean, put it off?," exclaimed Bernardo Tzalkin. "What do you think this is—a game? How can you stay calm when so many guests are coming! We won't be able to show our faces in public." His voice cracked into a sob.

She made another attempt: "Maybe we could just celebrate the girl's occasion? And put off the bar mitzvah until the boy is better. . ."

He dismissed her suggestion with a wave of the hand, as though no response were necessary. He ran over to the telephone, and spoke into the receiver with a broken, nervous voice. Have the doctor come immediately! One of his children has a high fever, and he is very worried! Having gotten a reassuring answer, he hung up the phone and began pacing the room again, looking at the door repeatedly, starting at the slightest noise, anxiously awaiting the doctor's arrival. At the first ring of the bell, Bernard Tzalkin ran into the entryway, opened wide the door, and welcomed the doctor in. The doctor sat down calmly by the bed and began a lengthy examination of the patient, checking his throat, feeling his pulse, tapping the boy's back with his fingers, listening to his lungs. The parents stood near the bed, following nervously with their eyes the doctor's movements, waiting impatiently for him to utter some word, offer a diagnosis. The doctor shrugged his shoulders, as though to allay their unfounded fears, and said in sparse terms, "There's no danger. The boy has a bad cold and will have to stay in bed a few days to sweat it out."

Bernardo Tzalkin stood there as though he had just been drenched with a bucket of cold water. Perplexed, at a loss for words, he tried to ask the doctor whether the boy could possibly get out of bed the next day for just an hour. It was his thirteenth birthday... He attempted to explain that there was to be a big party. All the guests had been invited. Everything was ready. The boy would have to make a speech, or otherwise the whole celebration would be ruined.

The doctor refused, shaking his head. He could not understand how it could matter so that the boy give a speech and thereby risk his health. Bernardo Tzalkin interrupted the doctor with a small voice, begging his authorization, trying to make him understand: "For us Jews, it's a big occasion. He's been practicing the speech for a long time." Maybe the doctor could prescribe some pencillin shots, for example, a high dose, so that the next day the boy would feel well enough to be taken to the hall, just to recite the speech before the guests. Then they would bring him back home to bed.

The doctor, a good-hearted man of Spanish ancestry, smiled and patted Bernardo Tzalkin on the back, showing he now understood. He uttered a quick "*Está bien*" and left the room.

The next day Bernardo Tzalkin stood outside his house, waiting nervously as his wife helped their daughter arrange her hair and gown before a mirror. The white silk drew tightly at the waist, before falling into slight pleats. With each movement the gown rustled, as though expressing the dreams and longings of the girl, about to take leave of her fifteen childhood years.

Bernardo Tzalkin kept looking at his watch, fearful it was getting late. He saw all the guests sitting at their tables and straining their eyes in anticipation of the hosts' arrival. And here they were still lingering. The injections prescibed by the doctor the day before had wrought the desired effect. The boy felt better, thereby vindicating Bernardo Tzalkin. After all, what would the entire party have been like without the bar mitzvah speech?

All of a sudden he noticed the door opening. Out stepped his daughter, bedecked, shining brilliantly. His wife followed, leading by the hand their son, swaddled in warm clothing. He opened up the car door quickly and took his son by the other arm. Together, they helped the boy into the car.

Bernardo Tzalkin was overtaken by cheer. Here he was, taking his son to recite the long-awaited bar mitzvah speech. The celebration was to go forward exactly as planned.

Upon entering the catering hall, he remarked how his son began hesitating, tottering, and seemed about to fall over. The boy's usually ruddy face went pale and gaunt. His eyes were sunken in and surrounded by bluish spots. Bernardo Tzalkin gave a shiver, taking fright lest his son's health worsen and keep him from delivering the bar mitzvah speech.

The band entoned a joyous melody. Merriment and laughter poured over the hall. The honorees were welcomed with great festivity; applause broke out on all sides. Hands stretched out to wish the family happiness. Bernardo Tzalkin was entranced by the music, the jolly faces that shined at him from all directions. The ceremonious music swept over him like a warm wave, embracing and caressing him, making him forget all his cares. The fears regarding his son dissolved. He remembered only that today was a celebration in honor of both his children, a double celebration he had made as sumptuous as possible, renting out the most luxurious hall, arranging for the finest foods—an occasion people were not likely to forget. They would all comment on his unrestrained generosity, his brilliant social standing. And soon his son would recite the bar mitzvah speech.

—Translated by A. A.

34
The Refugee

A SHORT STORY BY SALOMÓN ZYTNER

It turned out to be quite complicated for *señor* Reichman to bring over a remote cousin, the sole surviving member of his family in the Polish *shtetl.* He bragged about it at every opportunity. After all, getting that cousin from Europe had cost a fortune.

The first letter he had received described what had become of everyone. The cousin was the only remnant of a family whose branches had been so extensive. He alone could bear witness to the terrible fate they had undergone. Aimlessly, he wandered through the abandoned *shtetl* as in a graveyard.

That letter shook Reichman to the core, driving away the tranquil bonhomie he was known for. He became reflective, even mournful. The hustle and bustle of his business, the fortune he had amassed, all suddenly seemed worthless. His eyes moistened, his stare grew glassy. He decided then that he would bring that cousin over, no matter what it cost. This became his principal aim in life. He would spare no money or effort. His mood became exalted.

On the morning *señor* Reichman prepared to meet his cousin at the port, he beamed with joy, smiling to himself unceasingly. Dressed in his finest, he paced back and forth in the bedroom. He glanced impatiently at his wife. Would she ever be ready? Finally, they could leave. He ran out to the car, and opened its door hastily. They got in, the car started and drove wildly through the streets, until they saw the tall buildings of the port.

Upon meeting his cousin, *señor* Reichman was perplexed and reduced to silence. He looked in astonishment at his cousin, as though beholding one of nature's oddest wonders. This young man, whom he had never seen before, seemed to him strange, distant. This was the sole remnant of his family. He threw himself at the new arrival, hugging him tightly as though afraid to lose him. Then he took him by the arm and guided him like a child saved from a calamity.

He sat next to the newcomer on the way home. From the side, he threw sympathetic glances that allowed him to examine the young man's pale face and sad eyes. From time to time he gave him a friendly pat on the back and announced to him, "Don't worry about a thing. You won't have to do anything, not even lift a finger!"

And to encourage him further, he added, "Here, in your new country, you'll forget about everything, you hear? You'll feel as though you've been born again. This is a free country, where everyone can live as he likes. . ."

He stopped himself, unable to find a convincing illustration of his point. He thought for a while, then stated with great pathos: "You can stand in the middle of the street and curse the president himself, and nothing will happen." He felt triumphant for devising such a fitting example.

They approached the house. The mirrored surfaces on the outside walls, reflecting the sun, shone in many colors, like fragments of a rainbow. A rounded balcony, adorned with plaster moldings, gazed arrogantly upon the street and the neighboring buildings. A palm tree with green, fan-like leaves majestically stood watch over the still-new house. It spread cool shadows over the symmetrical flowerbeds, and made the home seem even more magnificent.

From behind the lowered window shades the house issued forth a feeling of complacent tranquility. *Señor* Reichman proudly pointed to the house and said, "This is my very own home. I myself built it a few years ago."

They went inside. All the Reichmans' friends had already gathered around the table. He had told them that his cousin was arriving that day. With tears in his eyes he introduced the young man as his "sole surviving relative." He took him by the arm in a gesture that clearly stated, "Today, I alone have the right to speak to him and enjoy his company. I spent enough time and money to bring him over."

He guided him through all the rooms, pointing out the furniture. There were the richly-upholstered chairs that seemed to open their arms wide to welcome honored guests, and the crystal that winked with a shimmer from the glass cabinet. The gleam was blinding.

Señor Reichman caught the newcomer's glances of admiration and surprise at his cousin's riches. Seeking to explain it all, he put his hand gently on the young man's shoulder. "You see, during the war, we here in the Americas had it good. People became wealthy overnight. We sold warehouses full of merchandise." He neighed with laughter, adding, "Now things are slower. We're going through a bit of crisis in this country, like after a war. . ."

Señor Reichman stood with his mouth open, in disbelief, as the young man hastily freed himself from his hold. His cousin's eyes were filled with scorn and pity. He flung the door open and quickly strode outside, as if to get as far away as possible.

At a loss for words, *señor* Reichman looked at his wife, who was busy with the guests. Her smile suddenly disappeared, and was replaced by a clasping of the lips. She became serious and shook her head in vindication. Why hadn't he listened to her? Why had he so single-mindedly poured time and money into sending for this relative, who had just made a fool of him in front of everyone? She grumbled at him with contempt: "That's the thanks you get for all you've done for your dear little cousin. No effort was too great to get him out. That's your reward, and it's well deserved."

He pretended to ignore her words. He went back to the guests, who stared in amazement. He felt insulted and ashamed. In order to smooth over the incident, he put his finger to his forehead, and said in a tone combining pity and regret: "You shouldn't be surprised at the refugees. They've been through so much. What suffering. . . They're not quite all there. . ." And to erase the bad impression, he took out a pack of cards and began dealing them to the visitors.

The refugee strode out quickly, as though shot from his cousin's house. He felt a menace upon him, goading him like a whip, forcing him to bend his back. His pale, drawn cheeks had taken on an ashen color. The nervous twitch in his eye had turned into a constant spasm, like that of a dying animal.

He felt deep waves of unrest rising within him, knocking at the limits of his consciousness, about to invade his entire being. His cousin's cynical comment about his ill-earned wartime fortune, his neighing laughter, his boastfulness—all this brought into relief the horrors and pain he had lived through. The unspeakable suffering and oppression in the ghetto, the loss of all his loved ones, the despair, the transport to the camps—all suddenly surfaced from the depths of his soul. In contrast, he pictured his fat-faced cousin, neighing, patting him on the back, and repeating: "You won't have to do a thing. Wouldn't you like to freeload off me for a while?" The words went through him like sharp little spears. He felt humiliated and dejected. The smoldering images that had been pushed into the recesses of his mind had now returned, to rob him of his calm and throw him into despair. He quickened his pace, and strode further.

"No, I cannot accept his help!" he almost screamed, as his whole body shuddered. To accept such aid would be to defile the memory of his loved ones. While his cousin here had peacefully wheeled, dealt, and made a bundle, his family in the old country had been wiped from the face of the earth. All those in their *shtetl*, where Jews had lived for generations, now numbered among the martyrs to the glorious Name of the Eternal One.

—Translated by A. A.

35
A Banquet in Mexico City

A SHORT STORY BY HANAN AYALTI

[*Hanan Ayalti (b. 1910 Sapetkin, near Grodno, Belarus; d. 1992 New York) was the pen name of Khonen Klenbort. In 1929, he left for Palestine to become a* haluts *("farming pioneer"); he published his first novel in Hebrew, but thereafter wrote in Yiddish.*

In 1933, Ayalti arrived in Paris to study at the Sorbonne; in 1936, he was a newspaper correspondent in Spain. He returned to Paris in 1940 and fled to the south of France just before the Nazi invasion. After a short period of internment in a Vichy concentration camp, Ayalti managed to get to Uruguay in 1942. In 1946 he settled in New York, where he became editorial secretary for the Zionist publication Der Yidisher Kemfer. *Translations of his stories appeared in such significant American journals as* Commentary *and* Midstream.]

Right there in Mexico City our plane goes and breaks down. They asked us to be good enough to get out, and tell us that in exactly twenty-four hours we'll be on our way again. What can I do? Nothing. I go out in the street and look for Jews, and not just plain Jews, but Jews from Lipsk and especially those Jews from the Scissors and Iron Workers Party, since I come from Lipsk myself and was a Party member there way back many years ago in the revolutionary days of 1905.

So I walk up and down the Avenida de los Incas, look at shop windows, and wonder: "Jewish or not Jewish?"—when all of a sudden who comes walking along the avenue toward me but Sheindele the Beauty.

"Sheindele!" I shout, but she doesn't recognize me, and when she finally does recognize me, she drapes herself around my neck and begins to spout Spanish words, like *señor* and *señora*. And this goes on for about fifteen minutes on the clock until she realizes I don't understand a word of what she's saying. Then she asks me in plain Yiddish: "What are you doing here in Mexico?"

"I'm flying further south," I say. "My plane broke down, so I have to wait here twenty-four hours."

"Never mind!" she says. "In our Mexico, if they say twenty-four hours, it's at least forty-eight. No matter; everybody's flying, doing things, running around. Only my Haskell, the nincompoop, still gets dirty in the factory."

While she's talking, I remember how Sheindele the Beauty got married to Haskell the simpleton, and how all Lipsk was buzzing for days. But I can't recall exactly what happened because Sheindele won't let me.

"What do you think?" she asks. "*Don* Jaime, the factory owner, going to be President of the Party at the expense of my Haskell, who's still a proletarian."

"Who?" I ask. "*Don* Jaime? Hymie the hat maker?"

"Who else?" she says. "That's him, Hymie the ham-eater, cursed be his father's son. Only here, in our Mexico, he's a manufacturer of men's hats and president of all the labor organizations—Scissors and Iron, Workers' Schools, Progressive Culture, and so on and so on."

Now, I remember how Sheindele the Beauty had carried on an affair in Lipsk with Hymie the ham-eater for two and a half years, until one fine morning he wakes up and runs away to the Americas. But I don't say a word, because I also remember how once, about a quarter of a century ago, Sheindele gave one honorable citizen of Lipsk such a smack in the teeth that he had to spend three weeks in bed. And I can't allow myself such a luxury, as I have to catch my plane in forty-eight hours.

"But now that's all over!" says Sheindele. "We're going to give them an ultimatum: my Haskell is going to become a peddler. Let them find another proletarian for the Party."

To make a long story short, from all this talk I am getting weaker and weaker in the stomach as I haven't had any breakfast yet. I ask Sheindele where you can find a decent hotel and she says she'll take me to one herself. And she takes me there—on foot—at least an hour and a half on the clock, and the whole time she talks about Mexico and Lipsk and the world in general, so that when I finally do get there I'm practically dead from hunger. I order a few cups of coffee with fresh rolls and butter, and an omelet, and whatever else you can think of, and then I go up to my room, and right into the bathroom, for when you fly through the hot countries, you perspire a great deal, and it's good to take a warm bath and a cold shower, especially if you've just had a two-hour talk with Sheindele the Beauty, whom you haven't seen for at least twenty years.

I'm standing in the bathroom covered with soap from head to foot, when all of a sudden the telephone rings. Who can be calling me here in Mexico? Half dead, half alive, I run, begging your pardon, all naked, and grab the receiver. At the other end there's a woman's voice.

"Do you recognize me?" asks the voice.

"Who are you?" I ask.

"Woe is me!" she says. "Don't you know me? I'm Esther the *rebbitzin*, Yoshe the rabbi's wife from Lipsk."

At this point I feel faint, for you can be as extreme a freethinker as you like, but you just don't stand and talk to a rabbi's wife in such a state.

"Wait a second, one minute, please!" I shout, and run back and throw over myself all the towels I can find, but as this is still not enough, I wrap myself up in a bedsheet and so, dressed like a corpse in a shroud, God help us, I go back to the phone.

"Hello, *rebbetzin*," I say, "How are you? How is the rabbi, *reb* Yoshe?"

"*Reb* Yoshe," she says, "is getting old, but God be praised, we can't complain. And besides, our Ladies' Auxiliary would like you to give a lecture."

"Why a lecture?" I say. "Who am I?"

"Why not?" she answers me. "A Jew who flies through Mexico City and stops in a hotel must be a delegate, an emissary, a cultural ambassador, or some kind of troublemaker, it seems to me."

"With the greatest pleasure," I say, "but my plane leaves in forty-eight hours."

"Never mind!" she says. "In our Mexico, if they say forty-eight hours, it won't be less than ninety-six. Anyhow, come right over."

Although by nature, I am, so to speak, an atheist, still nowadays, you know, by sentiment, by custom, there is such a thing as Jewishness— so in a hurry I rinse myself off, get a taxi and set off for *reb* Yoshe's.

I get there, we greet each other, we sit awhile, and then I ask: "Who gave you my telephone number?"

"What do you mean *who*?" asks the rabbi. "My wife went to *don* Gabriel's to buy a wedding ring."

"Our Ladies' Auxiliary is making a wedding for a poor orphan girl," explains the rabbi's wife.

"*Don* Gabriel? Surely you mean Gabriel the watchmaker," say I, interrupting the rabbi's wife.

"The very one," she says. "He has, Praise God, a fine jewelry business, but he still mixes in as one of the Comrades in the Scissors and Iron Party."

"You see, the Party needs at least one intellectual," says the rabbi, defending him, "and he is the Party Secretary."

"Oh, now I understand it all," I say. "Sheindele the Beauty must have been to see him. I ran into her this morning, and she told me—"

I want to tell *reb* Yoshe the whole story, but motioning with his hand he says, "Forget about it. It's an old story. It happened already in Lipsk. *There's nothing new under the sun. . .*"

Although by nature I am, so to say, an atheist, I have a weakness for a nice Biblical saying, and especially since *reb* Yoshe is by now grizzled and gray, he could, it seems to me, have heard this saying from King Solomon in person. And *reb* Yoshe says to his wife, "Go, my wife, make a glass of tea for our guest, and meanwhile I'll tell him a story of what happened in Lipsk some forty years ago."

"I have just been appointed rabbi in Lipsk," *reb* Yoshe begins, "when a few days before Purim I say to my wife: 'Esther, we must prepare the presents for the poor.' I see that she is somewhat hesitant, and I ask her a question: 'Are there many poor people in town?'

"'I don't know,' she says.

"'What do you mean you don't know?' I ask, and the matter becomes quite serious, as I know wherever there is a poor bride or a needy woman in labor, Esther is the first to lend a hand.

"'They say there are no poor people in Lipsk,' she says.

"'What do you mean no poor people?' I say, ' and what of charity? It is written: *Charity shall deliver us from death.*'

"And I make up my mind," says *reb* Yoshe, "to investigate the matter carefully. The next morning immediately after prayers I start a conversation with several of the honorable householders, and it comes out that it is true, that the Jews of Lipsk are no great plutocrats, but there are also no poor, no people completely dependent on charity. It has happened! In the meantime people see that we are talking of civic affairs and quite a crowd gathers around us and everyone lends an ear. And I argue my point with them. 'And what about Purim?' I argue. 'Does it mean that there is no one here who obeys the commandment, *Gifts to the poor?*'

"A young fellow comes to the fore and begins, 'What's the excitement, rabbi? If there are no poor people, that's good—all the better!'

"I look at him and see right away that he is one of the modern-minded youth, and I put a question to him: 'What do you mean, "That's good?"' I ask him. 'It is clearly written, *For in the country, there shall always be poor*—eh?'

"But the young fellow, Gabriel, is a watchmaker, that is to say, an intellectual, a scholar as well, and he soon finds a counter-argument: 'It is written, *In the country,*' he says, 'but in the country there are enough poor people, and they come to us in the city, too, and beg from house to house.'

"'But it is also written in the Talmud, *The poor people of your city take precedence,*' I say, trying to corner him.

"In short, we debate these fine points about the needy, the destitute, indigent, abject, and plain poor people till all of a sudden he comes out with a statement: "You know, rabbi,' he says, 'why should we argue? If we were to send gifts to Hershl the fisherman, not only for Purim, but for an ordinary Sabbath and even in the middle of the week, it would be the greatest of good deeds. So what if his daughter, Rivke, has strayed from the right path? Better that such things didn't happen. . . especially since she is an orphan without a mother, and her father isn't at home all week long, since he goes away to fish in the lakes.'

"I take my prayer bag under the arm," continues *reb* Yoshe, "and see clearly that *One good deed engenders another,* as this is not merely a matter of *sending portions to one another* but of marrying off a bride, providing bridal garments for an orphan girl and so on and so forth."

To catch his breath, *reb* Yoshe takes a pinch of snuff, and before he can sneeze, his wife comes in from the kitchen and takes over the recital.

"That Purim," she says, "there is a banquet fit for a king at Hershl the fisherman's. The townspeople send in all sorts of delicacies: *homentashn,* strudel, calf's foot jelly, sweets and sours, fried livers, and whole quarters of chickens.

"Late that evening," she says, "a few important townspeople come over to Hershl's and they send for the bridegroom, a coachman. And, as in honor of Purim he's quite tipsy, he actually comes. At first, he absolutely denies the whole business; it is a tale made of whole cloth. But after a few more drinks, his tongue loosens: 'It is known to one and all,' he defends himself, 'that it is a good deed to make love to an orphan girl. But let bygones be bygones.' And if the town would furnish him with a horse and wagon, so that he wouldn't have to work for anyone else as a coachman, he would consent to stand under the canopy.

"In short," says the rabbi's wife, "the same evening they were officially engaged, before Passover they collected money not only for matzah but for a horse and wagon, the wedding was celebrated on the Great Sabbath, and before the new coachman could earn his first few pennies the town notables sent in matzah and farfel and chicken fat and whole barrel of borscht—enough to last until Shavuoth and the day after Shavuoth, the young wife took to bed and gave birth to a son. He was given the name Haskell. The town notables celebrated the *bris*, and their wives sent in cooked chickpeas, good luck charms, and fat chicken soup. It was clear to all and one that God is the father of orphans. Good heavens, the water is boiling!"

And before she can come back with the tea, the telephone rings. The rabbi's wife lets the tea stand and runs to the phone. She motions to me that someone wants to talk to me. I take the phone and hear a deep voice: "Hello, how are you? *¿Cómo le va?* This is *don* Jaime, the President of Scissors and Iron. Do you recognize my voice? I had a hard time reaching you on the phone."

"How come?" I ask him. "Is it so hard to make a call in Mexico?"

"No," he says, "but the rabbi subscribes the American company."

"What do you mean, the American company?"

"When you come over to my place I'll explain it to you. My chauffeur is already on his way. He's driving over in my new Chevrolet to get you."

And before I have a chance to say good-bye, a tall Mexican is already standing by the door looking at me with a pair of black

burning eyes, and motioning with his hand for me to go along with
him. But the rabbi's wife complains that it is a sin to leave a glass of
tea with sugar. So I pick it up and start to drink it in a hurry, and at
the first gulp I burn my tongue. Before I know it we are both sitting
in the Chevrolet and chatting in Spanish. That is to say, the chauffeur
is talking, because in the first place, I've burnt my tongue, and in
the second place, I can't speak any Spanish. I only understand, and
then I understand only one word, *señor*. And the car, meanwhile,
like an arrow shot from a bow, speeds through streets and alleys,
and we are already in a suburb, and, as in a dream, villas and gardens
and palms flash past the eye. And as in a dream, I recall Haskell and
how we went to Hebrew school together.

When Haskell first came to school the boys used to point at him
with their fingers and call him a name they didn't understand:
"bastard." Haskell quickly took a dislike to the school, the rabbi, and
learning altogether. He used to run away to the stable where he had a
good friend, his father's horse. The horse would look at him with its
big eyes and shake its head in thanks when Haskell would give it a
little hay. But his mother didn't want him to grow up a coachman,
and as he didn't want to go to school at all, he was apprenticed for a
three-year term to a boot maker.

Later we met again in the Scissors and Iron Party. There Haskell's
standing had greatly improved since in the first place, he was a
proletarian, which was quite a distinction in the Party, and in the
second place, modern ideas were held in high regard by the comrades,
and Haskell up to this time was the only one in Lipsk who had been
born, for all intents and purposes, as a result of free love.

In the meantime the chauffeur pulls up in front of a beautiful
villa, and in the garden by the door I see the Hymie the hat maker.
He leads me inside and gives me a great welcome. Then I ask him:
"What kind of American company?"

"We have two telephone companies here," he says, "a British
company and an American company, and if you have a telephone
from one company, you can't put a call through to a telephone of the
other company. And since the rabbi and his people are subscribers of

the American company, the people in our Party are subscribers of the British one. Besides, the British have a Labor government. But speak of the devil!" he shouts, as the telephone begins to ring. He picks up the phone and I hear him talking to someone.

"What?" he says, "he wants to become a peddler? The nerve of that simpleton! No, we can't allow it. Yes, get into your car at once and come here. We'll talk it over."

"That's Comrade Gabriel," he says to me. "You do remember, Gabriel the watchmaker? And do you remember Haskell? Just before the elections he wants to give up being a proletarian. This Saturday we have our general meeting and elections. You'll stay for that, won't you?"

"With the greatest of pleasure," I answer, "but my plane leaves in. . . ninety-six hours."

"Never mind!" he says. "When they say ninety-six hours here in our Mexico, it's at least a hundred and. . . well, at least a week."

At this point, the door opens, and in comes Comrade Gabriel,

"Well, what do you say?" he asks, out of breath.

"What do *you* say?" the President answers him.

For a while they are both silent and then the President says, "What's the reason he is taking such a step just before elections? He is, after all, our last proletarian. I'll tell you what: we won't give him any credit. How can he become a peddler without credit?"

But Gabriel, the Secretary, brushes off the idea with a wave of his hand. "If we won't give him any credit, then the Zionists will, or even the Communists. Why not? Aren't there millionaires among the Communists? They would do anything in the world to give us a slap in the face."

"What can we do then?"

"We'll have to call an emergency meeting."

And they sit down by the telephone and call all the members with British telephones, and then they go out and look for an American telephone, and before you know it, it is night already and we are eating supper at *don* Jaime's. Soon the Mexican chauffeur appears, and we get into the car and drive over to the special meeting.

First they welcome the guest. That's me, and they say I am the pride and joy of Lipsk and its environs. Then they all begin to talk and say this and that and make suggestions, then they offer a resolution, which is unanimously adopted, that Comrades Jaime and Gabriel should go as a delegation to Haskell, and not so much to him as to Sheindele, since everyone knows that the whole trouble started with her.

And by the time I get back to my hotel it is already half past three in the morning, and the Mexican porter quickly makes up his mind where such a guest has been running around the whole night, and taking me up in the elevator he winks at me and says, "Beautiful *muchachas* we have here in Mexico, no?"

"Yes," I answer, "beauties, one and all."

Early in the morning they wake me up and tell me that two *señores* are waiting for me downstairs. I go down and fine Comrade Jaime and Comrade Gabriel standing the by car. They tell me: "You have to come along with the delegation."

"What's going on?" I ask.

I am told I am being taken to Sheindele.

"Why me?" I ask. "Who am I to go to Sheindele?"

"You are a guest," they say, "and you are the pride of Lipsk and its environs, so she'll have a little respect for you."

Don Jaime drives the car and the Secretary and I sit in the back seat and I feel that he is shaking like a leaf.

"Why are you so nervous?" I ask him.

"A fine business," he answers. "I only hope we come out of it in one piece, as Sheindele still bears a grudge against Jaime from the old days. The old days in Lipsk, when he was called 'Hymie the ham-eater.' That is, she still bears a grudge against me, too, but a little less of one, as after all I came after it was over."

"What do you mean, after it was over?"

"Surely you remember," he says, in a low voice, "that for two and a half years Hymie the ham-eater carried on an affair with Sheindele, and all of a sudden he disappears somewhere in the Americas. Well, there is the devil to pay. Sheindele weeps and wails, and I come over to console her—you know what I mean? But she can't have any great complaints against me—just the other way around. As soon as I find out how things stand with her, I marry her off to Haskell, for it is better to have a simpleton for a husband than to have none at all, and if you can't go up, then you have to come down."

And talking like this we come to Haskell's house, and we find Sheindele all alone and she receives us in the kitchen where she is just starting to prepare lunch. And I see at once that the pot of water on the stove is already quite hot as it is puffing like a steam engine. The discussion starts off slowly. They say this and that, and then the President says, "But you have to understand, Sheindele, darling, that we are not asking for anything for ourselves. It is a matter of an ideal, a principle."

At this point Sheindele's eyes begin to blaze, and she stamps her foot.

"Shut up, you villain, you scoundrel! That's exactly what he said then; 'Sheindele, darling, it's only a matter of principle. We'll get married anyhow.' Thank God I came out of it whole, for how close did I come to being left behind with such a. . . a principle?" She points with one hand to her belly, and with the other she grabs the pot of water that has started to boil over.

Comrade Gabriel sees that it is a bad, bad business and takes the matter into his own hands.

"So, what do you say, Sheindele?" he says.

"What should I say?" she says. "I'm not saying anything. Speak up, if you have something to say."

"I propose," says Comrade Gabriel, "that the Party pay Haskell a bonus of three hundred pesos a month, and that he stay on as a worker in the factory."

"Three hundred pesos?" she says. "Over my dead body!"

"Three hundred and fifty," he says.

"A plague!" she says.

The negotiations go on for about two hours on the clock, and it is finally settled that the Party will pay Haskell five hundred pesos a month on condition that he will keep working in the factory. Meanwhile,

Sheindele throws noodles into the boiling water and we get ready to leave. But before we step over the threshold, she calls us back.

"And the banquet?" she asks.

"What banquet?"

"What do you think?" she says. "For you manufacturers the Scissors and Iron Party and the Labor Committee holds banquets every Monday and Thursday, and my Haskell, the real worker, gets nothing?"

"Good," agrees Comrade Haskell. "Let there be a banquet."

"When?" she asks.

"A week from next Saturday, God willing," he says.

"Good," she agrees, and turning to me, she says: "You'll be sure to come."

"With the greatest of pleasure," I say, "but my plane is leaving in exactly one week from today."

"Don't worry," she says, "in our Mexico when they say one week, it's at least twice as long. And everybody from Lipsk must be invited to the banquet," she says. "*Reb* Yoshe and his wife, too."

"The rabbi?" sputters *don* Jaime, jumping up. "No, not that! This is a matter of principle!"

"Again a principle," says Sheindele, brandishing the pot of steaming noodles.

"All right, all right: *reb* Yoshe, too," says Comrade Gabriel, smoothing things over.

So there we are the banquet and Haskell is sitting at the head table among the most important guests, so you hardly notice him. The Secretary makes a speech, and we eat gefilte fish and roast chicken, and we drink brandy. *Reb* Yoshe alone doesn't touch a thing, he only talks about current problems and preaches a sermon on the text, *For in the country, there shall always be poor.* Comrade Jaime also makes and speech and he says: "We are actually celebrating an anniversary, since it is exactly thirty years since Haskell became a proletarian." He drinks a toast to his health, but when he sits down he whispers to his neighbors: "The nerve of that bastard, eh?"

It seems that Sheindele hears this for I see that she gets up and stretches out her arm, and as she can't quite reach the President, all of a sudden she punches his wife in the teeth, and since I'm sitting to Sheindele's right, I get the first blow from the opposition, and the blow is so hard that everything grows dark before my eyes, and soon it gets dark in the hall, and blows and chairs begin to fly. I hear *reb* Yoshe saying, *One good deed engenders another*, and soon I hear nothing, and when I start to hear again I realize that they are speaking Spanish around me, for although I do not understand Spanish, I do understand the word *señor*, and I open my eyes and see that I am lying in a hospital in Mexico City.

About an hour later Sheindele comes to visit me and tells me that my plane has stayed here exactly two weeks and just took off today, and that they tell her in the office that I will get a seat in about two weeks.

"But don't worry," she comforts me, "in our Mexico when they say two weeks, it's at least a month, and in the meantime you can come to the banquet for the new Board of Directors of the Scissors and Iron Party, which we elected at the last general meeting."

—Translation revised by A. A.

36

The Memo from the Thirty-Six

A SHORT STORY BY HANAN AYALTI

[*This story is based on the legend that there are always thirty-six just men by virtue of whom the world exists and without whom the world could not continue.*]

When all the Jews of the town of Sapetkin were exterminated, one of them was left alive. Todros, the water carrier—he was left alive. The Lithuanians with their whips and the Ukrainians from the other side of the border didn't bother him; the Polish peasants wearing stolen Jewish boots kept away from him; even the Gestapo chief turned his head and pretended not to notice Todros when he passed by.

Apparently this was because Todros was one of the hidden saints, one of the Thirty-Six.

If they had killed Todros, there would have been no more world, God forbid; no more Lithuanians with whips, no more Ukrainians and Poles wearing Jewish boots, no more Gestapo even.

But Todros wasn't satisfied. So he set out through desolated cities and towns and had the following announcement published in the proper places: "As of this date, Todros the water-carrier convokes a Great Assembly of the Thirty-Six. And at once, without delay."

For, according to their constitution, every one of the Thirty-Six and convoke a general assembly. That is to say, he can convoke it when times are really bad.

And times were really bad. And how bad!

They asked, "Where is it to be held?"

He answered, "In a small forest near Treblinka."

So the Thirty-Six assembled in a small forest near Treblinka. There were all sorts: scholars with long gray bears, small-town artisans with broad backs, as well as a few Galician doctors. There was even a rabbi from New York State. All he could understand was English. Nobody knew how he got there. At any rate, he didn't come by airplane.

Somebody with a long beard began to justify God's ways saying that "God can never err nor doth the Eternal perfect justice," and that "Man cannot be more righteous than his Lord." As proof he cited opinions all the way from Moses, our master, to the Gaon of Vilna and the author of the book *Ye Who Desire Life* (of blessed memory).

But Todros wouldn't stand for that: he was a simple Jew, he said, and he just couldn't get so much Torah into his head. "And it seems to me," he added, "that this time they have really gone too far."

"Then what is there to do?" they asked.

He said, "One of us has to go up there himself, 'not through an

Angel and not through a messenger,' and ask 'Watchman, what of the night?'"

So they said to him: "'Let the letter-reader be the messenger'—meaning, that he—Todros, that is—ought to be the one to go. But since he was no scholar and knew nothing of the holy tongue, they decided to give him a memorandum to take along.

So a committee of scholars sat down and wrote a memorandum with goose quills on parchment to the Master of the Universe: "Such and such being the case, 'The waters having come in even unto the soul'—'How long, oh Lord, how long?'" At the end they even put in a couple of practical considerations: "If there are no more Jews, who will praise God? 'Not the dead shall praise the Lord'. . . etc. . . etc. . ."

So Todros stuck the memo under his coattail (so that if the Poles were to catch him they wouldn't convert it into uppers for a pair of boots) and set out on his way.

He went along with a large company. There were thousands of souls in the heavy smoke pouring out of the Treblinka chimneys: men, women, young folk, old folk, children—everybody. There were even a few apostates; and around the edges of the host flew one proselyte with a singed beard who looked like a former Subotnik—a member of a Russian sect that observed the Sabbath. Todros attached himself to the crowd and flew along.

At first they all related what had happened to them: how they had been thrown into trains, which were later sealed; how they had been given towels and led into a room. . . But no one listened, because they same thing had happened to everybody. They all knew about it. It became a little jollier the second day. They began a political discussion: Zionists argued with Bundists, Bundists with Communists, Communists, and some left-wing Zionists quoted Ber Borochov. Pious Jews discussed and studied a page of the Talmud they knew by heart.

Todros knew nothing about politics and since he wasn't a scholar either, he listened to the women. They began to tell all about the pickled cucumbers and casks of beet soup they had left at home. The richer housewives listed their jars of preserves and bottles of cherry brandy. Old grannies clutched their Yiddish prayer books.

When they arrived at the Gates of Heaven a brigade of angels began to sort out the souls. Some were to go to Paradise and some to Hell. The atheists at once protested, "What's the idea?" They raised a row. "We were good enough Jews for the crematorium, why shouldn't we be good enough for Paradise?" A Socialist suddenly recalled a long-forgotten text: "All Israel have a share in the world to come."

A Jew who had lived through a couple of dozen *selektzies* in various camps sighed in a low voice: "Who could imagine the same thing would be happening here?"

Todros didn't have the time to hear out the entire debate. He was concerned with those who were still alive and hurried to the Throne of Glory. As he approached, a secretary got in his way: "Where do you think you're going?"

So Todros explained to him that the Thirty-Six had assembled and composed a memorandum and how he had to deliver it to the Master of the Universe, in person.

"Hand it over!" The angel stretched out his hand from under his wing. "It will be all right. I'll pass it on."

"No!" Todros stood his ground. "This time it is not to be through an angel and not through a messenger. . ."

The secretary knit his brow. He didn't want to start up with the Thirty-Six.

"The Master of the Universe is not at home," he said coldly. "I suppose you think that yours is the only world He has on His mind? There are— God preserve them from the evil eye—thousands of stars and suns, big worlds and little worlds, like sand on the shore of the sea."

"What do you think, that all He has to do is sit all day on the Throne of Glory and wait for your prayers?" interrupted a blond, plump angel girl, who was sitting at a typewriter and typing lists based on last Rosh Hashanah's balance sheet.

She really didn't have a hard job at all, that blond angel. All she did was stick long columns of names into the typewriter and, without looking, type along every column the same two words:

By Fire
By Fire
By Fire
By Fire

But her heart was sad. A mere matter of five thousand years before, her sweetheart, a handsome young angel, had gone down to the sinful Earth and there had fallen in love with one of Adam's daughters. Can you imagine: he even got friendly with her and she bore him a child. At any rate, he stayed down there.

Todros, the water-carrier, didn't want to mix into the love affairs that went on between the inhabitants of Heaven and Earth. "When will He be back?"

"Tomorrow."

"Oh, well, there is nothing to be done about it," Todros though to himself. True, he knew that by tomorrow there'd be a few good trains arriving with Jews aboard in Maidanek, Auschwitz, and Treblinka, but there was nothing he could do to help them.

So he waited. Gradually evening stole in. The stars shone down on the heavenly streets and avenues. The nightingales started singing in Paradise and couples kissed in the dark alleys. The gleaming sword automatically turned at the Gate of Heaven, reflecting the gleaming moon now on one edge and now on the other.

Todros lay down behind the paling and fell asleep at once.

Tired out after his long journey. Todros slept late. When he opened his eyes, the sun was already high in the sky, and it was nine o'clock. "Oh, oh, I've overslept." Todros said, taking it to heart. He knew that every morning at nine o'clock with true Prussian punctuality the gas chambers in Auschwitz and Maidanek opened. Around them the angel mothers put their radios on high, so that the screams from below might not disturb the heavenly peace and frighten the angel babies in their cradles.

"Perhaps we will soon be able to avert the decree before noon," Todros thought to himself, and set out, stepping quickly along. On the way he encountered an elderly angel carrying two tremendous sacks on his back.

"Is the Master of the Universe at home yet?" Todros asked.

"No, not yet."

"What are you carrying in those sacks?"

"Good deeds," the angel sighed. "I am carrying them from the Gates of Prayer into the storage-hanger. But it's a useless labor: they won't appear at the Judgment Day anyhow, for their owners are already in the camps, awaiting their turn."

Todros waited until noon. The angels began to stream into the restaurants. For lunch they ordered gefilte fish taken from the Leviathan. Afterwards they ate steak cut off the Wild Ox and drank down foaming glasses of the Messianic Wine. While they were having coffee and announcer broadcast over the radio that between the afternoon and evening prayers the saint of our generation, the brilliant, etc. Rabbi Samuel Aaron ha-Cohen, who had just come from the Auschwitz ovens, would deliver an interesting, authentic account of his adventures in the other world, at the same time preaching on the text: "The world reposes on three things: on Torah, on worship, and on acts of loving kindness." In addition, a chanteuse from the Jewish theater on Earth who had been in the Warsaw ghetto would render the verse: "Give thanks unto the Lord for He is good, for His mercy endureth forever."

Todros was very fond of singing, but he had no time to go. Instead, he hurried to the Throne of Glory. The same secretary who had got in his way the day before came out to see him, looking surprised.

"Is the Master of the Universe back yet?" Todros asked.

A peal of laughter rang through the office. Even the serious-looking Chief Secretary smiled.

"What are you laughing at?" said Todros, puzzled. "You said 'tomorrow' yesterday yourselves, didn't you?"

"Apparently you don't read the Psalms," said one of the interns, nodding confidentially to the blond secretary. "For if you did read the Psalms, you would know that 'A thousand years in Thine eyes are as yesterday.'"

Todros started up. "Yes, yes, I have often read the verse, but I'm a simple Jew and don't know the meaning of every Hebrew word I read."

"When we say 'tomorrow' around here we mean in a thousand years around," the secretary explained to Todros. "Do you want to leave your memo with us?"

"No!" Todros stuck the parchment behind his coattail. "It'll get lost among all your papers and you won't be able to find it in a thousand years around."

And he set out on his way back to the sinful earth, to render an account of his mission to the Great Assembly.

Todros was alone on his return trip. For who is so crazy as to go down to the sinful Earth from Heaven nowadays? True, he angels were still talking about their fallen comrades of yesteryear, and the kindness of Adam's daughters. But what's the point of visiting Earth when the cities are in ruins and you can't even get a hotel room to spend the night?

The journeying back and forth took a long time and when Todros arrived at last at the small forest near Treblinka he found nobody there. In the distance he saw people walking around with large sieves and shaking their hands, like peasants sifting the chaff out of the grain. Curious, he drew nearer and saw that they actually were Polish peasants. So he asked them: "What are you doing, my good people?"

"We are sifting through the ashes," they explained. "Sometimes a gold tooth turns up, and sometimes even a wedding ring."

So Todros understood the Jews had been burned to death. Oh well, no use crying, they were burned to death, and nothing could be done about it. Blessed be the true Judge! But where there the other thirty-five saints?

Todros looked around and saw that the world continued to exist: the peasants were looking for gold teeth in the ashes; the corn was growing splendidly, for the earth was fat with the dead; and they were dealing in inflated currency in the town of Treblinka: with gold rubles and green dollars.

So he understood that the Thirty-Six must be somewhere about.

For the world would have perished without the Thirty-Six: the peasants would have found no wedding rings in the ashes, the corn would not have grown, and there would not even have been any business dealings in the inflated currency.

So he went on. He sought the Thirty-Six in D. P. camps of all four zones: English, American, Soviet, and French. But they were nowhere to be found.

He saw German fräuleins kissing American soldiers and hausfraus hauling up the fancy credenzas from their cellars and setting them up in their rooms; and he understood that his comrades must be somewhere about. For by virtue of whom were the German fräuleins kissing American soldiers in return for free nylons, if not by the virtue of the Thirty-Six?

So he went on. He went on and on till he came to a great expanse of water. And there a lot of Jews sat waiting. Someone told him that just the day before an illegal ship had sailed off, carrying Jews to Palestine. There were thirty-five of them, all told: small-town householders, scholars with gray bears, a couple of Galician doctors, and one rabbi who spoke only English.

So Todros understood that those were his comrades who had just sailed for Palestine. So he signed up for the illegal emigration, too, and sat down and waited.

He waited for one day, and two, and three, till on the twelfth day he saw everybody running towards the waterfront. So he got up and ran, too. There on the water was a ship that had just arrived. It was the very same ship on which the Thirty-Six had set out.

Apparently, the ship had been turned about in mid-voyage because the lower deck was fenced off with barbed wire and there stood British soldiers armed with rifles, revolvers, and other such weapons.

Todros wanted to go aboard the ship to give a report on his mission as soon as possible. But no one was permitted to come on board. What was he to do? He finally disguised himself as a correspondent of *The New York Times*. Then they let him on board.

The comrades were overjoyed when the saw him, for they were sure he had managed to avert the death decree. But, looking more closely into his face, they understood that something had gone wrong.

"What happened?"

"The Master of the Universe is not at home! When I asked for Him, they said that He would be back tomorrow—but in Heaven that means a thousand years around!" Todros rushed through his report, anxious to get rid of his mission as soon as possible.

"Certainly!" exclaimed one of the gray-bearded scholars. "Why the verse states explicitly, 'For a thousand years in Thine eyes are as yesterday."

"Yes, yes!" Todros agreed at once. "That's exactly the verse they cited."

And the next morning the ship carrying the Thirty-Six, the barbed-wire fence, and the armed soldiers sailed off in an unknown direction. Todros didn't go back on shore again, and no one knows to this day where the ship sailed to.

The memorandum, however, has turned up. Todros, in his great haste, had apparently mislaid it, and a fisherman came across it in the sand. He brought it to the village teacher, who could make no sense of the script. The parchment passed from hand to hand, until it reached the archeological institute in the capital. From there it strayed into the archives of the International Commission for Nuclear Arms Control, where it is to be found up to the present day.

—Translation by Jacob Sloan revised by A. A.

Sources

Argentina

Alpersohn, Mordechai (Marcos). *In Argentine. Musterverk fun der yidisher literatur.* Ed. Samuel Rollansky. Vol. 31. Buenos Aires: IWO, 1967. 32–41.

———. "Dos gautshl 'Yismekh Moyshe.'" *Dertseylungen fun feld.* Buenos Aires: n.p., 1943. 41–46.

Bendersky, Borekh. "A gut-oyg." *Geklibene shriftn.* Buenos Aires: Ikuf, 1954. 138–44.

———. "Farshterte shabosim." *Geklibene shriftn.* 145–48.

Bloshtein, Hirsh. et al. "In kegnzetslekhe rikhtungen." *Antologye fun der yidisher literatur in Argentine.* Ed. Salomón Suscovich et al. Buenos Aires: Di Prese, 1944. 83–85. Biographical information courtesy of Gennady Estraikh.

Chasanovitch, Leon. "Dos rezultat fun tsvey tsendlik yor." *Der krizis fun der yidisher kolonizatsye in Argentina un der moralisher bankrot fun der Ika-administratsyon.* Stanislav [Polish Galicia]: Bildung, 1910. 6-14. Courtesy of Joseph Katriel Shub.

———. "Broyt un ere." *Argentinish 1: Der kholem fun feld. Musterverk fun der yidisher literatur.* Vol. 66. Buenos Aires: IWO, 1975. 305–9. Courtesy of Joseph Katriel Shub.

Hirschbein, Peretz. "Di boyer fun a yidisher tsukunft." *Fun vayte lender.* New York: Tog, 1916. 62–69. Courtesy of Omus Hirshbein.

Nomberg, Hersh David. "Me benkt in Buenos-Ayres." *Gezamlte Verk.* Vol. 6. (Warsaw: Kulturlige, 1928). 49–54.

Pinzón, Mimi. *Der hoyf on fenster.* Buenos Aires: Ikuf, 1965. 60–67. Courtesy of Izi Shafer.

Rabinovich, Yoysef (José). "A mentsh un zayn popugay." *Antologye fun der yidisher literatur in Argentine.* Ed. Salomón Suscovich et al. Buenos Aires: Di Prese, 1944. 746–48.

Rollansky, Samuel (Rozhanski, Shmuel). "Lekoved Yon-kiper." *Argentinish 2: Tsvishn shtotishe vent. Musterverk fun der yidisher literatur.* Vol. 70. Buenos Aires: IWO, 1976. 283–86. Courtesy of Esther Rollansky.

Rubin, Moyshe. "Iber an ibergerisener retsue." *Argentinish 2: Tsvishn shtotishe vent. Musterverk fun der yidisher literatur.* Vol. 70. 204–9.

Schussheim, Aaron Leib. "Ven dos lebn hot bazigt dem toyt." *Yorbukh fun literatur, kunst un gezelshaftlekhkayt fun yidishn yishev in Argentine.* Buenos Aires: Farlag Yidish, 1945–46. 199–202. Courtesy of Jorge Schussheim.

Wald, Pinye. *Koshmar.* Buenos Aires: n. p., 1929. 20–29.

Brazil

Botoshanski, Yankev (Jacob). Director's Prologue. *Ibergus* by Leib Malach.
  Buenos Aires: n.p., 1926. N. pag.
Malach (Malekh), Leib. *Ibergus*. Buenos Aires: n.p., 1926. 11–14, 24–26, 31–32, 76.
Kucinski (Kutshinski), Meir. "A Mulatke." *Nusekh Brazil.* Tel Aviv: I.L.Peretz,
  1963. 128–33. Courtesy of Wolf Kucinski.
Palatnik, Rosa. "Af tnoim." *Kroshnik-Rio.* Rio de Janeiro: Monte Scopus, 1953.
  108–14. Courtesy of Felipe Wagner and Ita Szafran.

Chile

Goldchain, José (Yoysef). "Er hot zikh arufgearbet." *Fun a vayt land.* Santiago:
  S. Segel, 1949. 44–48. Russian translations courtesy of Bruce Holl.
———. "Zi vil es zol zayn vos beser un shener." *Fun a vayt land.* 59–61.
Obodovski, Yoyne. "Shloyme Likht." *Tshilenish. Musterverk fun der yisher
  literatur.* Vol. 54. Buenos Aires: IWO, 1972. 181–85.
Vital, Noyekh. "Gold." *Shtot un feld.* Buenos Aires: Litvish-yidisher farband in
  Argentine, 1946. 101–8.

Colombia

Brainsky, Salomón (Shloyme). "Nisoyen." *Goldene keyt* 21 (1955): 113–22.
  Courtesy of Simón Brainsky.

Cuba

Berniker, Pinkhes. "Yezus." *Shtile lebns.* Vilne (Vilnius): B. Kletskin, 1935. 169–86.
Dubelman, Abraham Josef. "Der 'kurandero.'" *Der Balans.* Havana: Havaner
  lebn, 1953. 33–39. Courtesy of Eugenia Dubelman.
Zeitlin, Aaron. "Der gayego." *Lider fun khurbn un lider fun gloybn.* 2 vols. New York:
  Bergen-Belsen Memorial Press, 1967–70. 2: 322–23.

Mexico

Berliner, Isaac. "Kloysters" accompanied by illustration by Diego Rivera. *Shtot
  fun palatsn.* Mexico City: Der Veg, 1936. 72–75. The translation by Mindy
  Rinkewich, "Churches," and the illustration by Diego Rivera, from Isaac
  Berliner's *City of Palaces* ([Basking Ridge, NJ: Jacoby, 1996] 42–44), are used
  courtesy of Jacoby Press.
Corona, Meir. "A bank aza." *Heymishe mentshn.* Mexico City: Yidisher Kultur-
  Klub in Meksike, 1939. 61–65. Courtesy of Ayala Corona.
Glantz, Jacobo. "Yontef af di gasn: Ershte antisemitishe manifestatsye." *Trit in di
  berg: Lider un poemes, 1926–1936.* Mexico City: Khurbn, 1939. 54. Courtesy
  of Margo Glantz and Sulamita Schoenfeld.
Weisbaum, Abraham. "Yente Tinifotski" and "Yankl Fayfer vert an aristokrat." *In
  meksikaner gan-eydn.* Mexico City: Hemshekh, 1959. 97–103, 130–35.

U.S.A. (Texas)

Gurwitz (Hurvits), Alexander Ziskind. "Vi San Antonio hot oysgezen mit tsvey un tsvantsik yor tsurik." *Seyfer zikhroynes fun tsvey doyres.* New York: Posy-Shoulson Press, 1935. 2: 171–73. Courtesy of Robert E. Gurwitz.

Uruguay

Zytner, Salomón (Shloyme). "Di bar-mitsve-droshe." *Der gerangl.* Montevideo: Yidisher shrayber- un zhurnalistn-fareyn in Urugvay, 1955. 19–26. Courtesy of Susana Zytner de Frisberg and Rosa Zytner.

———. "Der griner." *Der gerangl.* 65–69. Courtesy of Susana Zytner de Frisberg and Rosa Zytner.

Ayalti, Hanan. "A banket in Meksiko-Siti." *Der tshek un di eybikayt.* Montevideo: B. Reznikovich, 1950. 31–49. The translation "A Banquet in Mexico City," appearing in Ayalti, *The Presence is in Exile, Too* ([Montgomery, AL: Black Belt Press, 1997] 39–50), is used courtesy of Daniel Klenbort.

———. "Der memorandum fun di lamed-vov." *Der tshek un di eybikayt.* 113–25. The translation by Jacob Sloan, "Memo from the Thirty-six," appearing in *The Presence is in Exile, Too* (31–38), is used courtesy of Daniel Klenbort.